T0193418

BECK & CAUL
SPRING 1919

ERIC BAYSINGER

authorHOUSE®

AuthorHouse™
1663 Liberty Drive
Bloomington, IN 47403
www.authorhouse.com
Phone: 1 (800) 839-8640

Published by AuthorHouse 09/04/2019

ISBN: 978-1-7283-2385-5 (sc)
ISBN: 978-1-7283-2384-8 (e)

Library of Congress Control Number: 2019912217

Print information available on the last page.

BUNK

3/19/19

When I got back from chow, one of them flyboys that came aboard at Breast was in my bunk, fixin' to puke. I quick grabbed a bucket and he retched into it. It was an awful mess and he was very pale and sweaty, but once I got him squared away, I seen he was not a bad lookin' fellow: black hair, brown eyes, strong jaw, and a sort of lop-sided widow's ~~peak peek~~ peak. I fetched a rag and wiped off his mouth, which is wide and even. He thanked me and I told him to stay put, then snuck him some coffee and a boiled potato from the galley. He kept those down pretty well, lettin' me hold the cup to his mouth and feedin' him with a good clean fork. Kimball from the bunk above mine gave me some guff, but he's just jellous because him and me have fooled around before. I told him to go lay an egg and he shut up. Every spot on the ship is crowded with doughboys and pilots gettin' out of the war so me and Tom (that's the flyboy) squeezed in together for the night and talked some more. He told me he's from Pittsburgh and asked me where I'm from, but I didn't want to tell him I'm just some dumb hick from the hills, so I told him I'm from Waynesburg. His hair smells like Brilliantine.

Thursday, the 20ᵗʰ of March

Damnable ocean! The waves never cease and neither does my gut. Four days out from Brest and still no "sea legs" whatsoever. Give me the blue unending sky filled with German guns rather than this gray unending roil! Zeb, the red-headed swabby whose cot I collapsed onto, says we have to endure five more days on the water. Poseidon take me and this whole damned destroyer, only end my suffering! Zeb gave me one of his blank notebooks to write in and thereby pass some of the time that I don't spend hurling my half-digested meals into whatever container is at hand. He says his father is a veterinarian, so he's accustomed to caring for sickly creatures. His hand on my belly last night had an anodynic effect.

3/21/19

When I was done with duty, I got Tom to come up top with me. He was worse off for awhile, but I taught him to keep his eye on the horizon and that helped. We've been tradin' war stories. I told him about sinkin' the U-58 and takin' all its crew prisoner, but mostly I don't have much to say for myself in the last three years except that I mopped a lot of decks, listened to about a million radio messages and sent a million more. Tom, on the other hand, has seen a bunch of action: he's got two kills from dogfights he was in and lived through just as many crashes. Kimball and some of the others keep razzin' me for takin' him in tow, but I don't pay them no attention. We'll be back in the U.S. soon and I won't be seein' them no more, so to hell with them! Only wish it wasn't the end of my time with Tom too. He allmost makes me wish I had signed up with the "army of the air" (called "laugh-I-yet" in French) instead of the Navy. Only problem is, I can swim a hell of a lot better than I can fly!

Saturday, the 22nd of March

Zeb has gotten me more or less accustomed to the pitch and roll of the Fanning, *at least to the point that I can consume most of what is prepared in the galley. When I eat or speak, Zeb smiles all the way from the furrows in his cheeks right up to his eyes, which I would describe as a leafy green. He repeats some of the unfamiliar words I use and tries to employ them himself later on. He claims to have been graduated from high school, but I suspect that is not the case. What do I know? Perhaps he is the very flower of education in the bottom left corner of Pennsylvania.*

We continue to bunk together, there being no other square yard both suitable and available for slumber. Zeb keeps one arm wrapped tightly around my chest and with the other braces himself against the hull so that we do not spill out of bed. He talks in his sleep, rambling about his duties as one of the ship's radio operators mostly, but one time he mumbled my name and nuzzled the back of my head. Despite all that I sleep quite peacefully.

It would be pleasant to stay in touch with him, but, having survived the horrors of combat, no doubt we shall return to the wheel ruts worn out for us by generations past, I to Prouwder House and he to whatever hollow of Greene County lent him to the war effort.

Sunday, the 23rd of March

One of the crew made a lewd suggestion to Zeb about our comradeship. Apparently it's one thing to "pal around" with a shipmate, quite another to befriend a pilot, soldier or civilian. Zeb maintained a stony silence until the other man dared to cuff him on the cheek. At that, Zeb delivered a devastating fist to the man's solar plexus and laid him out. He "decked" him, in other words! I must say it was an admirable blow, but then Zeb came quite unexpectedly unhinged, kicked him in the back, and would have stomped on his neck if I hadn't pulled him in one direction while onlookers dragged the mouthy bastard in the other. An officer was consulted: now Zeb is confined to quarters until we reach port.

3/24/19

Still stuck in my bunk. Tom hasn't come around much, but he did bring me lunch and supper and we talked while I ate. He ain't sore about what I done, but I can tell he thinks less of me now. I promised not to fly off the handle like that again, but I feel bad all the same. He's educated. He don't know how it is when you got a dad with a well-used razor strop and two older brothers ready to take you apart for any queer thing you say, but now I got to live up to a higher standard and I will. I swear it! Tom's only six months older than me, but he seems about ten years more worldly. I hope he will come back and bunk with me our last night on board. With Kimball or fellows I met in Queenstown, Lisbon, or Ponta Delgada, it was just a quick tug and goodbye. Cuddling with Tom is something better even though I keep my hand above his waist and outside his clothes.

Monday, the 24th of March

Zeb's confinement has left me to my own devices for distraction and I've therefore fallen back into the despondent state in which I boarded the Fanning. The war itself served as the Great Diversion, one I expected not to survive. Good men fell all about me, but the Grim Reaper spurned me no matter the height from which I threw myself at him.

Zeb seems determined to remain at my side after we reach Philadelphia tomorrow. I wouldn't mind conducting him around the City of Brotherly Love, I suppose. It seems a fair recompense for the devotion he has shown me during this voyage. We'll stay in Father's suite at the Bellevue-Stratford and then I can take him around to some of the places I have enjoyed in summers past.

3/25/19

In Philadelphia. I wanted to find us any old flophouse, but Tom made me follow him to the biggest and fanciest goddamn hotel in God's creation. I'm sittin' on the very edge of one spindly chair in his father's ~~sweet suit~~ suite, scared I'll break or soil something. The stiff-backed S.O.B. at the front desk was lookin' pretty put out with the pair of us when we first walked in, Tom in his flying ace gear and me in my whites and cap. I hung back, ready to leap out the door if the cops was called, but after just thirty seconds of talkin' with Tom he changed his tune and scraped and bowed while we signed in. A bellhop came to carry my duffel bag and Tom's suitcase into the elevator and then up and up and up we went until here we are in a room so high I can't bear to look out the window. Tom, on the other hand, can't get enough of the ~~vue~~ view.

Bellevue, that's the name of the place! He stares out the window all the time, first down at the street and then up at the clouds. Tom used the telephone to call his father. He was still at work when we got here and didn't expect to come home until late so Tom and me ate down in the hotel restaurant, which was very fine.

There are two beds in this place and I figured me and Tom would share one. It's none too big, but after my bunk it would've seemed ample enough, only Tom fixed himself up on one of the couches in the parlor. Guess we ain't gonna be bedmates no more.

Tuesday, the 25th of March

Steady land underfoot at last! Even better, I am once more soaring among the birds and can barely restrain myself from crawling out onto the hotel ledge. Poor Zeb looks as out of place here as a bison on Beechwood Boulevard. We dined in the hotel and he ate with gusto, but the rich cuisine did not sit well with him after three years of beans, potatoes, and scrambled eggs. I haven't his gift for healing and sent him off to Lowell's old bed with a teaspoon of baking soda in a cup of water, as Belle used to do for us children.

There appears to be an "amnesty" in effect in the hotel restaurant's dress code: Zeb and I were seated without being taken to task for our uniforms and a few other military men were there as well. A great patriotism pervades the city. Two young ladies came by our table to kiss Zeb and me on the cheek while their father shook our hands and stammered something about his past service. He also stood us a round of bourbon and wished us well.

My own father came home just past midnight smelling

not of his office but of liquor. He was unsteady on his feet, but somehow well-practiced at being unsteady. He knew just what furniture to brace himself against, those being pieces from which all breakables were long ago removed. The valet who took his coat and hat was adept at supporting him without being overt about it. Had I not been there I'm sure Father would've been undressed and put to bed per his routine, but seeing me thwarted his efforts and he fell over his own feet down onto the floor of the vestibule with a piteous sob.

I knelt and embraced him as he wept on my shoulder, but these were not the grateful tears of a man whose son has returned from war alive; they were rather the tears of a man who still grieves the death of a more beloved son years ago. This is the heartache brought on by the morning star after the sun itself has been snuffed out. I'm glad Zeb did not witness this.

When Father had recovered himself, his valet and I got him situated in one of the parlor chairs. The deterioration in his appearance is profound. Five years ago —even four— he had no more gray hair than I and in general he struck one as a man in his prime, full of vigor and healthy color. He strode quickly and, while never possessing a cheery nature, seemed all-capable and effectual. Now he appears closer to sixty than his actual fifty. His nose is blossomed, but his cheeks are sallow and there is a minor but constant tremor in his right hand. Remember that these observations were made in low light when my own eyes were blurred by teardrops I barely kept from shedding. What will Father look like in the scalding light of day? If he did not own the company he works for, I suspect he would have lost his position by now.

More grief was piled on: Crowne is dead. Father reported that he and Cousin Rose were yesterday on a rescue near Biloxi, something about a capsized boat. After Crowne had saved many souls from drowning, the unworthy bastards turned on him for being with a white woman and lynched him on the very shore to which he had dragged them! They dared to rough up Rose herself and she apparently made her narrow escape only by diving back into the water and swimming out of reach. Father says everyone is expected at Prouwder House without delay so that a new duo (or trio) can be chosen to continue The Work before a week has elapsed. Oh, that this convocation had taken place while I was still in France or out on the Atlantic! I'd rather have been lost at sea, alone or even with all hands on board, than see on whom this awesome responsibility will fall next. It is undeniable that my rash actions of four years ago hastened Crowne's death and I never even knew his Christian name. I guess I will now learn it from his headstone.

Father says we're to leave on the earliest train tomorrow morning. No tour of Philadelphia will be possible, but I hope to convince Zeb to join us on the journey west. Despite the circumstances I'd like to prolong our time together; he lightens my mood and will make an awful trip more tolerable. If it weren't unseemly, I would crawl under the covers with him now.

3/26/19

Well, I sure ain't where I expected to be tonight! Thought I'd be parted from Tom and all alone in a flophouse or the Y.M.C.A., but here I am in my own bed back at the farm and right next to me is Tom Caul himself! Here's how all this come about:

We all got to Pittsburgh in the early afternoon. Tom had been awful antsy on the train. Me and him sat opposite his dad and it seemed like every five minutes Tom was up again and stridin' around our car or even into other cars. I went with him when I wasn't dozin' off. He made small talk about the countryside and the history of trains in Pennsylvania or asked me this and that about my family, but nothin' calmed him down. He was just rattled the whole way. When we got to Penn Station he only got worse. We was all outside under the rotunda where people was streamin' back and forth among carriages and taxis and private automobiles. There was a car there special for Tom and his father, with a showfur even, and Mr. Caul shook my hand and wished me well, then climbed in. I stuck my hand out for Tom to shake, but he only barely took hold of it, lookin' all around and rubbin' his mouth and the back of his neck. Then he shut the car door and told his dad he'd see me off on my train only I hadn't even bought a ticket yet and his dad said there was no time for that, to hurry up and get in, but Tom waved him away, grabbed me by the elbow and rushed me back into the station. He quick bought two tickets to Waynesburg, then hid himself and me on either side of the door to the rotunda and waited until his dad had given the signal to drive off, then Tom sort of slumped against the wall.

I didn't know what to make of this, but there wasn't a whole lot of time to ponder it because our train was startin' to load up so Tom and me got on board. I asked him about his family emergency and he said he had a few more days before he had to go home and that it probably wouldn't involve him anyway. Only once we was underway did I realize he had let the shofer take his suitcase and hadn't gotten it back. I said this to Tom, but he didn't seem to care. He just stared out the window or drew figures in his breath on the pane of glass.

We got to Waynesburg towards nightfall and I had to fess up that my family don't actually live in town but out on a farm just past the village of Sycamore. Tom didn't seem too surprised and didn't cuss me out for lyin' to him. We hoofed it all the way to Mom and Dad's door and wasn't they surprised to see us! Mom near doubled over with tears of joy and even Dad and my brothers clapped me on the back. We all had whiskey and Dad told me some bad news, which is that the Spanish flu killed my uncle Lenny and aunt Pearl last September. Mom and Dad took in their four kids. My brother Ezra also lives in the house with his wife and their two kids, my brother Clement is in a cabin by the barn with *his* wife and *their* girl, and my sister Sarah's just down the road with her husband, so there's Becks up to the rafters, as you can see. Cousin Kevin is the littlest, so he's on a cot in Mom and Dad's room. My sister Rebecca and our cousin Esther are together in Rebecca's miserable cubbyhole at the end of the hall, just about as tightly packed together as Tom and me was on the *Fanning*. We took my old bed, which is fine, but my cousins Aaron and Henry are in Clem's old bed right next to us so we have to be quiet, just our pens scratchin' away in our journals by kerosene lamplight.

Wednesday, the 26ᵗʰ of March

As one must surmise, I have decided to continue journaling. On the sea it was merely a pastime, but now I have become accustomed to the practice and I rather think it's a good idea. I am, after all, a superior writer and my life is worthy of chronicling. Perhaps someday I shall publish a version of these pages for the benefit of the masses.

I abandoned Father at the train station downtown and rode away with Zeb into the wilds of southwestern PA. His father is not a veterinarian, as he maintained, but rather a simple farmer and now we're in his parents' home on that farm. We're back to sleeping double in a single bed, as on the destroyer, and, with his two little cousins slumbering mere feet away, it's even more like the Fanning. *All that's missing is the undulation of the ocean. No doubt Zeb will throw his arm across my chest when we turn down the lamp.*

As crowded as the Beck homestead is, Prouwder House is no doubt worse, or soon will be. In 1915, when Rose and Crowne took over The Work, every living descendant of Jan Prouwder came when summoned: sixty-three aunts, uncles, great-aunts, great-uncles, cousins both first and second, some "removed" and all "moved in". Every bed was occupied and further accommodations were made in the library, the nursery, the conservatory, the various studies, et cetera. Staff were told to double up for the duration and I had to squeeze my cousins George and Peter into my own bedroom, which is not the house's largest by any means. I can bring to mind the stench of George's feet at will, as well as Peter's penchant for rummaging through my things. In comparison to either of them, Zeb is quite an affable bedmate. His skin is freckled and wherever he has been sweating a fine layer of residue remains. His perspiration is not malodorous but somehow more like a bundle of hay torn coarsely through the middle and he gives off a tremendous amount of body heat. I imagine I could pass the rest of my life sharing a bed with him and not complain about it, like Lincoln and his great friend Joshua Speed.

3/27/19

Up around seven to pancakes and good coffee. What a joy! Mom and Ezra's wife Jessie made us fresh batches of both. Dad and my brothers was already hard at work fixin' the tractor or seein' to the ewes that are lambin'. Tom and me took Dad's Model T and drove the kids to school in Nineveh. There we saw good old Miss Barnes! She made a fuss over us in our uniforms and had us do a little "show and tell" for the pupils. I could hardly get a word out I was so fixated on not using any of the cuss words I learned in the Navy, but Tom gave a right fine speech on his adventures as a pilot and kept it clean and simple. The kids had a lot of questions and I think a lot of them thought he was a Beck like me and my sister and cousins. Funny to think of Tom Caul as "Thomas Beck" or me as "Zebediah Caul". What a strange world that would be!

Not as funny is that we run into Nellie Edgerton's mom and she was quick to say Nellie is still unwed. I'm not goin' to call on her, but she's sure to come by the house right away now.

Thursday, the 27th of March

This afternoon Zeb and I hiked the length and breadth of his family's property. It's about one-third the size of the Prouwder estate, much more rugged, and replete with deer, turkey, and rabbit. Zeb's brothers have a collection of firearms. I wish I had my suitcase with me here so that I could make them a present of my Lebel revolver as I'm unlikely to need it in the future.

Zeb's father, for his part, is less interested in guns and hunting than in harness racing. He took us out to the barn to show off his sulky and the stallion that pulls it. They are his pride and joy, far more so than the farm itself. Zeb does not seem to share either passion and when I asked about his own hobbies, he led me to his bedroom and from the back of the topmost shelf in his closet produced three novels and one sketchbook. The novels are Verne's "Around the World in Eighty Days", Defoe's "Robinson Crusoe", and Melville's "Moby-Dick". The sketchpad he showed me contains illustrations of key scenes and characters from the novels, which were gifts from the teacher whose class we entertained this morning. "Why do you hide them?" I asked. He replied that his brothers would tear them up if they found them, as they would do with his journal. I had a great swell of pity for him. It made me want to take him away from here, perhaps out west where we could be trappers or gold miners or bandits.

My mind turns toward Prouwder House and the tumult it must be in. The mansion will be creaking all over and hearing many more footsteps than usual. It will smell the bayou dishes that the Prouwder-Doucettes insist on and the clashing tobaccos Great-uncles William and Henry bring with them. Through keyholes and transoms, it will spy on the aged and the newborn. Perhaps replacements for Rose and Crowne have already been selected and they are even now speeding somewhere on a mission of mercy. Russell? Phyllis? Earl? A Prouwder-Booke? A Prouwder-Lundt? There's just no telling who it will be. Rose took riding lessons on the estate, but she knew Crowne only as one of the stable boys before Fate threw them together in The Work.

Mother will be angry that I've dallied down here, but this is a reverie of simple work and sylvan joys. I'll stay a few more days and nights. There can be no harm in it.

3/28/19

That Nellie Edgerton came by, eager for me and her to pick up where we left off three years ago. She wrote me a passel of letters while I was away and I made sure the other fellows seen 'em or even read 'em. She mostly complained about how little I wrote her and made mention of Hiram White every chance she got. Each time he took her for ice cream or came callin' she was sure to write about it, tryin' to make me jellous, but the joke's on her 'cause I never cared one whit who she seen or what she done with him!

She made a big show of helpin' Mom and the other women cook up two big pots of stew and a tray of biscuits, but all that was mostly done by the time she showed up anyhow and she spent more time spyin' on me from the kitchen than mixin' or stirrin'. Mom had to ask her several times to move out of the way and even Jessie looked put out with her. My sister brought her family over so when it came time to eat, everybody got a bowl and a biscuit and tried to find some chair or stair step to eat on. Tom and me are still sort of guests of honor so Mom insisted we sit at the dining room table next to Dad. That meant Clem had to hunker down at the fireplace and he scowled at me for it all night.

I kept scoochin' my chair closer to Tom's until we was thigh to thigh, but Nellie on my other side kept pawin' at me and sayin' how good it was I'm home again and makin' cow eyes at me until I wanted to thunk her on the forehead with my spoon. After supper she didn't help wash up, but pulled me out to swing on the porch and I pulled Tom out with us so there we was all three on the swing, uncomfortable. Nellie even took my hand in hers, bein' forward as she is, and I put my other arm around Tom's shoulder, but she didn't take the hint. Mom and Dad will be on me to marry her, just you wait! I can't stay here!

Friday, the 28th of March

Zeb's sweetheart visited this evening. She's a simple and affectionate soul, but I think Zeb got used to the fiery ladies of the Azores and the fair colleens of Queenstown during his service and can't be satisfied with a small town American girl anymore. After a hearty repast and a turn on the porch swing, he insisted on climbing the massive hill behind the house. It's deceptive: what initially appears to be the summit turns out, upon reaching it, to be less than half the actual height. Miss Edgerton turned back in a pout at that point, but we trudged on until, out of breath, just we two stood under the vast Milky Way. It was penetratingly cold so we huddled together in the coats and blankets we'd brought with us and discussed the future.

Zeb confessed he finds the prospect of remaining on the farm stifling and hopes to make a different life for himself in Pittsburgh, perhaps in the steel mills or in some other trade where a strong back is valued. I expressed my surprise at his low expectations for himself and gave him a frank assessment of his talent at sketching. "Why not pursue work in illustration?" I asked him. The idea seemed to astonish him. We spent several minutes imagining courses he could take, a student's room in a boarding house, and the romantic deprivations he'd have to endure for the sake of his art. Zeb insisted I be a part of his nobly tragic career, starving and shivering alongside him as he sketched, perhaps serving as life model for a series of drawings which would bring him fame, albeit posthumously.

When all the details of our speculation had been worked out, we shook hands on the deal. Zeb rested his head on my shoulder and told me I was the best friend he's ever had.

3/29/19

Got up when Clem come in our room and lifted up one end of our bed then dropped it back down again. He said the sheep needed fed, "so hop to it!" I got no problem doin' the work, but Tom's meant for finer things and it irked me to see him puttin' on one of my old pair of overalls and some beat-to-hell farm boots, but the only other clothes he has here is his pilot gear. We ate quick, then got goin'. One stupid ewe was wedged all most upside down against the fence and it took both of us to get her back on her feet and then we stank of wet wool. We washed up at the pump. Tom smiled the whole time 'cause all this is new to him, but let me tell you, there's nothin' to smile about when you do this every day as I have done. Same stupid sheep, same sickening smell.

No sooner was we clean than Clem ordered us into the pig shed to shovel shit. I know he waited for us to wash up just so he could make us dirty again! I can toil from sun up to sun down, but I sure as hell can't take Clem the Clod givin' me orders anymore after I spent three years dodgin' death from the Kaiser's submarines! The clincher was when Tom and me had already started shovelin' and Clem come up and shoved me and said, "Put your back into it, Sailor Boy!" I swung my shovel around and cracked him on the head with it and I think I could just about have driven the blade right through his goddamn neck except that Tom yanked the thing out of my hand and threw it outside. I stormed off down the road and Tom didn't catch up with me for about five minutes. He wanted me to come back to the house, but I told him I was leavin' for Pittsburgh and he could come with me or stay there and rot. He talked me into stayin' by the side of the road while he went back to the house to get our stuff and say his goodbyes. That's the kind of fella he is: even when someone tries to knock him down in pig shit he says, "Thanks for lettin' me stay here." I ain't never goin' to be as good a man as he is, no matter how I try.

When he got back he had a five-dollar bill and said my mom pressed it into his hand for me. She was cryin', he said, and terrible upset about the fight and us leavin', but plenty's the times Clem or Ezra boxed my ears or pushed me around and I didn't do nothin' about it and she didn't cry then but this one time I stand up for myself she gets weepy! Even so, I had to go behind a tree and wipe my eyes 'cause what son wants to make his mom cry?

We could've waited for the narrow gauge to come right by the house, but I didn't want any more trouble, so Tom and me walked all the way into town. We went to the train station and bought tickets, then changed out of our overalls back into our uniforms in the men's room. I seen Tom had packed my books and sketchpad along with a few leftover biscuits. There was time to kill, so we walked around the college. I showed him the high school even though I only finished eighth grade and never went there. Maybe here in Pittsburgh I can find a teacher to pick up my schooling where Miss Barnes left off. I'd like to write right and talk to Tom on his level someday.

As I say, I'm here in Pittsburgh, only not at the Y.M.C.A. as expected. I tried again to say goodbye to Tom at Penn Station downtown, but the whole trip he had been thinking hard and wouldn't let me talk about finding myself a place in a boarding house so I made up my mind just to go my own way, awful as that would be, only he shoved me into a taxicab instead. I said Y.M.C.A. to the driver and he griped that we could walk it quicker, but Tom told him to "pipe down and drive" so the man set off, only when we got there Tom didn't like the looks of it and wouldn't let me out. He had the driver go then to another one across a bridge and all the while Tom was working his jaw back and forth and squinting like he was trying to figure something out. He barely glanced at the building this time before saying it also wouldn't do and the driver complained some more about us wasting his time, so Tom ~~through~~ threw a dollar at him and ordered him *back* across the same river and then away from downtown all together.

I didn't make a peep since Tom now had a full head of steam going and I didn't want him to blast me too! (He gets bad tempered sometimes, I seen.) We followed Second Avenue a long while. I know this because Tom didn't tell the driver where we ~~was~~ were going, only which road to take, where to turn, and the like. We went alongside the river. The Monongahela, I think. Mostly mills on the right side and small but nice houses on the left. It got a bit swankier when we turned onto Greenfield Avenue, not that the houses were any better, but they weren't cheek by jowl with factories pouring out black smoke anymore.

We climbed up quite a ways and then we were on a flatter and nicer street called Beachwood, then up again a street called Forward and then down down down into a wood and over a creek. The last hard climb brought us through a large stone wall and an iron gate. The driver stopped and turned around to stare at Tom. "You could've told me we were going to Prouwder House from the start and saved your breath, you know." Only he made it sound like "Prodder Hoss". Tom gave him another dollar and told him to pull up under the "poor coacher" or something. We couldn't even see the house from where we were and it wasn't quick that we came in sight of it either, but when we did it was like the Bellevue Hotel all over again! I could barely squeak, but I asked Tom was he or was he not "Tom Caul" and he said he was "Thomas Prouwder Caul", that being his middle name. Key-rist! I reckon tomorrow I'll just up and pay a call on Mr. Carnegie or Mr. Mellon, then take tea with Mr. Frick while I'm at it!

I didn't want to get out of the taxicab and Tom and me had a tussle. I told the driver to take me back to town, but Tom calm as could be just hauled my duffel bag out from between my legs, dropped it on the pavement under the overhang, and then started leveraging me out of my seat as well. It was quite a show for the driver and some folks that had gathered at the windows of the house and we were evenly matched for a while since I braced myself on the frame of the car door, but then Tom pinched me hard on the back of my arm and I landed on the pavement like a horse apple on a dinner plate.

A servant come outside and fetched my bag, then welcomed Tom and told him his mother was in her ~~chamebar~~ chaimber. Tom nodded and let the man go ahead of us, then right into my ear he said I should call him "Caul" or maybe "Caulie" from now on because that made us sound like school chums. "And I shall call you 'Beckie'," he laughed. I gave him a sharp look. The driver was still there, listening in. Tom told him he was dismissed in a way that even Captain Carpender on the *Fanning* would have hustled at hearing!

The inside of the house is no less fancy than the outside. We followed the servant into a hallway. Everywhere you look is polished wood and red carpet. There are black statues and white busts, plus paintings of other people hanging on the walls from long red cords. The ceiling is arched and practically as high up as the roof of our barn. It's painted green part of the way, then breaks into little corn-yellow squares. I held onto my bag tight because there was all kinds of stuff you could knock off the tables. Next to us was a staircase and under every tread was a carving of a wave or maybe a gust of wind. Every baluster (I asked Tom for that word) was twisted around and around like the horns of some sheep I seen.

We went through a set of doors which were slid most of the way into the walls and it was a big parlor. Here the ceiling was even higher and a few windows stretched almost all the way up the walls. Some people ~~was~~ were sitting and standing around in there and I guessed they were kin, here for the family emergency Tom told me about. Three pretty young ladies come over and hugged Tom around the neck and he introduced me to them only

I don't remember their names exactly except that they all ended in –een. One was in a pink dress, one in light yellow, and the last in light green. (Tom says their names are Ernestine, Josephine, and Pauline.) Tom said they were his "Doucette" cousins and asked them to entertain me while he went to see his mother. He briefly greeted some other relatives, then run up the stairs behind us.

The girls pulled me over to a table of sandwiches and punch, each of them chattering away without listening to each other and each fixing me a plate and cup until I had three plates and three cups to try to hold onto. I was pretty hungry and thirsty, so I did all right by what they gave me. They led me around the room and pointed out portraits of dead folks, pretty much ignoring the live folks that was there. After we made a complete circle of the room, the girls kept talking and I found a sturdy-looking chair to sit down on. I seen my duffel bag was still in the hallway and I wanted to fetch it, but my hands were full of cups and plates, so I decided to just kick it slow across the floor back under my chair only that got the attention of everyone in the room and they all stopped talking to watch me. I wished Tom would come back quick.

I sat quiet and felt sicker and sicker. This was even worse than the Bellevue because at least there I could imagine scraping together a few years wages and renting its cheapest room on my own, but at Prouwder House you have to be one of the family or, I guess, one of the servants to stay there and I definitely ain't am'nt either of those! Just when I had talked myself into hoisting my bag onto my back and skedaddling back through the hallway to the free world, Tom and his mom come into the parlor. They didn't see me at first because I was in the corner to their left mostly behind a giant spread of peacock feathers, but then Tom spied me and introduced us. "Mrs. Prouwder-Caul" smiled kind of small at me and offered me her hand. I figured I wasn't supposed to shake it hard, but I didn't want to kiss it either so I just kind of pressed it and she seemed okay with that. She's pretty much as gray as Tom's dad and she's taller than my mom, but heavier too and her nose tilts up so you can see farther into her nostrils than you might want to.

The Doucettes had three questions for her at once and called her Aunt Maude. One was about supper, one was about the piano which I hadn't even noticed because the room was so big, and the third was about how much longer something called "the convocation" would last and could she go into town to see a motion picture? Mrs. Caul excused herself, spread her arms wide, and herded the girls over to the piano. She'd started talking to a servant about the punch when Tom told me to pick up my duffel because he'd gotten us the last bed in the house.

I'd need an entire spool of twine to show how we got up here to our bed. We walked away from the parlor, up a staircase (not the one Tom and his mom come down), turned a corner past a long row of windows, up another smaller staircase, then wound up at the bottom of a third staircase and at the top of that was a door Tom unlocked with a key I guessed his mother gave him. In here there's a bedroom with one big bed, a smaller room with bookshelves and chairs, a bathroom joined to both, and another room that's got windows on three sides. They mostly look out on the roof of the mansion, but you can also see lots of woods and hills and a little stream running down to the Mon River. It's cozy enough for a couple nights, I suppose. After that I'll have to be moving on to my own place, wherever that turns out to be.

I asked Tom what his cousin meant by "convocation". He said it was nothing important, just a sort of election. His mom runs the house, but two or three other people are in charge of doing a kind of charity work, he said. Not everybody who is here now lives here all year long. They kind of cycle in and out. Mostly it's just him, his mom, her brother and their mom, *her* two brothers, plus Tom's sister and their cousin Rose. There's cooks and maids and ~~shofers~~ chauffeurs (I asked him how to spell that word, but it makes no sense, I think) and butlers and groundskeepers. There's more than a hundred rooms in the mansion, if you can believe it! It would be fun to explore them all, but I reckon I won't get the chance.

We stayed in our set of rooms until supper time, then washed up and headed back downstairs. Tom locked the door behind us, which seemed funny to me. I asked him why he done that and he said this was the only door in the whole house that *could* be locked so we should take advantage of it. That hardly made sense to me, but he pointed out as we went along that, sure enough, most doors had a keyhole, but no keys. Instead, every door that was big enough to walk through had a red ribbon hanging on the knob, either on the inside or the outside. If it was on the outside, Tom said, that meant someone was inside and you shouldn't open the door without knocking, especially the toilets (only he called them "powder rooms"). This seemed just about the looniest thing I ever heard, but I kept my opinion to myself because a man's home is his castle so he can run it any way he wants. I guess I mean Mrs. Caul can run it how she wants.

There was people everywhere we went. They were all kin or servants and greeted Tom as "Thomas" or "Master Caul". Me they greeted as "strange guy in a sailor suit", by which I mean they only eyeballed me and made funny faces because they didn't know who I was. One guy handed me his empty teacup, but then took it back quick as if I was only pretending to be a servant and was really there to steal the china. Only once we reached the dining room did Tom start introducing me. His father was there at the table and he nodded at me, but scowled pretty hard at Tom. Tom greeted a very old lady wearing more lace than I saw in the whole parlor and called her Grandmother. They smooched each other on the cheek and she made an apology that "Mr. Booke" (her husband?) couldn't join them. Tom then shook hands with men he called Great-uncle William and Great-uncle Henry. Me he introduced as "Beck" and all three old faces peered at me with the same confusion I'd seen on the way there. Other aunts and uncles and cousins made my ~~aquantance~~ acquaintance in pretty much the same way. The children were friendlier and I stayed back with a bunch of them and answered questions about ships and sailors while Tom's father pulled him aside for a "private" chat even though I could hear quite a bit of it. "Damned reckless to have run off like that," he said, and "why did you bring *him* here?" Tom was facing away from me so I didn't catch much from him. "Hardly the appropriate time," his dad went on.

Supper was a buffay and the kids I was with dragged me over to where the plates were. Between them and all the clinking of forks and dishes and glasses I couldn't hear anymore from Tom and his dad. I suppose I could have heard more if I'd tried because of all the years I spent listening for the faintest sparks over the wireless, but the main message from Prouwder House was "You're not welcome" and that message I'd already received loud and clear.

Why *did* Tom bring me here when he could have tossed me overboard at Penn Station and sailed on his way? My folks was confused about him comin' to the farm with me, but that was Tom's doing too. What does he want with me? I'd ask him now, but he's writing in his own journal and has a look of pure consternation on his face so I feel sorry for him and won't try to add to his worries. Tomorrow I'll bum cab fare off him if he can't give me a straight answer though.

Saturday, the 29th of March

An unpleasant start to the day and trouble here at the end as well. Beck and I are at Prouwder House, namely the "apartment" on the fourth floor. It's a Spartan space, miserably hot in summer and painfully cold in winter, dusty and neglected, but it contains the last unoccupied bed in the mansion.

Beck attacked his brother this morning, perhaps fracturing his skull and certainly causing a great flow of blood, but at least he was prevented in his attempt to decapitate him. This necessitated our hasty departure from the family farm. I hadn't wanted to return to Prouwder House until April 1st, but this was an unavoidable stop for us. Once this convocation is over, perhaps he and I can travel on somewhere and see the whole wide world. Europe will not be on our itinerary anytime soon; it will need a few years, I calculate, to pile the rubble back into cathedrals and replant the poppy fields. The American West must come first, then Mexico and South America, perhaps the Pacific islands.

I feel more strongly than ever a compulsion not to be parted from Beck. I thrust him into my taxicab at Penn Station, made a pretense of inspecting two of the hotels belonging to the Young Men's Christian Association, and then forced him back out of the taxicab under our porte-cochere. Whereas his family welcomed me cordially, mine has shunned him, interrogated him, or studied him from afar like a zoo animal. He's borne up under their rude treatment with his usual cheer and native grace. I will have to make it up to him once we are free of this place.

The convocation, Mother reports, has not gone well. That is to say, no one has been selected yet and the mood in the mansion reflects that: the servants are exhausted by the extra work, the adult Prouwders are testy, and the children are bored. Mother is on constant duty, arranging entertainments, settling disputes, and keeping her eyes and ears open for any sign a choice has been made. She chided me for "hiding out" in the country, but conceded that my cousins Stuart, Mitchell, Greta, and Ruby will not return from their service in the Great War in time to be candidates for the Great Work. Someone must *hear a cry for help soon, she asserts, if the whole family is not to come to ruin.*

That is her usual exaggeration, of course. I think it's rather the chosen who have come to ruin: Crowne lynched and Rose apparently so traumatized that she has not left her boudoir at all; my brother driven to depravity and my sister made mad; Belle hobbling around our kitchen, Uncle Louis a melancholy wreck, and Frank Candell a corpse; not to mention Great-uncle William, a deaf-mute widower by forty. I say to hell with The Work! So what if all our worldly wealth is taken from us? I for one would labor in poverty with a smile on my face as long as Beck was with me and no one else in my family was placing himself in danger for ungrateful strangers. I'd welcome the hoe, the bridle, or the scythe if it meant companionship and peace of mind.

Some twenty-six hours remain until the supposed deadline. Mother and many others may be in quite a state, but Beck and I shall just stay out of the way. I'll lend Belle a hand in the kitchen. She's been more a second mother to me than a servant. Uncle Louis I'll try to cheer up as Beck does me. Perhaps I'll even press my way in to see Rose, albeit briefly. She must be getting over the horror of Crowne's death by now and will want some light conversation.

And Beck. We'll have a walk around the estate and I'll be more forthcoming about the high regard in which I hold him. We'll make plans for the day after tomorrow, perhaps plot our course on a map, and pack suitcases for our lives as adventurers. He's put away his diary now. I'm tempted to read it as it must now touch upon my family and home, but neither of us will go back on his oath of privacy. When I douse the light, Beck will turn and wrap his arm around me. Perhaps this set of rooms is not so miserable as first I thought it.

3/30/19

Slept good enough, but got cold in the night. This bed is bigger than any Tom and me have shared so far, but we ended up cuddled tight just to keep warm. I think he has dreams about flying and crashing because he sometimes tenses up like he's got his hands on the gun of a plane and he'll keep fighting like that until I soothe him a bit. The war's been over four and a half months now, but I suppose it's not something you can get over quick. We got up and took a shower and what a pleasure that was! Real hot water and no end to it! I grew up getting bath water that had already been used by my dad and brothers and it wasn't any warmer than the air above it. Pure misery, but with indoor plumbing like they got here at Prouwder House I could see bathing even two times a week! Tom scrubbed my back and I scrubbed his. He's a couple inches taller than me, which makes him six foot even, but he let me wash his hair too and we had a laugh about that. He's in pretty good shape for a fella that crashed a couple of planes. There's a scar down his right shin and another on his right hip that looks sort of like the sun with rays coming out of it. I showed him one under my left nipple where I got jabbed by a sharp stick that I was using to feel my way along the bottom of the creek one time. I got other small ones on my right hand because I put it through a window in the well house once, just being stupid and het up. Tom said I had more small ones across my "dairy-air", but those are just marks from whoopings. All us kids have those.

Wish I had something to put on besides my uniforms and overalls. Everybody here is dressed up all the time.

Tom and me shaved and he gave me some of his 'ode to Colone' (who I guess was a famous barber maybe). We went down to breakfast, which was ham and eggs and toast. Tom said good morning to his grandma and she kissed him on both cheeks and said what a great surprise it was to have him back from "that awful European war". Tom introduced me to her again, just like he did last night, and she gave me the same funny look like she couldn't decide if I was fish or fowl, relative or servant. Tom's mom was there, but she hardly sat down at all. Instead she moved from one table of relatives to the next, seeing how everyone was doing. Most of them look worried, for some reason. One guy had sharp words for her, but I couldn't make out what he was saying. He jabbed his finger toward her, then threw his napkin down on the table and stomped out. If they just have to choose people to do charity work, I don't see what the trouble is. It can't be that hard to hand out food in a soup kitchen or write checks for the poor, can it?

Tom said he'd have to spend some time with his kin today, so I wandered around on my own a lot. Now that I knew to look for them, I seen those doorknob ribbons everywhere. Where I could, I went into rooms to see what I could see. I don't even know what some of them were for, but there was one for music, a library, a gymnasium, a nursery, even an indoor swimming pool! I also got outside and walked around the house. It's just about the most complicated thing I ever seen. There's hardly any long stretch of it without it denting in or jutting out and a lot of balconies touch each other on their corners. The whole thing is mostly three stories, but it rambles on and on and I don't think I seen even half of it yet. It's not a bad looking place, just jumbled, like toy blocks that have spilled out of their case and left as they fell. Some of the windows look like eyes, surprised or sleepy or spicious. There are windows in the roof too. It's mostly made of green shingles, but elsewhere on the house there's brown, yellow, orange, and red. I counted five buildings that ~~ain't~~ aren't joined to the house. One's a stable for horses, one's a stable for automobiles, and the other three I don't know what they are yet. Seems to me the house is like half of Noah's ark because it has one of every kind of room.

I saw Tom again at lunch. I'd snuck into the kitchen to beg something off the cook and avoid all them relatives. She limps faster than most people run, but she stopped dead when she saw me and said, "Well, you can't be a Prouwder with all that red hair, so you must be Tommy's guest. Have a seat over there, honey."

I sat down at a small table out of the way and the cook, whose name is Bell, got one of the eight or nine girls working there to fetch me a plate and another got me a napkin and a third got me a glass of milk. Like magic, a ham sandwich was built on my plate as I watched. Bread was laid down, mayo was spread on it, and then came slices of ham. When Bell come near, my mouth was full, but I asked her how she knew I was hungry and she smiled, "Nobody comes in here unless they want to be fed or put to work. What's your name, honey?"

I hadn't decided if I was "Zeb", "Zebediah", "Beck", "Beckie", or "Sailor" before Tom come in and Bell threw her arms up in the air and burst into whoops of joy. All the girls stared at her like owls, but she ignored them and gave Tom just about the biggest hug I ever seen. It made me feel funny, like why haven't I ever given him a big hug, but it's not like we been apart three years, so I don't know why I should feel that way. Bell put him right down at my table and promised him a sandwich which I seen she made all by herself. Tom looked troubled and said he'd been talking to his Uncle Louis and had a few questions for Bell too, but didn't know how to ask her. "They're of an intimate nature," he said quiet. If Tom didn't know how to say something, I sure as heck couldn't help him, but if it had to do with nature maybe I already knew the answer. I seen everything there is to see down on the farm, from rutting deer to foaling mares, plus shenanigans going on behind barns or just outside the light of a campfire, not to mention all I seen on ships or in port towns.

Bell came with the sandwich for Tom and gave him another hug around the shoulders. Even standing up she was barely taller than him sitting down. His eyebrows were turned up and his mouth was turned down so I plunged in and told Bell what a swell meal that was and how happy her husband must be with her cooking. "Husband? Never had one!" She laughed loud and then leaned in close to my ear. "I had *two!*" She turned her attention back to what the other cooks were doing and scurried off towards the big black stove.

Tom still looked bad, so maybe that wasn't what he needed to know, but he didn't try to talk to her himself. His hands were shaking and he didn't take any bites of his sandwich. It was just like back on the *Fanning*. He looked seasick, like Prouwder House was another destroyer rolling around on the ocean. He asked me, "Do you want to stay here?" I said I guessed we could take our sandwiches outside or up to our rooms, but wherever he went, I'd follow along. I meant it nice, but his jaw tensed up and he looked me over like an old pair of pants. Was I worth patching up or should he just throw me onto the quilting pile? In a minute his normal face come back and he pushed his plate over to me. "Eat up. Spend some time in the library. Any book you want, you may have." I asked him where he was going and he said he had more relatives to "question", then he left.

You can't believe how many books they have here! I found the library and read pretty far into "Adventures of Huckleberry Finn" before sundown. I wasn't very hungry 'cause of all I ate and how I didn't do any work all day, so I skipped supper. That was probably not very polite of me, but why should they waste food I don't need? They didn't even notice I was gone, most likely. I went back to our rooms, but the door was locked so I just sat on our staircase and read some more and wished I had my sketchpad. There's a lot of parts in Twain's book that are out on the Mississippi and I would like to draw them.

Tom finally come back pretty late. He stopped on the bottom stair and looked up at me kind of strange. It seems to me I only got two or three different looks, but his face is like a stereopticon with a whole box of cards to go with it. Deep in thought, I guess he was. He come up to the stair below mine. I stood up to get out of his way, but he didn't push past me. Instead he hugged me hard around the waist and buried his face in my belly. Poor fella! He must have been wore out from all his kinfolk. I get like that too. Too many people around and I start wanting to hide out in the barn loft. It's kind of like this set of rooms, a place to be alone with just yourself or one other person.

We're in bed now. Tom ~~ain't~~ ~~isn't~~ hasn't hardly said a word all night. He wrote furious fast in his journal and practically threw it across the room when he was done. He asked me what I want to do tomorrow and I said I'd probably better be moving on and finding work. He nodded kind of glum and laid his head on my belly again so I'm rubbing the back of his neck and head while I write. I don't know what's up with him tonight, but I have a thought about him maybe. I don't know where I'll be heading in the morning, but I'm done writing for now. I'm going to turn off the lamp, touch and kiss Tom all over, and see what's what.

Sunday, the 30th of March

I must make a momentous decision, but I cannot consult Mother or Father. They would be horrified. I have spoken to Uncle Louis, Belle, and Cousin Rose, albeit in a roundabout manner. I do not want to shame them by speaking more bluntly. My sister Hyacinth could shed more light on the matter at hand, but she is too unpredictable in her comings and goings and may bear me a profound grudge which would color her advice. Beck is here, of course, writing in his own journal, but I dare not reveal to him the scales on which I'm balancing the further course of his life. Even God cannot guide me now since sin is the unavoidable outcome of both my choices. My only council must therefore come from my own thoughts as laid out in this entry.

After rising, Beck and I showered "barracks style". He fairly danced with delight at the steady stream of warm water.

In general he is admirably doglike in his appreciation of simple pleasures, although he is no simpleton. The hours I left him alone today he filled by reading Twain, but I saw that he had also selected a copy of Darwin and another of Gibbon from the library. He washed my hair this morning, a task he somehow made more sensual than utilitarian. He is no simpleton and, perhaps, no naïf.

On my own after breakfast, I sought out Uncle Louis. As befits a Prouwder-Booke, I found him sitting among the tomes in his personal study. His solitary window faces north and he had not switched on any light so it was a gloomy space in which to hold a conversation. He was as melancholy as I've ever seen him. This business of the convocation has taxed him, apparently. I made general comments about the family and the well-being of various people. He responded in kind, taking pains to praise my mother for her stamina and organizational skills. I saw a chance to address the issue which was the purpose of my visit and said, "Yes, she's bearing up well, especially since no one can foresee how long the convocation will last." Uncle gripped the arms of his chair tightly and replied that we must *have a resolution before another dawn breaks over Prouwder House because to wait any longer would be fatal.*

"So say Grandmother and her brothers, but surely you don't believe all our fortune could be wiped out in one fell swoop like that!"

Quite grim-faced, he chided me for being inattentive. Not 'ruinous', he had said, but 'fatal'. I asked him what he meant and he demurred, saying only that I should seek out the very youngest descendant of Old Jan Prouwder and see to that child's good standing with its Creator or else by dawn its soul, rent from its flesh, would be the plaything of Old Scratch himself.

"You're putting me on, Uncle. You're telling me a tale better suited to a campfire, where monsters lurk just outside the circle of light!"

He asserted that he, my mother, and their sister Olivia had seen it firsthand when they were children: their infant cousin Wilbur, dead in his crib when a prior convocation had taken too long. Who, he asked me, was the youngest Prouwder now? I said nothing, but immediately thought of Gladys, newborn daughter of my second cousin Sally. She was barely one month old, almost too young, in fact, to have made the trip from Erie to Pittsburgh and one of the last to arrive.

"But how are people chosen for The Work?" I asked. "If the consequences are so dire, surely many of us or even all *of* us would volunteer at once! You and Belle and that Frank Candell did The Work for many years. Why were you three selected for that responsibility?"

Uncle sprang from his chair and said only that "God moves in a mysterious way, His wonders to perform." I persisted in questioning him, but after a few minutes I saw it was useless and took my leave.

Beck and I have vowed not to read each other's journal, but someday he may have overwhelming cause to do so. I hope I have made it clear so far that I find myself facing a matter of life or death; any decision I make, even without Beck's knowing consent, must be judged with that in mind.

I wandered about the mansion, chatting idly with my many relatives and wondering who knew what about The Work. As children we're merely told it's noble and good. Later we hear it is also necessary for the well-being of our family. As a boy I imagined we were part of the Underground Railroad or something similar. Unlike most Prouwders, I've always lived *here on the estate. My father, of course, has a home elsewhere, as do most of my relatives, but for me it was somehow both normal* and *thrilling to see Uncle Louis, Belle, and Frank dash off on a rescue through this room or that. "Rescue" was actually a word reserved for the ears of those who dwelt here permanently and I felt superior to cousins who hadn't even that scrap of real knowledge. Now I feel sick at what I have surmised.*

I discovered Beck in the kitchen near lunchtime. It's no wonder that he sought out refuge from the stares and cold shoulders of my family. I wanted to ask Belle about The Work, but she was very busy preparing a meal for sixty-plus house guests and Beck would have overheard all we said. I tried to put him off a bit by saying my questions were of an "intimate nature", but he remained. As it turned out, he happened to get out of Belle a kernel of information that set my thoughts racing: she joked that she had had not one, *but* two *husbands in her life, while I know for a fact that she has never married. Her mother and father came to see her when she was injured, years ago, and looked to die from it. They were introduced to us all as Mr. and Mrs. Harrison, which is Belle's name as well, obviously her maiden name. The two husbands she claims to have had can only be my Uncle Louis and Frank Candell, but what was I to make of that? Candell never mentioned a wife, at least not in any of the conversations I had with him. I admit he and I did not spend much time together, but I've always been close to Belle and, as for Uncle Louis, his wife is alive, well, and living over in Bloomfield! They have three sons together and, despite living apart now, are not divorced.*

I skipped the midday meal entirely and fell into discomfiting ruminations as I continued to walk about the house. At one point I was in the library, running my fingers over the spines of certain works by Flaubert, Tolstoy, Hawthorne, Hardy, and Zola. Beck entered without seeing me. I observed him for a while, impartially assessing his features and finding them severally unremarkable, but compelling as a whole. I recalled the various scars and marks I'd seen on his body that morning and wished I'd become his friend early enough to prevent them. I left the room by another door, undetected. Without willing it, I found myself in the wing of the mansion wherein Cousin Rose resides. Her parents and siblings being at lunch, I dared to knock upon her door and entered at the sound of her permission. She sat in bed and the strong light of the sun fell directly upon her. She looked grieved, but not unwell. Indeed there was a glow about her quite in competition with the rays coming through the window. Her cheeks were round and marked by color. Her hair, always golden, lay unrestrained about her shoulders. She was shocked to see me and rushed to draw the fluffy bedspread up over the mound of her belly to the fullness of her bosom. Her gown and pillows were carefully arranged to provide maximum comfort and back support, respectively. I took this all in, then averted my eyes.

"Crowne?" I asked. Out of the corner of my eye I could see her nod and begin to weep. I apologized for my intrusion, promised to remain silent, and withdrew.

The hallways and stairs whirled around me. Familiar corridors looked strange. Inchoate thoughts chased each other around the chambers of my mind. It occurred to me none of us was wearing black in a time of mourning, not even an armband. Had any provision been made for Crowne's family? What did my mother know? Had this always been the truth behind The Work? What did this mean for the convocation?

For baby Gladys and others yet to be? Who could be expected to bear this cross if ignominy, seclusion and injury were the only rewards?

I was nearly panicked and out of breath when I reached one of the balconies on the third floor. It overlooks a wide stone patio below and I recalled many times when I'd stood up there, eyes skyward, taking in the flights of birds and the drifts of clouds. It was there I'd first conceived the notion of learning to fly an airplane and there I'd decided to serve my nation as a pilot. Today, however, my focus was not on the ascent but on the fall. A fall indeed, from grace, from society, from righteousness. Not only for myself, but for someone else. How could I propose something so vile? I was certain to be rejected, either by one person or by all others. I clung to the railing and desperation clung to me. I had lifted one foot to the top of the railing when movement to my right caught my eye. There stood my sister Hyacinth, all in disarray. Her hair was only half done up, her dress torn in places, and her shoes soiled. She stared over the railing at some point midway between the balcony and the patio below. Her face was slack, but her voice shot between her lips like an arrow. "Lowell didn't do that," she said. "I didn't do that. Even when we most wanted to."

I brought my foot back alongside its mate and Hyacinth passed back into the house without acknowledging me further. I remained on the balcony past sundown and past supper, then returned to the apartment to find Beck grinning happily outside our locked door. The roiling in my stomach finally impinged upon my attention and, like a sailor advancing toward the bow of his ship while it crashes up and over each successive wave, I rose up the stairs to press my face against my boon companion's belly. It was giving and warm.

Soon I will lay my head there again, look into his trusting face, and, when darkness has hidden us from the sight of God, I will, with my hands and body, save the Prouwders and damn Beck's soul.

3/31/19

Tom and me woke to a cry for help.

HEARTH

3/31/19

Tom and me woke to a cry for help. We were tangled up in our sheets and each other's limbs, but the screams were so piercing we jumped out of bed and into our clothes like we were under attack by a U-Boat! That's how it seemed to me anyhow. Maybe Tom thought we were being strafed by a German fucker. We ran out of our rooms chasing the sounds. They were so loud I expected to find the woman doing the screaming around every corner, but Tom was leading the way and didn't stop running and dodging relatives or servants until we came to the little dining room where his mom, uncle, and grandma were eating breakfast. They all looked up at the ruckus Tom and me were making, but none of them was in any trouble and nobody was screaming either. I didn't know what to make of that and just kind of stood there with my mouth hanging open.

"Thomas is home!" His grandma clapped her hands together. "Oh, what a blessed surprise!"

"He's been home two days, Mother," Mrs. Prowder-Caul patted her on the arm. "Thomas, what's the matter?"

Tom hesitated. "We heard something, but I've lost it now."

Bell the cook rushed in behind us. "Lord! What a wailing! Louis, you hear it?"

Louis pointed sort of scared at the fireplace. What he meant by that I had no idea, but Tom and me went over to have a look anyway. It was just an unlit fireplace as far as I could tell except that the back of it looked blurry, like it was a whole lot farther away than the parts Tom and me had our hands on.

His grandma piped up again. "Maude, has Thomas been chosen? Does he hear the call?"

Mrs. P-C wrung her hands, but there was hope in her voice. "Do you, Thomas?"

Bell limped over and took hold of his arm. "Well, if you hear something, shake a leg or get out of the way and Louis and I will go, but you can't just stand there when someone needs help!"

None of this made any sense to me, but just then another scream came right out of the fireplace and whoever it was sounded worse off than before. Agonized, if you know what I mean. I asked Tom what we were going to do. He looked around at everybody, then said, "Follow me!" There wasn't anywhere to follow him, of course, but we ducked low under the mantle, stepped over the logs, and then it seemed we were in a long dark tunnel. Tom took my hand, which was a good thing because I couldn't see anything at all. I could hear him shuffling along in front of me and there was a kind of tight echo from our footsteps, but that was all. I asked him if he saw anything. "Yes. Up ahead. Get ready!"

Get ready for what, I wondered, but there wasn't time to get an answer because another moment after that we came out of the tunnel into the flames of hell itself!

Beck and I emerged from the darkness into a small kitchen being consumed by fire. He swore like only a sailor can and further startled the already terrified woman battling the blaze. She beat at the flames with her apron, serving only to spread them. They'd already leapt from a skillet on the stove to the cupboards and the ceiling above. There was no faucet or water pail in sight, so I began to look for a way outdoors in hopes of finding a pump, but just as I'd taken a few steps away, the woman lifted the lid off a large metal canister and prepared to throw its entire contents onto the fire. I tried to interfere, but I acted too slowly. Some two pounds of flour exploded in the blaze and ignited the curtains, the woman's apron, and her dress. All three of us were knocked backwards by the blast, but the woman got the brunt of it and fell to the floor. Beck reacted more quickly than I and tamped out the flames on her clothing. I scooped her up and yelled, "This way!"

We ran out of the kitchen and through the parlor, which were the home's only two rooms on this level. We gained the front door, crossed a small porch, and reached the street beyond. Neighbors and passersby had just begun to gather in reaction to the smoke pouring from the back of the house. Our appearance set them into fervent action. With cries and much alarm, they drew us away from the blaze. Someone took the woman from my arms and laid her down on the walkway across the street while others began running for water. A stout matron looked over our shoulders and began screaming about the woman's children. She pointed in horror at the home's second floor window and I whirled about to see two terror-stricken faces behind the pane of glass they were beating on and trying to open. I dashed back through the front door and found the staircase, then took the steps two at a time until I was in the front bedroom. The children at the window shrieked and an infant standing in his crib wailed mightily between coughing fits. Beck dashed into the room with flames at his back and shut the door against them. He said there was no escape in that direction and we both set to work on the window. It would not budge.

Beck picked up the room's only chair and made quick work of the glass. The influx of air fed the flames behind the door and we began to choke in the thick gray smoke. I threw the children's mattress over the sill and climbed out onto the roof of the porch. Each child that Beck passed to me was then taken into the arms of people on the ground. A claxon sounded from not far off and soon a fire engine raced into view. I stuck out my hand and helped Beck out of the house. Right behind him the entire home was beset by flame. We jumped to safety, but Beck had the wind knocked out of him and I landed with a bad twist to my ankle. Neighbors carried us out of the way. Amid the tumult the children's mother screamed even more loudly at seeing them rescued than she had at the first sign of their peril. Firefighters dashed to and fro. A haphazard bucket brigade was formed. The house was a certain loss, but quick action could yet save those on either side and that is what the crowd focused on.

An hour later someone had wrapped my ankle up tightly in makeshift bandages and Beck was breathing normally again. We wiped soot off our faces, drank the glasses of water given us, and received back pats of thanks from many in the crowd.

We stood up when we could and withdrew down the street to take in our surroundings: small wooden houses, here and there a tiny yard, horses, dogs, a few automobiles. There was the stench of burnt wood everywhere, but otherwise it was a modest, pleasant, and utterly unfamiliar road.

"Tom," Beck asked, "where in hell are we?"

I reckon you could say I've told some whoppers in my life. One time I was supposed to write an essay on Ben Franklin for Miss Barnes. When it came time to give it to her, I told her my brother Clem had thrown it into the oven that morning, but that wasn't true at all. I just hadn't written the thing because I was too lazy, but she'd had Clem in class and knew he was an ornery cuss so she believed me. Besides that, I can look pretty innocent when I want to. There's no way, though, I could ever get Miss Barnes to believe I walked into a fireplace in Pittsburgh and walked out into a house on fire in Chicago!

When Tom and me had gotten everybody out of the house, we seen we were on a street neither of us knew. It was flat land all around so it didn't look like Pittsburgh at all. We wandered to the nearest big intersection, which was South State Street. I wasn't familiar with it, but Tom stopped a fellow and asked him which way Lake Michigan was. He looked at us kind of queer and pointed due east so I guess that cinched it. Tom didn't seem all that shook up and when I asked him what was going on, he said, "This is the work." I asked him did he mean the charity work his family was waiting on someone to do and he said yes, that me and him had been "chosen" to do it. Right then and there I objected and said nobody asked *me* if I wanted to do work of any kind and what were my wages going to be if I did say yes to it? He looked like he had never thought about wages before in his life, which I suppose he hadn't, on account of who his family is. I don't know all that much about the Prouwders, but they're up there with the Vanderbilts and Henry Ford, that's for sure. It doesn't seem like they're tied to oil or railroads or automobiles, exactly, but they've got more money than everybody in Greene County put together, I figure, and here I am in the thick of them!

Speaking of money, it turned out me and Tom didn't have a penny on us. I certainly hadn't reckoned on a trip to Chicago when I pulled on my skivvies this morning and Tom hadn't either. "First order of business," he said, "is to wire home for funds." We set off toward downtown, asking people along the way where the nearest Western Union office was until we found someone who actually knew. People were pretty friendly, but they had an accent as flat as their land. It helped, I guess, that Tom was dressed pretty swanky even if he wasn't wearing all the fancy clothes he sometimes does. I was in my uniform, of course, and maybe that helped too, but I got to buy me some city clothes if we ever get back to Pittsburgh. Tom says this "rescue work" might happen every day. I sure don't want to go through another fireplace without at least five dollars in my pocket!

We got to the Western Union office only to find out that we *needed* money to *wire for* money. Wasn't that a pretty pickle to be in! Tom looked flustered and didn't know what to do except say again and again that he was a Prouwder, but the guy behind the counter said he didn't give a hang how proud Tom was, he still needed to pay upfront for his telegram. I took a different tack and looked the guy over. He seemed to be all alone there, trying to work the counter and the telegraph at the same time, so I said to him why don't he let me help him out with his workload in exchange for sending off our telegram and he asked me could I handle the number of messages they get and I said even if some of them came from a German sub I'd be quick as hell with them. We haggled over how much time I'd have to give him for the cost of one telegram and settled on one hour, which I think was robbery on his part, but he wouldn't budge below that, so I stole two pens and this pad of paper I'm writing on to even things out. The fellow said our money ($75.00) might come today, but most likely it wouldn't get there until tomorrow, so that left Tom and me with the whole rest of the day and the night to get through, still without a penny on us!

Beck proved himself indispensable to our efforts to secure funds for the trip back to Pittsburgh, but our more pressing needs, food and shelter, remained. We departed the Western Union office and strolled down to the shore of Lake Michigan. What a vast and thrilling inland sea! And so perfectly positioned not *under my feet!*

Chicago itself throbs like an overworked biceps, pushing the produce of the plains and Pacific eastward for consumption, then hauling heavier industrial goods over the waves to the farmer. I wanted a western journey for us and I got it, but I'd rather have been better prepared. Not even a pawn shop was of use as neither of us wore a single article of clothing we could do without, let alone a piece of jewelry. In future, Beck and I must each wear a gold ring against the need for cash in some far off place. I cannot fathom how he has so readily accepted our being transported by unknown means across a distance of four hundred miles. Perhaps the uneducated, being raised more with fairytales than with scientific treatises, simply expect fantastic occurrences and welcome them when encountered, even if they've picked up a copy of "On the Origin of Species" along the way. I myself, although accustomed to stories of other people's trips through closets, cupboards, and coal chutes, am amazed by the reality.

There was nothing for us to do but to seek out charity and this we found at the Salvation Army. These good soldiers of Christianity run a shelter where Beck and I finally broke our fast, washed up, and, many hours later, acquired rude cots to sleep in. There was a slight misunderstanding while we were having our shower bath in that an especially pious attendant objected to our scrubbing each other's backs. He reprimanded us and the lieutenant in charge saw to it that we slept as far apart as possible. Nevertheless, I silently promised this worthy organization a donation commensurate with the aid provided us.

Beck had rudimentary questions about The Work: wages were his chief concern (I deferred to my mother regarding those), but hours, duties, job title, and pension also came up for discussion. When we return to Prouwder House, I shall have to see that he doesn't start a unionizing effort among the servants!

4/1/19

Our money was there at the Western Union office first thing this morning. I say "our" money because, even though it came from Tom's mom, he gave me half of it. That's the kind of guy he is and none is better in my book. The fellow at the office tried to offer me a job there. I don't want to be four hundred miles away from Tom now, but maybe I'll look into telegraph work when we get back to Pittsburgh. Tom couldn't tell me much about this rescue work his family does as far as wages and pension go. I guess it's Mrs. P-C that handles all the money in the family. I'll have to ask her about it when we get back. I don't much like the idea of working for her, but that's better than Tom being my boss.

We had a lot of time to kill before our train, so we bought *The Chicago Tribune* and looked for ideas of what to do. There was a tiny article about the house fire we were at, mother and three children rescued, home a total loss, and so forth, but no mention of us. Oh well. I guess Tom and I are a two-person Salvation Army, but not as famous as the one that gave us food and lodging. I'm grateful to them, but they watched us like hawks last night. Well, tonight Tom and I are in a private sleeping compartment on the train, so I think we'll get to do whatever we want!

Mother's assistance arrived right on time this morning, $100, which is more than I requested. Beck and I took the opportunity to have a splendid lunch of chicken pot pie at The Walnut Room, which is located inside the Macy's department store on the seventh floor. Once more, patriotism (and a tip to the maître d') helped get us seated even though we were underdressed. I don't see much remedy for that in future rescues. We can't very well bring a change of clothes with us, although it occurs to me two knapsacks of necessities would indeed be *manageable. Rope, cash, bandages, a compass, a knife, perhaps my Lebel, all would be useful items to have on hand in an emergency. I shall have to seek advice on further contents from Belle and Uncle Louis.*

After lunch we visited the Art Institute of Chicago and saw a marvelous exhibition of Japanese prints from the collection of Clarence Buckingham. Courtesans, samurai, and actors mostly, along with hawks, cranes, and frogs. Beck asked me what I thought of every piece and seemed to commit my opinions to memory. Perhaps he'll regurgitate them as his own some day without realizing it. He bore me a look of adoration for much of the day and in the cinema this evening, while we were watching several Harold Lloyd pictures, including "Next Aisle Over", I actually had to pull my knee and hand away because he kept attempting contact even though we were surrounded by the public. He and I shall have to discuss this when we have completed our journal entries. He must be made to see our one night of indiscretion was a necessary evil so that we could take on The Work. He was, I realize, very enthusiastic about our intimacies, but I doubt he'll have any trouble putting that experience behind him, as I have done. Indeed, he is sure to welcome the nobility of our current undertaking, hazardous as it is, and relegate our physical friendship to the attic of his memory!

4/2/19

God damn Tom Caul! God <u>damn</u> him! I'm shakin' so hard I can hardly hold this pen. If I don't keep myself under control I'm goin' to bust up every stick of furniture in this lousy YMCA and punch my hand through every window too! And if I bleed to death from the cuts, so be it. That won't be the worst hurt I ever had in this cussed life. You think you know a guy pretty good, real good even, and then come to find out, you don't know him at all. He's just been playin' some April fool's joke on you the whole time.

I want to write down everything Tom and me done the other night so's anybody who ever finds this journal will see I had good cause to think we was more than just pals, only maybe I don't want to cause him shame. I got to remember he grew up rich in a famous family so that's a lot of pressure on a fella. Even a nobody like me knows it's hard to be one way if your family says you have to be another way and your brothers punch you to toughen you up until you feel like you're just an old leather feed bag.

On the other hand, it wasn't just me havin' fun that night. Plenty's the times Tom kissed me just as hard as I kissed him and plenty of other things happened too so you could say there's not one scrap of his body that I didn't visit that night and he did the same to me. But last night when we had done our writin' and got undressed I tried to get alongside him in his bunk and he pushed me away until I had fallen on the floor! Then he goes on to explain how we can't have none of that anymore and it was all just so's we could do these rescues, do I understand? I told him I goddamned well did *not* understand and what kind of a trick was he tryin' to pull on me anyhow?

After that he said a bunch of crazy things about how others who done this work slept together and somehow that made everything possible: hearin' people yell for help, goin' through fireplaces, and savin' them and then he said a lot about salvation and damnation, but I pretty much quit listenin' after that because I was so heartsick. I tell you, I couldn't have felt more wretched if I'd thrown myself under the wheels of the train. Tom went on, but I just picked myself up and laid down on my own bunk. He wanted to make things right between us, he said. I told him to shut up or I'd knock his teeth in. I shouldn't have said that, but in the morning it come to worse because as soon as we pulled into Pittsburgh I got up to leave and he got up too and said more crazy stuff about nobility and sacrifice. I just wanted to get away, but he grabbed hold of my arm like he was goin' to make me listen to him the way we had to listen to a sermon at the Salvation Army. I seen red like I've done before and shoved him clear across the compartment until he fell back on his bunk and hit his head on the wall and I left as fast as I could.

Now, like I said, I'm at the Y. I used some of the $50 Tom give me to get a room here. I've just been stewin' all day today, but tomorrow I'll have to get on with it and find work. I'm goin' to work hard and save as much money as I can, maybe get into a boarding house and then an apartment or even my own small house where I can be just who I am even if I'm never as good as Tom Caul. I got to quit writin' now because otherwise these pages are goin' to get blurry and smeared.

Wednesday, the 2nd of April

I returned to Prouwder House alone, to the great dismay of my mother. Some relatives had packed up and left while Beck and I were gone, but Mother convinced most of them to remain until the convocation's success could be verified. All clamored for word and she was obliged to tell them I and my companion had indeed been chosen, but that "Mr. Beck" had opted not to stay and do The Work. This led to recriminations and accusations that Mother had mishandled the entire convocation. Tempers grew short. I stepped in and pledged myself to the fulfillment of our family's duty. This settled most of them down, but now I shall have to carry on by myself. I don't think I will bear this burden very long, however: The Work will likely make "quick work" of me. That itself is of little concern, but I admit it vexes me to think I shall someday disappear through some door or passageway of Prouwder House and simply never return. No one will know where I went, whom I was meant to rescue, or what became of me. Even Lowell's fate there on the border with Mexico was at last revealed to us.

Beck's absence is painful not just because he would have been a great help in The Work. I must confess I had gotten quite used to his companionship and I now regret that I am here in "our" apartment alone, as if in solitary confinement. I am indeed a prisoner here even though rescues may take me all over the world. Today, for example, I was summoned to the woods around Prouwder House by cries for help and soon found myself back in the "tunnel" Beck and I traversed previously. At its far end the terrain, the temperature, and even the position of the sun were different. I was in some vast forest of redwoods and soon came upon a rather elderly couple in distress. They had been hiking when the man fell, rolled downhill, and became pinned by a large branch which neither he nor his wife could budge. It was a simple enough matter for me to lift the branch and free the man, but his knee was quite "banged up". I helped him limp up an incline to a rough road, with his wife following close behind. Not long thereafter came a logging wagon, which we flagged down. The team of lumberjacks was only too happy to take the exhausted pair with them into the town of Scotia. It was a fortunate outcome, indeed, as a night or two exposed to the elements could have done them in. They begged me to come along with them, but I declined and assured them I was well-suited to returning where I had come from. We wished each other well and parted.

Before my mission Uncle Louis had disclosed to me a vital piece of information which Beck and I did not know when we entered the fireplace in the breakfast room two days ago: rescuers can return to Prouwder House by means of the same "tunnel" they used to leave the mansion. Had Beck and I merely retraced our steps through the fire-wrecked house in Chicago, all would have been well. There would have been no need for Western Union, the Salvation Army, nor the long and disastrous train ride home. These are the pranks of providence.

I lie now on "my" side of this bed. I lie in another way as well: I desire Beck. His warm breath, the pliancy of his lips, the weight of his body on mine, all of it. It was no sacrifice to join with him but rather a "consummation devoutly to be wished". I am damned and have not now even my sin to comfort me.

It's raining. This apartment felt free when Beck was here, as if we soared above the rest of the house and all the world beyond it. Now it only feels exposed and desolate.

If I ever see Beck again I shall kiss him brazenly and admit I love him.

4/3/19

It's after midnight now so I think my date is right though I can't be sure I even wrote it right since the only light I'm writin' by is the one hangin' here under the "poor coacher" at Prouwder House. "Poor" and "miserable" are the right words. It's raining hard and I'm only barely out of reach of the drops. I'm crouchin' down beside the stone staircase Tom and me walked up together the first time I came to this mansion. I didn't right earlier about somethin' I should have because I was ashamed of it, but this is it: yesterday late afternoon I was in my room at the Y and started hearing calls for help. They was very far off. I went out of my room followin' them, first down the stairs and then clear out onto the street. They didn't seem any closer, but I could still hear them. I went as far as the intersection and then stopped. I knew somehow they was comin' from Tom's place and I just didn't want to go there. I thought he was probably sore with me for knockin' him down and maybe he'd given up on me helpin' him save people. I figured he'd told his mom and other relatives I wasn't good or noble enough to do their charity work and maybe they wouldn't even let me in the door if I did show up there.

I slumped on back to my room and laid down and even put the pillow over my head, but I could still hear them. It sounded like an old woman, not exactly in pain or panicked, but real worried and losin' hope with each yell. And me, skunk that I am, just ignored her. She went on for awhile, then stopped. It should've been a relief, but I knew they stopped because Tom had gone to help her and who knew what danger he was in now? I was even more miserable then than I am now. Earlier I walked far enough away from the house to see the light on up in Tom's apartment. He was pry writin', tellin' his journal what all he'd done that day, where he'd gone, and who he'd saved. Those Salvation Army folks could learn a thing or two from him about noble sacrifice. He didn't even want me the way I wanted him, but he went ahead and laid with me that one night so he could go save who ever needed him. I'm a turd on a skunk's butt for leavin' him to do all this work by himself! I wonder what he wrote about me, though I might burn with shame if I read it.

Well, not next time! I don't care if I have to crouch out here all night, then scamper off into the woods to hide come daylight. Next time I hear a call for help I'm goin' to march right on into this house and walk through a fireplace, even one that's lit, if that's where Tom leads me. I just hope we're never up nowhere high like that hotel in Philly. That place scared the by-Jesus out of me!

GYMNASIUM

4/4/19

Damned if what I least wanted to happen picked today to happen! But if I get ahead of myself I'll forget everything else, like how yesterday ~~me and~~ Tom and I made up and did some hugging and kissing in the woods around the mansion and then climbed up a tree in Sweden to rescue a little tyke who'd gotten his foot caught in one crook of the branches and then carried him back to the farm house where his "mor" and "far" hadn't even noticed he was missing from their brood yet! After some ale, bread, and cheese with them, Tom and I did some more kissing and hugging and fooling around in the forest before we came back to Prouwder House and he told all his relatives they could go on home because the convocation was "well and truly concluded".

We had the rest of the day and all of the night together alone and I think it was about the finest time of my life, but today after breakfast it got rough again. Not rough like fighting a fire or fighting each other, but rough like we had to talk to his mom and uncle Louis about my "position" here on the estate. We all met in

Mrs. Prouwder-Caul's study, ~~her~~ she at her desk, Louis on a "setty", Tom and I on chairs with no arms. Mrs. P-C allowed as how she was very grateful I had returned to the mansion and committed myself to the work. It was a "noble sacrifice" and a "Christ-like act of charity". She also said Prouwder House offered competitive wages to its servants and that I should choose a job in keeping with my interests and abilities. I tell you, I didn't rightly know what she was talking about. Wasn't I already doing the work they all found so noble and important?

"Thomas has told me something of your family's farm," she said. "Perhaps you'd be interested in becoming an assistant to our gardener, Marks, or filling a vacancy in our stable?" I knew this was that fellow Crown who'd been strung up while out on a rescue in Mississippi, only she didn't call him by name or say anything about *his* sacrifice. That didn't set well with me. The way I saw it, I already had a job going off hither and yon to save people from burning to death or dying up a tree where their mom and dad wouldn't find them until maybe they were already a little blonde skeleton. I looked at Tom, but he was blank-faced and silent. Mrs. P-C pulled a hanky from her sleeve and dabbed all around her mouth like breakfast was repeating on her, then opened up a ledger book on her desk. "What position shall I say you have for the purposes of our budget, Mr. Beck?"

I saw how it was. At Prouwder House you're either family or flunky. Since I couldn't be the first, I had to be the second. There was no column for "Tom's pal" in that ledger. His uncle said, "Perhaps night watchman?" I just shrugged and looked at how dirty my fingernails and uniform were. For a while the grandfather clock was the only noise in the room.

"Well," said Mrs. P-C, "let us pencil that in for the nonce. As for wages, Mr. Beck, we can offer you $115 per month. I expect that will meet your needs since your meals and housing will be provided free of charge for the duration of your employment. Your normal work week shall consist of forty-eight hours Tuesday through Sunday so that our regular night watchman, James, may have the Sabbath off. You'll report to him each evening at ten o'clock if you are on the premises. Time you spend on rescue missions from ten until six in the morning will naturally be deducted from the forty-eight hours you owe us, in increments of thirty minutes. A portion of your salary will be set aside for you to in order to provide a pension in your infirm years and a room here will be available to you so long as you live. As you can see, Prouwder House *is* a competitive employer. We take care of our own."

She shut her ledger and looked around at all of us with a smile of satisfaction that was a lot like how the boss at the slaughterhouse looked whenever my dad brought in a herd of cows or pigs, sort of "I got the better of you, but I gave you enough that my conscience won't pain me none." I shrugged again, but looked up quick when she started screaming. Tom and his uncle sat up sharp as well, only it wasn't really his mom screaming but somebody else, somewhere in the house. Mrs. P-C was startled by Tom and me jumping to our feet. "What is it? Louis, do you hear something?"

Louis squeezed his eyes shut and kind of scrunched

down in his seat, then pointed at the ceiling without lifting his hand from his lap. Tom threw his new knapsack over his shoulder and I did the same with my old duffle bag, then we bolted out of Mrs. P-C's study and headed for the nearest staircase. When we were on the third floor we listened again and Tom led us past servants' quarters and a nursery, plus a classroom and other rooms which had their doors closed. "The gymnasium!" he shouted. I could hardly imagine any house in the world big enough to have a gymnasium in it, but sure enough we came to a big room with lots of long windows, a high ceiling, and every kind of exercise equipment you could think of: barbells, dumbbells, a rowing machine, even a sort of leather horse-like thing for springing onto and off of. Nobody was in there and there wasn't any fireplace either, so I was stumped, but Tom pointed off to the end of the room where a big thick rope was hanging down from the rafters. We heard yelling again, clear as a bell, but there wasn't anybody on the rope at all.

"Climb on and hold tight!" He shimmied up the rope hand over hand and I followed. No sooner had my feet left the floor than everything went pitch black like it had in the fireplace and when I finally could see again, I sure as hell wished I couldn't because Prouwder House was gone and we were sailing through the air a whole lot higher than I ever want to be again. It wasn't just Tom and me on the rope either; some third fella looking every bit as scared as I felt was also there, hanging on between us and hollering to beat the band!

Friday, the 4ᵗʰ of April

The thick slack rope of the gymnasium was suddenly replaced by one thinner and tauter. I wrapped my arms and legs around it as securely as possible, then looked down. Beck had done the same, as had the young, dark-haired man screaming in between us. We were all at least five hundred feet above a generally flat landscape of fields both green and brown, narrow roads, and trees, mostly cypresses and pines, but no forests or rivers. Right below us were villages where farm wagons moved along or stood entirely still as their owners stared and pointed up at us. Children ran to follow us, but fell behind quickly. I saw that we hung from the nose of a steel-gray dirigible marked F 6. In the center of its underbelly was an enclosed cabin through the many front windows of which the airship's captain and crew shouted and gesticulated. Wind and large propellers on either side of the vehicle made it impossible to understand what they were saying, but their distress seemed almost equal to our own. Passengers likewise leaned out of the craft's windows and screamed or tore at their hair.

Beck yelled upwards to ask what we were going to do. He was clearly fearful, but not so deeply as the fellow between us, who seemed totally paralyzed with terror. I surmised he had failed to let go of this rope during the launch of the dirigible and now might not be persuaded to take any action at all until exhaustion inevitably cost him his life. I peered back up to where this mooring line was attached to the hydrogen envelope, but there was no safe retreat at that end. I then caught the attention of the captain and jabbed my thumb toward the ground. He only shook his head and by means of gestures seemed to indicate it would not be possible to land while we three remained suspended there. He then pointed straight ahead and made a jumping or falling motion. I couldn't see any landing area that would be survivable, but the captain then imitated swimming and I guessed a lake or river might lie along our flight path. He pulled his watch out of his vest pocket and then held up eight fingers. I nodded in comprehension.

"Beck, we'll have to jump for it! There's water ahead!"

He shook his head. "Hard as rock!"

"No better choice! How low is safe?" This I had to repeat in order to be understood.

"Six feet, but only IF you can swim!"

I gave Beck a sarcastic look and he thought his answer over more carefully. The man between us followed our discussion without apparently understanding it.

"Thirty feet. No more than fifty!"

I nodded and passed this idea on to the captain, who clutched the sides of his head in dread of bringing his airship that low without intending to land. At last he seemed to acquiesce and gave orders to his crew. We descended slowly but steadily. I studied the landscape and came to the conclusion we were likely on the northern side of the Mediterranean. Vineyards and what appeared to be olive trees passed below. The Captain and all the passengers I could see were as swarthy as our fellow denizen of this rope. He became more animated as we drew closer to the ground. I suspected he had grasped the idea that we were going to jump sometime soon and the prospect definitely did not appeal to him. He shook his head violently and began to jabber in what I eventually surmised was Italian. Two words came through clearly: "non" and "saltare". Our new friend was apparently dead set against jumping!

I calmed him as much as I could and got his name out of him, which was Ludano. He went on, I believe, to tell me about going out to see the launch of the dirigible and the sudden wind that had brought him to his current straits. I asked him about the villages and roads below us and he prattled on for quite a while carefully and then more boldly pointing out this farm or that, apparently giving me his opinion of the quality of wines and olive oils produced in the region, all the while mentioning 'Roma', which was no doubt the city I'd seen in the distance eight minutes before. Unfortunately, when I asked him the name of the lake we were now fast approaching, "Lago Albano", he was reminded of his dangerous predicament and the entirely unacceptable rescue we had in mind for him. He reverted to "non non non" and began to tighten his already weary grip on our rope.

Beck tried to show Ludano how best to fall into the lake. He mimicked as much as possible the need for protecting one's head, bending one's knees, hitting the water feet first, and saturating one's lungs with air before going under the surface. I wasn't at all sure Ludano could swim, which, of course, made our plan all the less likely to succeed!

Soon as I saw we were past the lake shore and all the docks and not liable to hit any unseen sand shoals I started getting ready to jump. It was hard to say exactly how far up we were; maybe forty feet? I hoped it was closer to twenty, but the Captain of the airship was probably none too keen on getting down that low, so it was now or never. I tugged on the Italian fellow's pant leg and he looked down at me, but other than that he was petrified. I couldn't say I disagreed with him, but we'd come there to save him and that was what we were going to do! I shouted up at Tom that the guy wouldn't let go of the rope. Tom saw it as clear as I did, but he didn't seem to know what to do about it either other than wrestle him free of his grip. Below us all kinds of people were scrambling along the shore and some fishermen were rowing hard to keep up with us. "Go!" shouted Tom. I nodded, took the biggest gulp of air I could, and let loose of the rope.

It was only about one second of free fall, but still I hated it. I went deep into the water and the handles of my old duffle bag dang near strangled me while I was also trying not to drown, but I got back up into air and started swimming, which was hard, seeing as I had my whole uniform on, including my shoes. I didn't even notice the rowboat beside me until two guys stuck out their hands to grab me. They leaned away and hauled me aboard. I hoped to be hearing two more big splashes into the lake, but when I finally was oriented again, I saw that the airship had crossed the whole lake, was climbing again, and still had two men clinging by a rope to its nose!

Ludano had not been able to let go of the rope. He clung to it in terror without realizing he might as well have looped it around his neck in a noose for all the good it was going to do him now. We rose and cleared copses of pines on the southern shore of the lake, then passed over other roads and farmhouses. The wind seemed to have picked up significantly, pushing the airship along and making our slender rope sway precariously. I realized it might be impossible for the airship to move against the wind at this point. Its propellers were outmatched by the size of the balloon they guided. How I missed my old Spad VII! In it I could have swooped and dived all around this ponderous gray whale of the sky!

Now Ludano moaned and gasped. He also began to slide down the rope. My own hands were cramped and tired; his were no doubt worse, aggravated by the primitive horror of falling. I looked at the Captain. His countenance was grim. By means of gestures, I suggested we come about and head back over Lake Albano, but he pointed ahead instead. Not too distant from us I saw another lake, much smaller than Albano and therefore a much harder target to hit, especially given the winds which seemed determined to push us east of the water. The Captain signaled two minutes and put his hands together in supplication. Even if there was another lake beyond this one, neither Ludano nor I would have the strength to hang on until we reached it.

I shouted down at my companion, but my words did not pierce the stupor his fear had put him in. I worried he might give up all hope of salvation and suddenly plummet onto the hard-packed earth below us. I would have to act for both of us. I began to recite the Lord's Prayer in Latin and Ludano followed suit. This occupied his attention and let me work my knapsack around in front of me inch by perilous inch. I opened it, then dug as well as I could inside it. Each time I took one hand off the rope I slid down the rough coil. Smears of blood marked my descent. I restarted the Pater Noster each time Ludano came to its end, but his voice grew wearier and more resigned each time. When at last I had what I needed, I saw we were as well situated above the water as we were going to get: higher than we had been over Lake Albano and dreadfully close to the unforgiving shore.

With a final "Amen" I lifted the knife just above my head and cut the rope!

Getting to dry land was a pretty awful time for me, not because the fishing boat ride was rough, but because I got to imagining all the bad places Tom might have ended up jumping or falling. To me it seemed the shore and everything beyond it was covered by rocks and tree stumps and fence posts. That's the way my mind goes sometimes, to the very worst thing possible. I didn't care whether he saved the other guy now or not. In fact, I wanted to slap that guy silly for not letting go when he should have. A crowd of people helped me from the boat onto a dock and an even bigger group met me on land. They were friendly, but just about as wrought up as people can be. They kept checking me for broken legs or arms, found I was all right, but also patted me so hard on the back that they almost broke my spine! They all pointed in the direction the airship had flown and got me into a wagon that took off in pursuit. I figured they were Italians because they all sounded and waved their hands about just like Salvatore, the cook on the *USS Fanning*.

It took us quite a while to get away from the lake. The roads were winding and there were more and more people in this caravan the farther we went. I wasn't sure I wanted to see what they were so eager to show me. I shook bad at the thought that we would come upon Tom's busted body along one of these foreign roads. Somebody threw a blanket over my shoulders, but it wasn't being soaked to the skin that was the problem. When we got high enough I saw there was a second lake beyond the one I'd jumped into and a little spark of hope fixed up in my heart. It still was a torment getting down to the shore though. I nearly leapt over the side to make a run for it when the wagon could barely fit between all the trees, but the crowd held me in place and we pushed on until we saw water and another big crowd waiting beside it.

That was all I could stand. I heaved myself over the side and took off running with the younger ones chasing behind me. They yelled something and the people in front of me did the same. They parted just in time for me to find Tom and the other fellow soaking wet and panting heavily on a bench at the near end of a short dock. I rushed up and took Tom in my arms and he hugged me back just as hard. The fellow we rescued cried out and hopped up on one foot. His other was wrapped up tight in make-shift bandages, but he didn't let that keep him from squeezing the breath out of both of us, kissing us again and again on the cheeks, and making the sign of the cross. Others in the crowd did the same and then glasses of red wine were poured for all three of us plus several of the onlookers. It was a cheery moment and never was I gladder to be alive, but then I saw a problem no train or money gram could solve very easy.

"Tom," I said over the loud chatter of the crowd, "how in heck are we going to get home from here without that rope to climb back onto?"

I pondered Beck's question and peered in the direction of the F6. I managed to ask Ludano what its destination was and received "Napoli" as his answer, so that would be of no help to us. I then asked the name of the lake we sat beside and bystanders supplied "Lago di Nemi". They went on to describe their region and all its wonders, apparently exaggerating the value of some and neglecting the beauty of others because a general row on that topic ensued among the townsfolk. Ludano drank his wine or favored Beck and me with languid looks by turns. He kept one arm around my shoulders, which caused the front of his shirt to part and reveal a silver crucifix hanging amid the dark hair of his chest. I impulsively picked it up. "Ludano, vogliamo pregare. Dov'è una chiesa con un campanile?"

He shrugged, then repeated my question to the crowd. They turned from their argument about sight-seeing to one concerning local churches. Emphatic gestures were made in various directions and soon the throng was divided into two camps as some proposed one place of worship while others favored another. Beck asked me what was up. I took some pleasure in keeping him in the dark and winked at him. Ludano noticed this and asked whether we were 'amici stretti'. "Amici molto stretti", I replied and bussed Beck's cheek, which caused him to blush. Ludano grew quite animated at this and kissed us both again.

In the end we were taken to the Tempio di Santa Maria della Rotonda, an interior hemisphere of gray-green with stained glass, mosaics and, most importantly for my purposes, a bell tower. In short order the priest was told our story and 'miracolo' echoed around the chamber. The Father blessed us three and importuned us to express our gratitude to the Lord and Savior. I assumed a prayerful position while eyeing the exits. Ludano knelt on my left and Beck did the same on my right. The crowd did likewise and we said our prayers. After several benedictions had been given, I made clear to the priest that I wished to see the bell tower as a reminder of our rescue from on high. He quickly consented and a faction of the crowd joined us in climbing the stairs, with occasional explanations of what we were seeing through the windows, until we reached the apex. More sight-seeing followed, with Ludano, although injured, being among the most enthusiastic onlookers. Beck and I moved around the tower, pretending to study the architecture, until we were out of the way and relatively unobserved.

"Well, now what?" Beck asked. "You aren't thinking we'll catch that airship from here on its way back, are you?"

"No," I answered with another wink. "When I say 'go', jump onto the rope leading to the largest of the bells. That one there, see?"

"Sure," he replied, "but shouldn't we be looking for a gymnasium instead?"

"I suspect the locals get all the natural exercise they need, but that will be our secondary plan if this doesn't succeed. Make sure your feet are off the floor. Ready? Go!"

We sprang for it, heard one enormous strike of the clapper as well as several cries of surprise, then found ourselves back in Prouwder House. We dropped to the floor of the gymnasium and stepped well away from the rope.

"Hey!" Beck exclaimed. "It worked!"

"I never doubted it." I checked the condition of my clothes and knapsack. Both were still damp. My pants, shirt, and vest were rumpled. My underclothes were likewise clammy and uncomfortable.

Beck inspected his own attire and surprised me by saying, "Let's go tell your mom we're back."

"Let's shower and change first," I objected.

"No. If I don't do this now, I might never have the gumption to do it again."

Intrigued, I followed him out of the gymnasium.

Despite being wet as a ship rat and twice as tired, I led Tom back to his mother's study. Well, I had to ask him for directions a couple times, but it was me that decided to go there and me that knocked on her door, which had one of those red ribbons on the outside knob. When she told us to come in, she was still sitting at her desk with that same ledger book open in front of her. There was a glass of tea next to that and an adding machine on its own stand beside her. When she saw us, she clasped her hands together and pressed them to her forehead for a moment. I heard her whisper, "Praise ye the Lord for His mercy endureth forever." She asked us where we'd been, then settled back in her chair to hear Tom's tale of the dirigible and our midair rescue. He made it sound almost fun, which it hadn't been in any way *I* could see, but that's the way he told all his war stories back on the *Fanning* too.

"Well, I am much relieved that you returned safely and grateful for your service, especially yours, Beck. Thank you."

She smiled at me so kindly I almost lost the nerve to say what I came there to say, so, just like the damn fool I am, I blurted it all out at once: "That's good 'cause I want $3600 a year and I don't want to be no night watchman 'cause if I'm goin' to be hangin' off of ropes and jumpin' into lakes or bustin' out windows in a house on fire that's all the job I think I should have to do and you can put me down as a 'rescuer' in your ledger if you need to and I want to be paid on the first of each month and besides all that I want people to say 'hello' to me when I pass 'em in the hall and also I want to get an education while I'm livin' here." I sort of pointed at the bookshelves behind her, but my hands were shaking so bad she might have thought I was having a spasm. "That's all. Ma'am."

Mrs. Maude Prouwder-Caul sat back up and gave me just about the cuttingest look I ever did endure, but she didn't say anything. She just frowned real stern, then picked up her pen and wrote in her ledger. From the front of it she filled out a check and handed it over to me. I saw that it was for three hundred dollars and felt almost as frightened as I had when Tom and I first found ourselves in midair over Italy, plus I was so parched I thought I could drink half the lake I'd fallen into!

"Mind your money well, Beck. There will be *no* advances on your pay and your pension is now *entirely* up to you. Understood?"

I nodded and tried not to let my eyes roll right out of my head. Tom took hold of my elbow and began drawing me toward the door. "Thank you, Mother."

Once we were back in the hallway and had closed the door behind us, I showed Tom the check and told him I had never had so much money all at once in my life before.

"You realize that's more than *my* monthly allowance, don't you?" He put his arm around my shoulder. "What are you going to do with it?"

"Some of it I'm going to send to my mom and dad. If I don't come back from one of these rescues, I want them to have a little set by so they can have a funeral for me."

Tom's eyebrows worried up his forehead, but then he smiled. "Well, Lord Beck, I think you should also invest in a new set of clothes. How about we withdraw to our rooms, bathe, have a *lot* more red wine, and then I'll instruct you in the proper use of a measuring tape!"

I allowed as how that sounded like a fine idea and followed close on his heels as we raced to the very tiptop point of good old Prouwder House.

CHAPEL

4/5/19

When the *Fanning* used to hit a storm out on the open ocean, the bow would ride up on the crest of one wave and then fall into the valley of the next. It was sickening when I was a newbie, but after a few crossings I got so I kind of liked it. Here at Prouwder House I'm a newbie again and today I'm sick like I fell all the way from our apartment to the ground outside and then got tossed up to the roof again.

This morning we got up, showered for the second time this week, and then I stayed naked because my uniform was too filthy to put on again. Tom teased me that he would leave me in the altogether the whole day, but then he went and fetched me clothes from his old bedroom. Even his skivvies are finer than my Sunday best. He gave me some B.V.D. knee-length drawers, coat-cut undershirts, plus socks with garters. On top of that he loaned me a pair of dark-green striped trousers with a matching vest, a silk necktie (also green), and a white shirt. All this just for breakfast! His collar cut into my neck bad, but that kept me from slouching as I sometimes do. In the Navy the important thing was to keep your balance and not crack your head open on a bulkhead. In Tom's clothes I thought I looked very presentable. He must have thought so too because he got kind of flushed like he didn't dare make time with a gentleman of my standing even though it was just his good old Zeb underneath that finery.

On the way to breakfast he showed me one of the chutes that go all the way to the laundry room in the basement and we dumped my uniform and farm clothes into it. I guess a servant usually does that for the Prouwders, but Tom won't allow anyone else in our apartment, so we put my things into the laundry chute ourselves. He said Saturday is wash day. When it's all done, a maid will leave it on the staircase up to our place. I figure she'll know whose things those are because nobody else would claim a sailor's uniform and a couple pairs of overalls. There's as much routine to learn here in the mansion as there was on the *Fanning*, but I'll get the hang of it soon enough.

By the time we got to the breakfast room, I was powerful hungry. Tom's grandma was there and when he went over to kiss her cheek she pointed at me and asked him who I was. She hardly seemed to listen to his explanation and hurried to tell him that Mr. Booke was under the weather and sent his regrets. Tom's mom and his three cousins were also there, as well as a woman I didn't know. She turned out to be his Aunt Olivia Prouwder-Doucette. I knew enough to just stand there quiet and respectful while Tom introduced me to her, but then she didn't say anything or put her hand out to me. She just smiled Miss Cheevus over her cup of coffee. She's a far sight prettier than her sister, I'll give her that, but it was awkward for me and it only got worse when Mrs. P-C said, "Beck, servants have their own dining area. Agnes here," she signaled the maid in the corner, "will show you the way." One of the Doucette cousins giggled, but I didn't see which one because my eyes had gone blurry with embarrassment.

Tom objected. He said I was his guest and should eat with them as I had before, but Mrs. P-C only smiled tightly and said, "*Yesterday* he was your guest. *Today* he's our employee." The maid appeared at my side. I looked at Tom, but he was in shock and didn't say anything else, so I followed her out of the room and down the hall.

Saturday, the 5th of April

After Beck had gone, I fell to fiddling with my butter knife. Aunt Olivia continued to smirk behind her coffee cup, then dared to scold me. "Don't pout, Tommy. It spoils your good looks."

The fury her remark caused in me was quickly turned into a resolve to do her great bodily harm at some opportune moment in the future: a beating, a shove down a staircase, a bullet to her brain. Something to tell one and all I will not tolerate such disrespect. I tilted my knife so that I could see her in its reflection and waited until she had noticed. "Good looks are so important to some ladies that they select their husbands on that basis alone without regard to character, intelligence, or fidelity." She scowled, but before she could riposte, Mother entreated us to stop baiting each other as it upset Grandmother. Nothing of the kind was in evidence, but I was famished and ceased fire so that I could serve myself from the tureen of porridge.

Mother went on to say she realized I had been on my own the last three years and was an adult man now, but Prouwder House was not a battlefield. The "one for all and all for one" spirit I'd grown accustomed to in France was ill-suited to the good management of a household as large as this. I might think her unkind to have sent Beck down to the kitchen, but didn't I see he'd be more comfortable there? Leaving him in some "no man's land" between family and staff was the true disservice. "Among the other workers," she continued, "he'll be able to dig in and make a trench for himself."

Olivia accused Mother of reading far too many newspaper accounts of the war. This made her cross, but she held her tongue and busied herself with arranging Grandmother's napkin for maximum utility. Ernestine, Josephine, and Pauline giggled behind their hands, which only flustered Mother more. I hoped Beck was finding his table companions pleasanter than mine.

When we got to the kitchen, Agnes led me to an area where other girls, women, and men sat eating, all in uniforms of one kind or another. Bell stubbed out her cigarette, said good morning to me, then pointed out an empty chair at one table. I guess she'd already heard Mrs. P-C had hired me and knew to expect me in the kitchen from then on. I wish somebody had told *me* that was the plan; they could have saved me a lot of embarrassment. As I sat down, Bell stood up and limped away toward the stove.

There's an awful lot of people at Prouwder House even though most of Tom's relatives have gone back to their own homes. For every family member here it seems like there's at least two servants and now four of them were looking me over as I sat down. I'll try to get their names right, but I sure wish they all had their names stitched on their shirts or something.

To my left was a real big guy with arms, chest, and shoulders like a blacksmith, but he said he was James, the night watchman. He looked a little tired because this was the end of his shift, but his smile was as bright inside his long black beard as his eyes were bright blue above it and he shook my hand real friendly. Next to him was Roberts, the butler. His beard was shorter and sort of red-brown. He had an English accent and a trim build. The next fellow was Charles, the chauffeur. He was the thinnest of them all and looked more like he ran with the Prouwders' horses than with their automobiles. He had hair as dark as James, but no beard. That left the oldest of them, Marks, the gardener. He didn't seem to have been listening to what the others said and I don't think he realized he didn't know me yet, but when Roberts got his attention, he introduced himself and shook my hand. He was very stiff all through his back and shoulders and pretty bent over too. I guess that comes from digging around plants so much, but my mom has always kept a garden and she's as straight-backed as a chair.

I guess I was lost in my thoughts too much because Charles the chauffeur said, "Well, do *you* have a name or should we just call you Greensuit?" James, Roberts, and Marks all looked on as I tried to come up with my answer. It seemed like there was some reason all their names ended in 's', but I couldn't piece it together.

"Becks," I said. "Is that how it's done here?"

"It's *your* name," Roberts said, "even if that *isn't* your suit."

I told him Tom lent it to me, which caused all of them to raise their eyebrows. "Tom lent it to him," Charles repeated to Roberts and then, for good measure, to James. He kept his face dead straight, but I knew he was making fun of me. If we was in the Navy, I'd have knocked his block off, but I'm trying to be more civilized here, like Tom is. James asked me what my job was and Charles said I was obviously Tom's clothes model. James told him to lay off, but I still had to come up with an answer. "Rescuer", I guessed, and then I told them how Tom and I had gone through the hearth to a house fire in Chicago a couple days before and later we climbed a tree in Sweden, plus there'd been a guy hanging from a dirigible in Italy. They all looked confused.

"Oh, that's enough of that," Bell broke in. She put a cup of coffee and a plate of waffles in front of me. "Yinz quit digging into Prouwder House business."

I guess she's got more authority in the mansion than you'd expect a cook to have because right away all the men at my table shut their yaps and got busy finishing off their breakfasts. Maybe she's important because she used to do the work that Tom and I do now. I got to admit I wouldn't mind having that kind of pull myself! With a snap of her fingers she dismissed all the maids and other cooks. They hustled around to clear off their tables and get their dishes washed. They were making a lot of noise, it seemed to me. It took me a while to realize it wasn't just the clatter of plates and silverware I was hearing, but also a whole bunch of voices yelling not *in* the house, but *through* the house. Bell stood still and listened as well, wiping her hands on her apron as she tried to make out where the sound was coming from.

"Outside. Towards the stable, I think." She looked at me and put her fists on her waist. "Well? What are you waiting for? Take as much as you can eat while running and get going!"

I did as I was told and ran out the kitchen door into the yard. In a minute or so I met Tom at the door to a stone storage building that ran all along the backside of the stable. He asked if I was ready and I said I was. We pulled our knapsacks on tighter, took deep breaths, and opened the door to find a whole troop of soldiers aiming their rifles at us!

Shouting and shoving were all I could discern of the room at first. Riflemen in light blue greatcoats, caps, and leggings forced Beck and me against one plaster wall and then down onto the bare wooden floor below a multi-paneled window. We found ourselves in one corner of a chamber perhaps thirty feet in length by twenty feet in width containing a few crates and wooden chairs. About three dozen civilian men and boys were likewise being pushed into place and while I assessed the situation, one youth was knocked to the floor between me and Beck, who cushioned most of the boy's fall. He was several years younger than we, perhaps sixteen or seventeen, and appeared to be in shock. The soldiers' shouts abated, as did the cries of alarm coming from their captives. Armed men in uniform equaled unarmed men in suits. I listened to what each group was saying. The soldiers, I determined, were probably Poles, due both to the nasal and fricative-heavy language they spoke as well as the distinctively asymmetrical caps they wore. The civilians apparently spoke some dialect of German. Perhaps we were in German territory that had been ceded to the newly reformed nation of Poland. I decided to find out more from the youth between Beck and me. "Was ist dein Name?"

He had some trouble turning his attention away from the scene developing around us, but after I had repeated my question, he said, "Abraham Bankausky."

I pointed out the window behind us. "Wo sind wir, Abraham? Ist das Warschau?"

He gave me a queer look. "Pinsk." I recalled reading in the newspapers that the Polish Army had invaded White Russia and taken parts of it over. Polish troops faced resistance from Bolshevik insurgents supported by Soviet Russia and Soviet Ukraine. Many borders in Europe were shifting in the wake of the Great War, of course. I relayed what I'd learned to Beck sotto voce. *He asked whom we were supposed to rescue here and I had to admit I didn't know.*

A spokesman for the captives rose cautiously at the other end of the room. He was somewhere in his forties, dark-haired, stout, and mustachioed. He first addressed the two riflemen nearest him, then engaged an officer of high rank who drew near. I couldn't hear everything they said and there were strong accents to contend with. I soon realized the spokesman was using Yiddish, which the Polish officer understood with even greater difficulty than I. Both parties mentioned America, but "Bolshevik" came up as well. The Polish officer was, in quick succession, engaged, dismissive, and then aggressive. He grew louder and louder while the spokesman tried harder and harder to calm him down. The officer, a solid man of perhaps thirty with blonde hair and a strong jaw, gestured for the spokesman to sit down, then ordered him to sit down. Without warning, one of the two riflemen struck the spokesman in the head with his rifle. He was stunned by the blow and fell to the floor, whereupon he received several kicks from each rifleman. There was an outcry from the other Jews. The boys among them, some clearly still in elementary school, wailed in shock. Abraham clutched Beck's arm. I wiped my hand across my mouth and chin, trying to come up with some sort of plan to rescue us.

The officer began inspecting one crate labeled USA. I asked Abraham what was in it. He told me it was American aid. Town elders were meeting to decide how to distribute it when the Polish soldiers rushed the building. This gave me at least the first step of a rescue plan. I rose and brought Beck to his feet as well. We should probably not have moved so suddenly for we startled the soldiers closest to us. They quickly surrounded us and pinned us to the wall. This got the officer's attention. He left off his inspection of the crate and approached us. Once he had taken in the quality of our clothing and some dissimilarities of appearance which set us apart from the other captives, he asked who we were. I introduced myself and Beck, (who, I maintained, was my cousin and assistant), purposefully playing up flaws in my pronunciation of German to reinforce the impression that we were indeed Americans. By the way the officer frowned and focused on my mouth, I suspected his command of the language was nevertheless inferior to mine. I also thought he might be put into a better mood if we abandoned the language of our common enemy in the war just concluded.

"Parlez-vous français?"

He nodded curtly and told me he was Major Aleksander Narbut- Łuczyński. I complimented his facility with the language and observed he must have spent many years in a francophone country to have achieved such fluency. He acknowledged having lived and studied in Belgium. I explained that I myself had been a fighter pilot for first the French and then the American air force. "Why are you here?" he wanted to know. I smiled as broadly as possible and indicated we were present to oversee the distribution of foodstuffs, et cetera. "Papers," he demanded. These I could not provide, of course, and my attempts to explain their absence failed. The major noticed the knapsacks Beck and I wore, then ordered them searched. Two soldiers tore them from our backs with more violence than necessary and opened them up. They contained several items –a coil of rope, a Bowie knife, a compass, matches, bandages, a small telescope, and my Lebel pistol– which were inconsistent with the humanitarian mission I'd claimed to be on.

"You are Bolshevik insurgents in league with these Jews," Narbut returned to German. I assured him we were not. He moved about the room, asking the others whether they knew us and, naturally, they were quick to disavow any acquaintance with us. Unfortunately, this only served to confirm to him that we were in secret collusion with the resistance. He accused us all of firing on Polish soldiers from the windows of this very building. No protestations to the contrary swayed him from his conviction, and then, from ours. He returned to our end of the room, but addressed all his captives. "I find you guilty of conspiracy to murder members of the Polish armed forces and sentence you all to immediate death by firing squad!"

I never learned French in school, but there was no mistaking what the major had said in German. I hoped we would all rush the soldiers and make a decent fair fight of it, but there was a lot of boys among us and the men there were probably their dads or brothers and didn't want them getting hurt. I looked at Abraham. His dark hair was slicked back and that made his ears stick out like the handles on a jug of moonshine. His eyes were dark too, but his skin was pale and his nose, thin and sharp, pointed down like an arrow toward his mouth and chin. He must have known everyone there, but he stuck between Tom and me. I hoped Tom could get us all out of this fix.

Beck and Abraham looked on as I began to plead with Major Narbut. I'd failed to convince him we were innocent of wrongdoing, but perhaps I could negotiate some outcome far short of a mass execution.

"Surely, monsieur le commandant, you cannot think these boys," I indicated Abraham and some of the other lads in the room, "are capable of killing strong Polish soldiers. These children can barely do up their trousers after taking a piss. You are no doubt a father yourself and know that a son will follow along, no matter what business his father is engaged in. Let these short pants go!"

The man considered my words and seemed moved by them initially, but, already a major, his ambition overcame his capacity for mercy. "No! Today's rock thrower is tomorrow's bomb thrower. I do not want my own son to die later at the hands of an enemy I neglected to eliminate now."

I laid my hand on the center of the man's chest in hopes of reaching his heart, but I was immediately struck by the end of one soldier's rifle. Thereafter I kept my hands in the air while pressing my case further. "You have seen through me, Commandant: I and my colleague have come to Pinsk to foment Bolshevism. It was our hope to stir up resistance to the Polish occupation, but you caught us too readily. These locals have told the truth: they do not know us because we only just arrived. Our mission has failed. Please, carry out your rightful judgment on us alone and let these others go."

Narbut drew nearer. "Many of my men have already been slaughtered. You are no wolf among the sheep. The lesson I wish to teach this town requires all their deaths."

I interlaced my fingers before him and lowered my voice. "You are a wise and perceptive man, clearly well-educated, and experienced in the ways of the world, whereas these Jews live in a place more outhouse than town." I had his attention; he regarded the captives with disdain. "You've heard of my family, yes? Then you know we have millions of dollars. Tens of millions. Forget this rabble. Having contacted my father, my cousin and I will gladly sit in your custody until the sum you set for our release is brought to you. A farm in Poland? Yours. A villa in France? At your disposal. Even a penthouse in London or New York! All that can be yours as well as glorious acclaim for the mercy you show here today."

I thought I had him, but somewhere outside two shots were fired and all reveries of villas and penthouses dissipated, leaving Narbut in this *room, with* this *threat to confront. He shouted something to his men and strode away through the only door.*

Tom was sweaty. Whatever he'd been trying to do hadn't worked and now the riflemen were jerking the muzzles of their weapons into the air and pulling the townsmen onto their feet. We were made to line up single file with our hands on our heads. Abraham fell in behind me and Tom behind him. We stuck as close together as we could. Abraham clung to the back of my vest and pressed his brow into the space between my shoulder blades. I couldn't understand what any of the soldiers were saying. They began pushing captives through the door the officer had gone through and then down a staircase. The first man went down voluntarily, but the second resisted. He was thrown head over heels down the steps. I couldn't see where he landed, but just by the cracks of bone on wood, I knew we had about twenty stairs to go down. I suddenly got the oddest idea that maybe we weren't soldiers and civilians or shooters and targets, but just a crowd of men on our way to a baseball game or a prizefight. I'd had crazy thoughts like that back on the *Fanning* sometimes, especially when we'd sunk that U-boat and took all its survivors on board with us. We were all pressed together back then too. German bodies and American bodies, squeezing past each other in the corridors and breathing the same bubble of air that stank of our sweat and farts.

The air outside the building should have been refreshing, but instead it just brought me back to stinking reality. The way Abraham pulled on the back of my shirt made it tight across my chest and his toes kept catching under my heels. I had to walk on the balls of my feet which was hard to do since the street underneath us was sometimes cobblestone, sometimes mud. People watched us file by, either from the sidewalk or from their houses or sometimes hurrying in fear from one to the other. I kept my eyes mostly on the ground, not just so that I wouldn't fall, but also because I felt too much shame to look the townsfolk in the face, like they knew I'd been sent there special to save everybody but was too stupid even to save myself.

My mind raced ahead of my feet. I tried to anticipate where we were headed, but, not knowing Pinsk at all, that was impossible. I hoped some opportunity to escape would present itself, but nothing obvious came into view. The riflemen hemmed us in on both sides and the street we followed was wide; we couldn't dive out of sight quickly. Even if Beck and I were able to escape, that left Abraham in danger, not to mention all the other men and boys we shuffled along with. I wondered morbidly why we hadn't been shot en masse inside the room we'd just left. I supposed that wouldn't have sent the merciless message Narbut desired. Likely for the same reason he had rejected the insignificant street just outside there. No, he would assuredly want a high-profile location, one the residents would associate with this demonstration of power, most probably the city hall. There'd be no better locale from which to project the change in regime more effectively. I even surmised our blood spatter would not be washed away, all the more deeply to drive home Narbut's point. What loomed over the low buildings and houses, however, was the town's cathedral. Its towers, cupolas, and arches dominated the marketplace beside it and what was perhaps a seminary, equally stolid, stood not far off. I had a wild idea that I could rally my fellow captives into a mad rush of the cathedral doors, under fire from the soldiers, but successful in our plea for asylum. We might be stranded inside for weeks while word got out of the daring young American shielding Jews among the Jesuits. Easter Sunday seemed like a good time for US troops to come and liberate us, at the behest of President Wilson himself, of course. I would ride through Paris in an open motorcar and wave to the populace that cheered and saluted me.

Instead, of course, I tramped along in the muck with other doomed men who saw no way out. We came to a stop at the cathedral while the major conferred with his subordinates on how best to proceed. To shoot us indoors was out of the question, I assumed. Isn't it peculiar that one may retain any sense of decency even after deciding to murder other human beings? The niceties are preserved. One soldier was sent off to our left, another to our right, and each disappeared around his respective corner of the cathedral. The one who'd gone to our right came back first and reported to the major. He pointed in his assigned direction and seemed to pantomime some long flat wall. We were all driven whence he had come and saw indeed that this side of the cathedral offered a vertical expanse devoid of nooks, doors, or ground floor windows and thus well-suited to our execution.

There were prayers among the condemned. The older Jews swayed forward and backward, chanting in Hebrew and comforting the young. Abraham shivered so badly that Beck and I had to grasp him under his arms to keep him from collapsing. He stared in hope and terror, first into Beck's eyes, then into mine. We were at the end of the line of men being shoved against the cathedral's foundation. It was the dirty white of winter, as worn as the dresses and shoes of the onlookers now gathered at a safe distance. Some wailed, some wept, some merely watched. They would undoubtedly go on wailing, weeping, or watching as our bullet-ridden bodies were thrown into a mass grave dug by the soldiers who'd slain us. I touched the wall. Beck, Abraham, and I would fall against it, leave swaths of blood upon it, then crumple dead at its base. No rest for us in the Prouwder estate cemetery, no service in the Prouwder mansion chapel.

I saw one possibility and quickly tightened my grip on

Abraham's arm, then brought his back, buttocks, and heels into contact with the cathedral. "Beck! When I say 'go', push Abraham as hard as you can through this wall!"

"Through the wall?"

I nodded. "Through this wall into the tunnel —don't let go of him- and then out the other end to the outside wall of the Prouwder chapel. Stay focused on that destination. Understood?"

"Why wait, Tom? Why not go right now?"

I eyed the soldiers. They were taking up their positions. "They might separate us if we look like we're trying to escape. Keep one hand on Abraham, one hand on this wall, and wait until I say go. Try to block him from their bullets. Push him ahead of us."

Beck did as I told him. We stood shoulder to shoulder. Abraham could barely see beyond us, but his face contorted in fear and he sobbed onto our sleeves. He gripped our arms to the point of bruising, just as we gripped his. All three of us watched the soldiers as the major issued his orders. They got ready, took aim...

"Go!"

...and fired.

Tom and I pushed through the wall. It gave as easy as the back of the fireplace had. I felt Abraham's arm in my hand and his hand was holding onto my arm just as hard. We ran through the pitch-black tunnel with gunfire and screams chasing after us. I'd only seen the Prouwder chapel from the outside, so that was an easier place to picture than if we'd been trying to show up inside it. Our feet echoed in the darkness and then hit bare ground again, which made me stumble and fall, but I was still glad to have escaped. I saw that I had a hold of Tom's arm and he had a hold of mine, but even when I looked all around us, no one else was there. No Abraham.

Beck and I felt all along the stone wall we'd just traversed, but it was utterly solid now. Solid and rough enough that Beck's fingertips bled from scraping at it and most assuredly solid enough to have broken his knuckles if I hadn't stepped in front of his fists. He howled loudly and bent over sobbing until tears and drool and snot ran onto the ground. When he was spent of immediate grief and could stand up straight, we checked the inside of the chapel, but there also we found no sign of Abraham or of any God that could tell us whom we'd been sent to rescue.

We stayed in our apartment pretty much the rest of the day. I barely got off the green velvet sofa in our big room. That was lazy of me, but I did make a sketch of Abraham that I think turned out ~~good~~ well. It looks like him, at least to me. I'm going to find a picture frame and hang him up so's he can look out a window and see the woods and sunset like Tom and I do. I'm going to hang it just as high as he was tall.

I passed on lunch, but at suppertime Tom went down to the kitchen and brought back two plates of ham and peas and we ate at the little table we got here. I didn't have much appetite, but Tom looked worried so I got some of it down my gullet for his sake. I guess he's smart enough to read my mind sometimes because out of the blue he said, "He isn't suffering now, Beck. He's passed beyond pain and want."

I nodded and then swallowed a bunch of tears down with some ham and a gulp of milk. "Maybe we were just there to see what happened. You think that could be?"

He said he didn't know, but I said if anybody ever asked, I'd sure as hell tell them everything I saw. I'd go all the way back there to Pinsk and find that building and show them the staircase they threw one guy down. Then I'd walk them along the streets we marched along until we got to that cathedral and then I'd say, 'There! Right *there* is where the sons of bitches did it!' I'd point out the bloodstains and maybe even help find the hole those soldiers threw their victims into. I'd get a shovel and help dig until we found the bodies and maybe then, if I still had the strength, I'd touch one of the younger ones and say to everyone who was there, 'Him! That was Abraham Bankausky. Write that down: Abraham Bankausky!' Damned if I wouldn't.

Beck made two requests as we turned in for the night: that I cease calling him 'Beck' and that I assist him in acquiring an entire week's worth of Navy uniforms. I consented readily and by way of explanation he said that he didn't mind my mother addressing him as an employee, but that he shouldn't like it if I did the same.

"*Zeb you shall be then.*"

The uniforms, he explained, were not only a practical choice, but familiar and distinct from everyone else's garb at Prouwder House. The washer woman would never mistake whose clothes they were, nor would other employees think he was "putting on airs". I liked the idea and told him so. I resolved to wear my pilot's uniform as well. Having seen up close the arbitrary groups men will partition themselves into and the deadly consequences of one group's disdain for the other, I am glad Zeb and I have chosen to affirm our solidarity at a time when we might have otherwise let ourselves be riven apart as 'employer' and 'employee'.

Perhaps it was not our mission to rescue Abraham, but his to rescue Zeb and me. Then again, perhaps that is only a sugar coating I have put on this very bitter pill of failure.

PRIVY

4/6/19

Outhouses stink no matter how big the property they're on or how rich the people that use them. The one on the Prouwder estate is a three-holer with three separate doors and a small window into each triangle-shaped cubby. It has a stone foundation, forest-green clapboard siding, and a dark gray shingle roof, just like the mansion. There are even lace curtains in the windows and a small pump with a cake of scented soap just outside. Only the stable men, the grounds-keepers, James the night watchman, and Marks the gardener use it nowadays. Everybody inside the mansion has a proper flush toilet to go to, like Tom and me.

Pretty or not, it stinks, and I wasn't happy about being called there this afternoon, but I figured we'd end up in the Australian outback or maybe Outer Mongolia. That's the way the tunnels have worked here, at least part of the time: fireplace into a place on fire, gym rope to the nose of a dirigible, cathedral to a chapel. Other times it's been a one-for-one swap: tree here for a tree in Sweden or a storage room here for a storage room in Pinsk. Today was one of those, an outhouse for an outhouse. I already described the one we walked into. The one we walked out of was a lot simpler, just as smelly, and stood at the far end of a small garden behind a small house. Right in front of us was a small girl, about four years old, crying hard. She didn't act surprised by us being there all of a sudden. She just wiped her eyes or let her tears fall onto the red-checked dress she was wearing. Her hair was all done up in light brown ringlets. Both her stockings had slid down to her shoes and one of those was untied. Tom took off his leather aviator helmet, crouched beside her, and asked what was wrong. She pointed back into the privy. "My kitty!"

I swore and Tom frowned at me, then put on his best smile and asked the girl to show us. She pointed down the single hole, of course. This made Tom flinch. He covered his nose and mouth with one end of his scarf and listened. Sure enough, little meows were coming up out of the pit in the ground. The shit pit. I walked off to get away from the smell and Tom followed me, leaving the little girl behind. "What do we do?" he asked.

I told him yesterday we couldn't save a *human being*; I sure as hell wasn't going anywhere that awful to save a *cat!* He said if we didn't, maybe the girl would get so desperate that she'd try to go down there herself and be in danger, but I looked at her and even at four years old she looked too smart to do that, so I just crossed my arms and shook my head. Our fight was interrupted by a lady with a face like a withered apple who opened up the door of the back porch and yelled, "Barbara Jean! What are you doin' out there?" and then "Who are you two?"

The girl went running for the house in another outburst of tears. Tom poured on more charm as he followed her and introduced us. He said we'd been walking past the house when we heard the girl crying and stopped to see what the matter was. Then he explained about the kitten. That prompted the old lady to swat the girl on the legs and send her bawling deeper into the house. "I've told her a dozen times not to take that cat with her into the privy, but she's so willful! Can you boys get it out?"

I'd hoped there was an older brother or a dad or even an uncle we could pass that rescue over to, but no luck. The lady said her son-in-law, Walter, wouldn't get back to Des Moines until Friday. He's the girl's dad, she said, and a traveling salesman that peddles hardware as far off as Cedar Rapids and Davenport. The girl's mom got done in by the Spanish flu last fall, so now it's just the girl and her at home most of the time. She didn't seem like a bad old woman, just cranky and rheumatic. Tom looked kind of panicked. This isn't the kind of rescue he wants to go on. Dangling for dear life under a balloon or crashing through windows in a smoke-filled room, sure, but wading through waste, no thanks! Back on my folks' farm he didn't seem so squeamish, but I guess he was trying to impress them or me with his willingness to work hard. Now he already has me in his bed and my family is out of the picture, so he doesn't have to put on such a brave face. "We'll see what assistance we can provide, madam," he promised. The woman frowned at being called 'madam' and told us to call her 'Mrs. Carter' instead.

Tom pulled me out of earshot. The old woman shut

the door and watched us through the screen. "Maybe she has a net on a long pole," he said. I said I was sure she did because she was just the type to go catching butterflies in her spare time. He didn't like the smart aleck way I said that and thunked me on the chest for it, but not mean. He said he had a rope in his new knapsack, but we both agreed there was no way we were going to snag a kitten out of the muck with a rope or a shovel. The idea of a rake gave us hope, so we asked the old woman for one. She said there might be one leaning against the side of the house. We found it, but only the rusty iron tines, not the wooden handle. Where that might be, she said, was anyone's guess. She hadn't done any garden work and didn't plan to, given the arthritis she suffered from day and night. We thought about asking a neighbor for one, but Mrs. Carter barely knew anybody by name. All her remaining kin except Walter and Barbara Jean were in Nebraska.

Tom and I returned to the outhouse and fell to debating which of us would go down in the pit. He said I was more used to working in manure. I pointed out that he was wearing calf-high boots, not ankle-high shoes. He claimed it would be cheaper to replace my shoes than his. I argued that he saw better in the dark than I did, even though I had no proof of that. My being two inches shorter meant, in his opinion, that I wouldn't have to crouch down as much as he would. I argued that his hands were gentler and better suited to handling a little kitten. He cheated then and said if I let him keep his hands clean he'd use them to rub my back and other parts when we got back to Prouwder House. I flushed red and agreed to go down in the crapper for him.

Mrs. Carter helped by finding a pair of boots Walter used for hunting and fishing. They weren't as tall as Tom's, but better than my shoes for the job at hand. I took them and my socks off, rolled my pants up as high as I could, which was just above my knees, and squeezed my feet down into the cold, hard rubber. The outhouse seat was hinged and, with a little work, we got it up out of the way. I sure was glad it was a day in early April, not mid-August! Down I went, not sure how deep the crap would be. It turned out to be just ankle high, thank Christ. I could hear the kitten easy enough, but finding her in the darkness was hard, partly because she'd wandered around looking for a way out and partly because it turned out she was black herself. Finally I got her by the scruff of the neck and held her up so's Tom could take hold of her using a rag Mrs. Carter gave us. Getting myself out of the pit was trickier because there was little I could cling to and the one time I tried jumping I banged my head on the underside of the outhouse and damn near fell over. With more effort and a whole lot more cussing, I finally managed to climb out.

I spat a lot, blew my nose, and got to the pump real quick so Tom could get water flowing over my feet and shins after I took the boots off. The water was terrible cold, but not as bad for me as for the poor kitten that had to be dowsed in it all over. Mrs. Carter gave me soap and Barbara Jean came out of the house to watch. Her crying had eased up and she was eager to cuddle her kitten once I'd gotten the half-drowned, half-frozen creature clean. I got my own shoes and socks back on, rolled my pants legs down, and then Tom and I made our goodbyes. They didn't have any money to spare, but Mrs. Carter gave us each a buttermilk biscuit by way of thanks. I couldn't eat mine because I was still working to get the stench out of my nose, so Tom ate both of them (if you can believe that!) as we pretended to saunter on down the road, Maury Street. When it looked like nobody was watching, we snuck back to the outhouse and went in.

Nothing happened!

Sunday, the 6th of April

To our great surprise, returning to the outhouse did not whisk us off to the Prouwder estate. Zeb and I simply stood there, crowded together in the stench and early spring cobwebs. We pushed on the back wall of the privy, but that didn't have the desired effect. There was nothing for us to do but exit and reconsider our options. Zeb suggested we try traveling individually, first I, then he, but to no avail. Had anyone seen us entering and exiting in this manner, they might have thought us mad or perhaps beset by bees. Next we snuck into the neighbor's outhouse, which was a much dicier undertaking, but that likewise failed and we deemed the chances of getting caught too high and the chances of succeeding too low to try other outhouses. In the end we merely sat down on the shore of a pond directly opposite Mrs. Carter's home and devised other plans. Obviously, we could purchase train tickets and get back to Pittsburgh in two or three days' time. Since we had sufficient money with us, there would be no need to wire Mother for funds. I found it puzzling, however, that we should not be able to go back the way we had come; in Chicago, of course, we simply hadn't imagined that the mysterious tunnel which brought us into that house fire would just as easily return us to the mansion, but that wasn't the case now. I rather thought something else was up and told Zeb so. He proposed sending a telegram and asking for advice. There were, of course, still several former rescuers to petition: Belle, Uncle Louis, Great-uncle William, Cousin Rose, and, if she could be found, my sister, Hyacinth. Any of them or all of them could have encountered just such a predicament and might have valuable counsel.

That was the course upon which we set ourselves. We rose from the bank of the pond and set off down Maury Street again toward what appeared to be downtown Des Moines. There we hoped to find a telegraph office and, if necessary, lodging for the night. We had not reached the end of Mrs. Carter's property, however, before we heard a piercing scream, such as can only come from a child's tiny but powerful throat! We dashed through the back porch to the door of the house, knocked loudly without getting an answer, then entered. There on the floor lay the old woman, with Barbara Jean in terrified tears beside her!

We didn't know if the old lady had fallen, had a stroke, a heart attack or what, but she was out cold! Tom tried to rouse her, but got no response. I saw the kitten cowering under the sofa as I picked the kid up and tried to calm her. She was mighty scared. I guess I would be too if my main caretaker was laid out on the floor like that. Tom listened to her chest and said her heart was beating. She was breathing also, but she looked bad. He told me to look for a telephone, but I could have told him before looking that they didn't have one. Most people can't afford the luxuries the Prouwders got, after all. There didn't seem to be much point in asking for a telephone among the neighbors either. This wasn't a bad area of town, I figured, but not the hoity-toitiest. Tom thought a local business might be the best option for finding help, but, this being Sunday, most of those were probably closed. We'd have to start with the nearest neighbor, hoping to get directions to a doctor or a hospital.

It wasn't clear which of us should go knocking on doors. I probably have more in common with the people around here, but Tom can smooth talk better than me and he had cash on hand as well. Barbara Jean didn't want to turn loose of me, so off Tom went and we watched him from the front door. Nobody answered at the house next door though I could have sworn I'd seen somebody at the window earlier. The house next to that was colored folks. Tom talked to the mom and dad and they sent their son galloping off on a horse. Tom came back with the mom and told me the kid was riding to Mercy Hospital to fetch help. The woman checked Mrs. Carter over and pointed out a goose egg on her temple, then got a pillow from the couch and slid it under her head carefully. From one of the bedrooms she brought a blanket and laid that over her, then we waited and made some small talk.

By the time the ambulance arrived, Mrs. Carter had come to, but she was very ornery and confused. She didn't know her neighbor, didn't remember Tom and me from the outhouse, and wasn't even too sure who Barbara Jean was. The orderlies asked her name and she told them it was Ann Eliza, but she thought she was in Blair, Nebraska, so they put her on a stretcher and loaded her into the back of the ambulance. Other neighbors had gathered in the street to watch or chatter, but nobody from right next door. One asked Tom who we were and he said we were Mrs. Carter's nephews, just back from the War. I guess that made more sense than the truth. He gave the colored lady a quarter dollar for her help and for sending her son off so quick. That was good of him, but in his place I would've done it more on the sly. Not everybody has to know it when you come into a little money. He said he was going along with the ambulance to get Mrs. Carter signed in proper and see to the cost of her care. Both front seats were taken and there was no room in the back, so he rode on the running board as the car chugged away. The neighbors went on back to their houses. That left me alone with Barbara Jean. She was quiet now and we went inside the house. Her kitten was out of its hidey hole and dashed around my feet as we came in, mewling for milk or something to eat.

The place was just one common room, a kitchen, and two small bedrooms. It looked like Walter was in one, while Barbara Jean and her grandma shared the other. A few toys lay on the dresser alongside a bottle of perfume, some powder, and ~~rooze rogue~~ rouge. In the other bedroom there was even less on the dresser. Walter probably took most of his belongings on the road with him. It was about three o'clock. I was bored already, but Barbara Jean entertained me by putting "Kitty" on the arm of the chair I sat in and bringing me both her dolls. She showed me how to unsnap each doll's dress and comb its hair and feed it 'oatmeal' from the baby spoon she had. I danced "Ruthie" and "Blackie" across my knees and couldn't get over how much this delighted the girl. She climbed up on my lap and smooshed the dolls together in a duet, then came out with "I'm hungry". I thought I could maybe get away with just ignoring her, but she said it again and looked me right in the face, so I got up and carried her around the corner into the kitchen. A little bit of scavenging didn't turn up much, but I spread some butter on a couple of saltines and she got most of those into her mouth except for half of one cracker that she dropped on her dress. This caused her to stomp in place and squeal until I pulled it loose, fed it to her, and wiped up the spot with a dishrag. I really hoped Tom would come back soon and bring Mrs. Carter with him, but that didn't seem likely. I have two younger sisters, of course, so it's not like I've never been around kids, but they're only a few years behind me. I've never had to take care of somebody twenty years littler than me! It was 3:20.

Tom didn't get back until almost six. Barbara Jean and I had eaten all the crackers by then and I'd given her a glass of milk from the bottle I found in the icebox. She was shy of Tom at first, but I was sure glad to see him even though it seemed he had taken his own damn time in coming 'home'. He said the doctor thought Mrs. Carter had fainted from low blood pressure and might be able to come home in a few days. We looked at Barbara Jean, who was teaching Kitty to play with yarn just inside her bedroom door and I whispered that I bet the cat had tripped Mrs. Carter up. No cat was to be trusted, my dad always said. Tom shrugged and began to ponder what we were going to do. "We cannot take her to Prouwder House, as we learned yesterday, and we cannot leave her here alone. That means we must locate someone to watch over her until her father or grandmother returns or remain here as her guardians ourselves."

I was already going stir crazy from just four hours in that place. Another five days would drive me right over the edge, so Tom took over for a while and I got out to stretch my legs. I'd started pissing in the outhouse before I even realized there was still no tunnel to take us home, but I rapped on the back wall just in case. Our rescue wasn't over yet, I guessed. We fried up potatoes and eggs for supper. They were burnt and runny. Neither of us had ever cooked much. Tom had Bell and a whole kitchen staff doing for him and I had my mom and sisters doing for me. In the service the closest I got to cooking was stealing Tom that coffee and boiled potato. Otherwise I steered clear of the galley because Cook never held back from knocking a guy over the head with his rolling pin if there was any messing about with his pots and pans. Tom said he and the other pilots sometimes built an open fire to roast geese or ducks they shot and they boiled every vegetable they could lay their hands on, but mostly they bought meals from local farmwives or restaurants. Barbara Jean ate without complaint, then scrambled up on the countertop to a cabinet where Mrs. Carter had stashed some molasses cookies. We didn't know how many she was supposed to have, so we let her have two.

After that there wasn't much to do. The kid had a few books and wanted them read to her so we took turns doing that. Tom and I have been writing most of the evening by the light of the one kerosene lamp. Barbara Jean fell asleep right on the rug where she was playing and we just looked at her for a while, wondering what we should do with her. Eventually we just took off her shoes and put her in bed with the covers over her. I guess he and I will take Walter's bed although it's the smaller of the two.

Monday, the 7th of April

The child awoke in the night, crying, and was difficult to comfort. She looked with dismay at Zeb, at her dress, and at me. She needed the chamber pot, tipped it over, and wept the entire time. We managed to get her into her regular nightgown, but she wouldn't be left alone in the room and wouldn't let either of us take her grandmother's spot on the bed either, so Zeb and I carried in the large chair from the common room and I dozed in it the rest of the night with only my overcoat as bedding.

This morning I had a headache brought on by the awkward position of my neck while I slept and I wished for bourbon, but Mrs. Carter is apparently an advocate of Temperance. She may also be a Baptist, as there are no playing cards in the house and no music either, although she allows herself makeup. I'd wonder what she does all day, but Zeb and I have been thoroughly schooled in that regard. Breakfast was more potatoes and eggs plus toast, better than at supper, but still bottom notch. We hauled in water to do dishes and also scrubbed Barbara Jean's face, neck, and hands. Thereafter I insisted we trek out to the grocer's. If we have to remain here four more days, I want to live as comfortably as possible. Zeb and I were the only male customers and attracted much attention, both for our sex and for our utter helplessness among the wares. We asked for sugar and got only a laugh from the shopkeeper, as it is still rationed. Belle seems to secure all that Prouwder House needs, but I have no idea how.

The clerk didn't know us, of course, but he recognized "Barbie" and offered her a mint candy. Her joy and our gratitude were oil for the gears, so to speak, because after that he was eager to make conversation with us, accepted our story that we are Mrs. Carter's nephews, and then prevailed upon us to settle her outstanding debts. Given the abundance of our purchase, we could hardly plead insufficient funds and, in any case, I was happy to pay her bill and be on our way. The rest of the day provided little stimulation and much drudgery, although I did strike out in order to send a telegram to Mother explaining our situation. The Western Union office stood not far from the brand new Hotel Fort Des Moines. I'm quite tempted to shut up the house and take Barbie and Zeb there to ride out Mrs. Carter's convalescence in what luxury the city has to offer!

Tom's a *junker*, as some of the sailors say. He's as keen for adventure as a hophead is for opium. I never noticed before that he can't sit still without at least a book in hand, so today was a trial for him. Me? I'm happy with any good piece of wood and the whittling knife I put in my new knapsack yesterday morning. Between turns at the stove or the dish sink or the outhouse, I was content carving out a little cat figure for Barbie Jean. She liked it very much and asked me for a puppy so I'll try to carve that out tomorrow. We went for a walk and found some kids for her to play with, but she got shy again and wouldn't join in. Too bad her mom didn't have a couple other babies before she went to her eternal rest. I wouldn't want to be an only child, even though my brothers were pretty mean to me! Tom says we'll have to scout out the nearest library tomorrow and buy playing cards as well. It's a kind of vacation we're having, not trapped on the Prouwder estate and not fighting for our lives in war or rescue.

Tuesday, the 8th of April

Zeb and I introduced Barbie to the lending library on the riverfront. I gave Mrs. Carter's address as our own and we received borrowing privileges. I took out "My Ántonia" by Cather for myself and "The Wonderful Wizard of Oz" for Barbie. She cannot read yet, of course, but I'm already tired of the few books she possesses, drivel for the most part, and I want to raise her expectations of literature. Zeb got Burroughs' "The Land That Time Forgot". We ate lunch downtown, a welcome respite from our own culinary efforts. I must admit, however, that Zeb is getting more adept at frying eggs: breakfast was quite tolerable, despite the absence of coffee.

Heard back from Mother. I flesh out her telegram here: she reports no cries for help have been heard at Prouwder House since our departure on Sunday, so we must be doing God's (?) will. We are to wire for more money, if need be, and hire a girl to clean, cook, and wash for us while we're away. I mentioned this suggestion to Zeb and he scoffed. He is, for some reason, adamant that he and I can fend for ourselves. We shall see whether he maintains that opinion tomorrow when we are obliged to do laundry!

4/9/19

My hands are awful red and chapped from washing clothes today. I don't think I've ever done harder work even though I've shoveled shit, sheered sheep, bailed hay, mopped decks during maelstroms, and pulled calves out of cows! I look kinder on my mom every day. It isn't a showy strength she's got, like when a man arm wrestles another man or splits a log with one chop of the axe, but after scrubbing up and down the washboard hour after hour and also mixing together ingredients for molasses cookies, I can barely lift my hand up to blow my nose! Tom clucked at me from the couch, saying again that we maybe need to hire a maid, but now my heels are dug in and I'll never say die until this house is spit and polish!

Little Barbie cried some for her grandma today so we promised to take her by the hospital tomorrow and visit, if they'll let her in. Tom paid the neighbor's son to ride back to Mercy and find out how Mrs. Carter is. The doctor wrote back and said she is weak, but stable. A couple of the neighbors have come by to ask after her and "check in on the little girl". The colored lady, whose name is Mabel, brought a loaf of homemade bread, which is very tasty. The neighbor right next door hasn't come by to say hello and I don't even know if it's a man or a woman or a couple, but somebody's been watching us sharp. I saw whoever it is peeking through the curtains today while I was hanging socks and pants and other things on the line to dry. I wonder what he or she thought of Barbie helping with that chore.

The sooner we get out of here, the better, for Barbie's sake too. I think we've spoiled her a bit, giving her candy and constant attention. Tom gets after me for it, but he's just as bad, reading to her until late at night and talking about buying her new dresses and hair ribbons! If I'd ever asked for something that wasn't handed down to me from my big brothers, my dad would've switched me hard, but my mom always snuck me an extra oatmeal cookie when nobody was looking because she has a sweet tooth just like me.

Barbie was fussy at bedtime the first couple nights. She just wouldn't stay in her bedroom alone, so Tom and

I carried Walter's bed in beside Mrs. Carter's and put Barbie in it while we share the big one. Now she's fine all night except for needing the chamber pot once or twice. We wash her good in the morning, including brushing her teeth, and I do what I can with her hair. Out of the blue she started calling us Uncle Tom and Uncle Zeb.

Tom and I have no privacy. When we get back to Prouwder House, I bet we hump like bunnies. I've been putting my shoulder to the wheel while he's been keeping his feet up on the couch. I figure Mrs. Prouwder-Caul pays me to be a rescue worker, so this house keeping stuff is my duty, but when we get home, I'll see to it that Tom puts his feet up on my shoulders a good long while!

Thursday, the 10th of April

The road to hell, as they say, is paved with good intentions. Today we took Barbie up to see her grandmother in the hospital. I had assumed she wouldn't be let in on account of her young age, but luck was with us and the good Sisters of Mercy permitted the visit. I can't say either was especially overjoyed to see the other. They haven't really been living together that long, of course; only since Mrs. Carter's daughter passed away. I imagine she is as fatigued by the conditions on Maury Street as we are: no friends, much labor, plus her advanced age and joint pain. Barbie, for her part, probably doesn't find Mrs. Carter a loving substitute for her mother and she rarely sees her father. I wish I could create a better situation for both of them, but, of course, millions of people suffer much worse and carry on living.

In any case, the visit has caused an immediate problem: Mrs. Carter, still in a state of confusion brought on by the fall and the blow to her head, cast doubt on our being her nephews. (Of course I should rather say that, despite *her injury, she rightly knew we are not her nephews!) An attending nurse heard her discredit our identities and became suspicious. She summoned the nun in charge of the hospital, who then summoned the priest doing his rounds there, and they questioned us extensively. Since Zeb and I do not resemble each other, I thought it better to maintain that he and I are first cousins, not brothers, but even of that it was difficult to convince the Sister and the Father. It did weigh in our favor that I have paid for "Aunt Ann Eliza's" care, nothing a stranger would be likely to do, they agreed. Nevertheless, the priest, in an attempt to assuage the Sister's concerns, promised to visit us at 'home' tomorrow and stated that, if he finds Barbie's care in the slightest bit unsatisfactory, he shall contact the authorities and have her placed in an orphanage until her father comes to claim her!*

4/11/19

I told Tom Thursday we should just hightail it out of the house and set up with Barbie in a hotel somewhere, but he said that would only look even more like we were up to no good and we had better just stay put and make a good show for the priest. It felt like I spent all of Friday worrying and peeking out the windows just like the neighbor next door does to us. I made sure Barbie looked her very cleanest, polished her shoes, and even ironed her dress, with only a little burn to the hem in back. Tom bought her hair ribbons and he put one in over her left ear while I put one in over her right. Supper was some green beans I found canned in the cellar, pork chops, more of the bread from Mabel, and oatmeal cookies for dessert.

I made an extra chop for the priest and good thing I did because not only did he show up as if I'd rung the dinner bell, but he brought along his brother, who's a cop! I quick cut Tom's chop in two while I was out in the kitchen and set two more plates on the small foldout dining table in the common room. Kitty got curious at all the good smells, so I trapped her in the cellar with a bowl of milk big enough to drown in.

We ate after the priest, Father O'Farrell, said grace. He and Officer O'Farrell managed to stuff their faces without stopping their inspection of the premises, craning their necks into both bedrooms while chewing or checking for dust on the countertop while fetching more bread. The priest pinched Barbie's cheek and she made a face, but he didn't notice because the cop was asking Tom about the War and what it was like to fight German pilots. Tom's a storyteller like no other and once he got to talking I thought we were home free. Barbie helped me clear away the plates when all the food was eaten up and she showed off the cat and dog I whittled for her. I started to relax about the whole thing, held Barbie on my lap, and picked at my teeth with a sliver of wood, but Tom started to lose the O'Farrell brothers' attention more and more. They looked from one of us to the other nervous-like and kind of tapped on the table like they were waiting for something more. I began to think it was money they were after, in the guise of donations to police pensions or maybe help for mission work, but before Tom could get out his billfold, Officer O'Farrell wondered out loud whether we might have a drop of whiskey as "a pair o' teeth".

Not a drop in the house, I realized! Mrs. Carter didn't

keep any liquor around, for whatever reason, and we sure as heck didn't think to buy a bottle for this evening. The O'Farrell brothers sat up straight then and became "officious", as my dad would say about Waynesburg's mayor. They began to lay out the reasons Barbie couldn't stay with us and would be better off as a ward of the city until such time as her father could reassert his parental rights and so on and so forth. It all happened so quick! Before I knew it, they'd rushed Barbie out the front door and were packing her into the police car. I was thunderstruck, Tom was in shock, and Barbie was sobbing, kicking, and punching both men. I wished to hell we'd run away with her, all the way back to Pittsburgh maybe, because this was a lot like what happened to Abraham and I thought I'd rather get shot in the back than let these two bastards shunt Barbie off to some lousy orphanage!

Just as I was about to commence swinging my fists around, out of the house next door came a middle-aged woman with a full head of steam and a mouth powered by it. "Oh no!" she said, "You ain't takin' that little girl away no how 'cause I been watchin' these fellas the whole week doin' the laundry and cookin' and carin' for the child better than her grandma ever does!" She lit into both the O'Farrells with fire and damnation and hell to pay if the girl's dad come home to find his little one fallen into the hands of papists and her and all the Maury Street Baptist Church would rally behind him on a march to City Hall to have their heads if they didn't turn her back over to her lovin' kinfolk right this instant!

Now I'm not like some people. I don't care if a person's Catholic or colored or poor or can't speak English. The way I see it, the Mother in charge of that Mercy Hospital is as close to a saint as I'm likely to see on Earth and Mabel is every bit as good as Tom or me, but this woman's tirade against the O'Farrells must have struck some deep old fears in them because they up and handed Barbie back to us without another word and drove off quick.

"It's good that you don't switch the girl," the woman said when they were gone. "I never liked gettin' switched." She didn't say anything else, just went back into her house and peered at us through the curtains again.

That was a mighty close call, as you can see, and it took Tom, Barbie, and me quite a while to settle down into normal breathing that night. Tom said he thought the O'Farrells had intended to take Barbie all along, no matter what, but then they'd seen an opportunity for a free meal so they waited until it was over to carry out their plan. Maybe Tom could've bribed them, but their taste for liquor got the better of them and they missed out on the money they could've gotten. In the end we fell asleep around 9:30, happy enough. Late in the night, on the other hand, Tom and I woke up with a gun pointed at us!

Saturday, the 12th of April, dawn

Dark bedroom, two figures, one of which has taken Barbie into its arms, the other of which bears a pistol aimed at my forehead. An unpleasant awakening, to say the least. These must be the O'Farrell brothers, I think, come after all to take the child into their custody, but the armed figure asks who we are and what we're doing in his house, ergo, Walter the traveling salesman!

I start, calmly, with our names. Identifying oneself

indicates innocence and it's simply easier to shoot strangers than 'Thomas Prouwder Caul' and 'Zebediah Beck'. (That Polish major, Narbut, for example, did not ask the names of his captives.) I then request permission to light the lamp beside the bed and am told not to make any funny moves. In my most unfunny way, I shed illumination on the situation. Walter, as I surmised, but the person holding Barbie is a woman! Quite a mystery! Zeb and I keep our hands where Walter can see them and I begin the story of how we came to inhabit his home, leaving out, of course, all mention of tunnels and Pittsburgh and divine rescue missions. To the rightful man of the house I weave a tale of random passersby, servicemen recently discharged, who came to the aid of his family in the hour of its need. Walter lowers his weapon. Barbie explores the face, coat, and hat of the woman who holds her. She is plump, but patient with the girl and asks for the blanket off her bed before settling down with her on the couch away from the confrontation.

Walter tells us to get dressed and retreats a bit, but doesn't turn his back to us. Zeb and I put our uniforms on once more, including footwear. He follows my lead as I sling my knapsack over my shoulder; we may need to make a dash for it despite how civilly our conversation with Walter is proceeding and I don't want to leave any of our belongings behind. We join the others in the common room.

Where's his mother-in-law, he wants to know. I clarify that she is still recovering from her fall and mention that I have seen to her hospital bill. This is no time to downplay the money I've spent on his family's behalf. He introduces the woman as his new wife, Minnie, lately of Davenport. She says it's nice to meet us and Walter tells Barbie this is her new mom. Barbie seems doubtful about this, but she doesn't pull away. Kitty jumps up on her lap and both pet her.

Walter doesn't mean to be rude, but it's been a long drive and Minnie's tired. Thanks for all we've done, but . . .

His pistol, muzzle down, swings towards the door. Time for us to be going, I agree. Zeb obviously longs to say goodbye to Barbie, but she's distracted. He idly touches the wooden cat on the small table next to the big chair and then nods that he is ready. With Walter's permission, I say, Zeb and I will make use of the outhouse before hitting the road. He consents, but keeps a cautious distance as we exit through the back door, then locks it behind us. He watches us find our way past the garden that might get cultivated after all and notices a light on in the house next door. There's a figure at the window.

Zeb and I enter the privy together and never come out of it again.

LESSONS

Saturday, the 12th of April, sunset

After our interlude in Des Moines, it seemed all the more urgent that Zeb and I learn as much as possible about The Work from the rescuers remaining at Prouwder House. To that end, and to quell our hunger, we descended to the kitchen to question Belle and obtain breakfast. Knowing her schedule well, I aimed to have us arrive when the peak hurly-burly of the morning meal was past, but preparation for lunch had not begun in earnest. Although Belle, so far as I had seen, never shirked her share of the drudgery, I was confident she would delegate the dish washing to underlings so that she could help out her favorite Prouwder, which I fancy I am.

There was leftover toast, coffee, and sausages when we came in. Belle was in her regular seat and smoking one of the two cigarettes she allows herself each day. Her auburn hair was momentarily free of the white headscarf that the kitchen staff wears. With her free hand she rubbed the hip that pains her and causes her to limp. We sat down at her table and she welcomed us back. At her signal, plates with generous servings were set in front of us and the other women left us three alone. I ate with great appetite and commented that it was grand to *have a break from Zeb's cooking. She asked where we'd been the last week and I gave her a synopsis of our time with Barbie and her family. She wanted to know what Zeb had made and then offered him hints on those dishes plus others he might try in the future. He took notes with sincere attention and I think that pleased her.*

"Have you ever had a rescue go on so long?" I asked, eager to learn as much as possible while she was available.

"Oh, sure!" she said and went on to mention weeks spent in Mexico, the Himalayas, and on the Mediterranean. "Even Paris! Yinz can stay an extra day or two, you know, after you're done with what you got to do."

"And back here," I continued, "there are no cries for help while a rescue is underway?"

She shook her head and said she hadn't heard anything, for example, while Zeb and I were in Iowa. "Ya got to take advantage of the situation when ya can. You're stuck on the estate all the time if you don't. When we was doin' The Work I saw more of Peru than of Pittsburgh!"

I wondered whether she missed rescues and she said no, not really. Some of it was fun, but it was also dangerous. She rubbed her hip some more and added, "Your Uncle Louis, his nerves are shot from it."

"And Frank Candell?" I asked.

"Dead."

"How did he die?" Zeb paused in his note-taking.

"Rockslide." Belle looked with some apprehension at what Zeb was writing down and fidgeted with the headscarf she'd laid on the table.

"Where?" I wanted to know.

"Out west somewhere. We didn't have time to find out.

Bunch of Chinese miners had used dynamite to open up a vein of copper. We saved all of them, but Frank went down the mountain with the boulder he was standing on." She rose and began putting her headscarf in place. "I should get back to work. You boys eat and just leave your plates where they are."

"One more question, Belle: why do you and Uncle Louis still hear the calls for help? Great-uncle William doesn't hear them and I don't think Rose or Hyacinth does either. They stopped hearing the calls when their partners in The Work died."

She retied her apron. "Mr. Booke doesn't hear anything. He's deaf as a post. I don't know about the girls. You'd have to ask them directly. Louis and me still hear the screams because most of our team is still alive, I suppose. It isn't the screams of strangers that keep ya up at night, anyway; it's the screams of your teammates."

She walked away, leaving Zeb and me to eat and ponder whom we would "interrogate" next.

I ate some of the tastiest sausage I've about ever had and wished I'd asked Bell for tips on how to fry them up. The ones I made in Des Moines were awful burnt. Tom said we should go see his uncle and great-uncle next. I decided I'd take notes during our talk with them as well and I hoped they wouldn't cut our conversation short like Bell had. She must have been mighty partial to that Candle fellow to get so upset, but I guess that's a foolish thing to say seeing as how I got so worked up over Abraham. If Tom died on a rescue, I figure that would be the end of me too. I wonder why Bell and that Frank never got hitched. Tom said he was a burly guy, swarthy, and rough so Tom steered clear of him when he was a kid. He was master of the stables and then became Mrs. Prouwder-Book's chauffeur when she bought her first automobile. That's Tom's grandma. Seems funny that she would be the first in the family to own a car. Bell and Louis look to be around fifty. I wonder if they'd still be doing this work if Candle hadn't died.

We wandered the mansion, trying to find Tom's uncle Louis or great-uncle William. Tom also made our wandering a sort of test for me. From the kitchen, he told me to find the way back to our apartment, which was easy. Then he told me to find the laundry room, but once we got to the basement, I was lost. There's a lot down there: laundry, boilers, a larder for canned goods, a butcher's space, coal room, sauna, even an indoor pool! These Prouwders seem set on having one of every kind of room.

From there we got more serious about our search and eventually found William and Louis, plus one more man, together in an office on the second floor. They were reading newspapers and stock reports that came out of a tickertape machine. Tom told me later that everything's in William's name since he's the oldest. He's up past seventy, I reckon, and stone deaf, like Bell said, but still sharp-witted. He had a little chalkboard to write on, but mostly he used gestures or finger spelling and the other man, who turned out to be his son Nathan, used them too, so we all knew what was being said.

The three of them looked at me kind of funny when Tom reminded them I was his "colleague", Mr. Zebediah Beck. I wondered for a second whether I still smelled like Mrs. Carter's outhouse. Tom and I were both in our uniforms and there were handshakes all around, then Tom made quick work of telling them about our time in Des Moines. He left out the part about me climbing down into the latrine and then he asked them whether they'd ever been stuck some place for a long time like that. Louis took up a long study of his shoes and kept moving his finger from one of the buttons in the leather couch to another, but William spoke up pretty quickly, that is, he wrote on his chalkboard and held it up for us to see: Krakatoa.

He went on, through his son, to tell us of his being in Sumatra and Java several times from May of 1883 up through the big blow in August. That's the one that deafened him, he said. Tom asked about his wife, Sarah, was she injured too? This made William mad and, even though it was very hard to understand him the few times he actually spoke, "No no no!" came through plain enough. He jabbed his finger at Louis, who looked even more down at the mouth while Nathan spoke for his father. "No! I never let Sarah come through the tunnel until I knew it was safe! Louis and that dad-blasted Frank Candle took Bell Harris along on every rescue and look what happened to her! Shot in the hip and almost killed by it! Sarah waited at Prouwder House until I fetched her through. Mostly she was there to bring me things I needed. I didn't let her come to Sumatra after the first time."

I was pretty surprised by all this. I didn't know, of course, what caused Bell to limp the way she does. I figured it was just old age. Ain't life peculiar that she's been shot, but Tom and I haven't been even though we were in the war! Not to mention how we were sentenced to death there in Pinsk and escaped without any bullet holes in us at all. The other surprising news was that one of us could stay behind or maybe go back to Prouwder House to fetch something we needed. We don't have to take all the necessaries with us, but instead we can come back to fetch bandages or a crowbar or a rake. That would have been handy to know in Des Moines. If all this was a surprise to Tom, he kept it to himself. He's good at that. His face doesn't tell you anything except he lets it. My face is more like the tickertape that kept clicking out of the machine: it's all there to be read with minute by minute updates.

I wasn't sure we'd get anything out of Louis now. He looked as browbeaten as all get out and hadn't said anything in his defense. I didn't know what Sarah had been like, but it seemed to me that anybody who met Bell could see she would've just laughed if Louis or Frank had told her to stay behind. Tom asked his uncle Louis whether he had ever been stuck somewhere the way we'd been in Des Moines. He just shook his head. Did he have any advice for us, Tom asked. Louis shook his head again. I didn't think we'd get anything out of him and Tom must have thought so too because he stood up, thanked all of them, and led me into the hallway. We found a window bench that was getting some of the late morning light and looked down into one of the grassy sort of courtyards Prouwder House has a lot of. We talked about why Louis had lied about spending extra time in Mexico and the Mediterranean. Tom figured it was on account of the dressing down William had given him, but of course

Louis didn't know we'd already talked to Bell. Maybe he was embarrassed by it or something. Tom seemed to think something about that, but he didn't share it with me. These Prouwders keep a lot of secrets.

Tom said we'd have to make a test during our next rescue and see whether one of us could come back and get something. I told him that would have to be him because I couldn't find whole rooms in the mansion yet, let alone extra knives or a hammer. Odd stuff was lying all about, he pointed out, and drew back the curtain behind him to show me a wool cap there. Next to a door down the hall was a spear, of all things, and even further off was a pair of snowshoes. I just figured the maids were lazy, I told him. He chuckled and said he grew up with stuff like that tucked all around, so he didn't think anything of it. I thought I'd never know where to go for what we needed if there wasn't any system. On the *Fanning* every spoon and shell and life-preserver had its place. Tom agreed that we'd have to bring "military order" to our supplies, ideally in one room of the mansion that was "centrally located".

Just then, Louis came out of William's office and seeing us, rushed off in the other direction. Tom and I looked at each other for a second, then set off like hound dogs after him!

It was unclear why Uncle Louis fled from us, but I was convinced he had something to tell. We caught up to him quite quickly, of course, but he didn't slow down until we had exited the mansion and reached a dilapidated cabin out of sight of the house. It overlooks Nine Mile Run and I played around it many times in childhood. Louis stopped at the front door, which now appears unopenable, and recounted how Belle, Frank, and he had gone to San Francisco after the quake. They had helped fight fires, pull survivors from the rubble, and tend the wounded. After a week of near constant effort, Louis had asked William to make a large donation to further recovery efforts. This William had refused to do, citing as precedent that his own father, Jacob, had likewise scoffed at monetary aid in the aftermath of the Krakatoa explosion. It was enough, William said, that Prouwders put their lives in jeopardy; there was no sense in spending down the Prouwder fortune to help the same people.

I knew for a fact that Mother made numerous and generous donations to charity and I said so. Louis maintained that had not always been the case. Frank Candell had been so outraged by William's stinginess that the two men had come to blows, with William getting the worse end of the altercation. In consequence thereof, Frank had been banished from the mansion except when responding to cries for help, and he was also relieved of his duties as stable master and chauffeur. At that time my mother took over control of the Prouwder fortune, although William retained legal ownership of the estate.

"Frank lived here after that. He was shunned and cut off from contact with Belle and me except for the times we were conducting rescues. We began spending more and more time together in far-off places, but he grew sour about his situation." In response to Belle's account of Frank's death, Louis shook his head. "The boulder he stood on did not give way: Frank jumped."

This was astonishing news. I was not yet eleven when my brother and sister took over The Work, merely nine when Candell was banished to this cabin. It cannot be said I knew the man well, but I would never have taken him for a suicide. It was an uncomfortable reminder of how I too had contemplated that act rather than accept the duties of The Work.

"You came seeking advice," Louis said despondently. "This is all I can offer: let no one separate you one from the other. A great deal of grief might have been avoided if Belle and I had moved out here with Frank. Grief that was not just ours, but yours, your mother's, and Rose's as well."

We left Louis at the cabin and returned to the mansion. Zeb quipped that he'd hoped for more practical advice: what to eat in the desert, how to treat frostbite, that sort of thing. I surmised we could find such knowledge in the Prouwder House library and proposed that we make such study part of our daily routine, but first I wanted to go to my cousin Rose and gain whatever insight she might provide us. While we walked to that wing of the house, I explained to Zeb that Rose Prouwder is my second cousin. Her father is John Prouwder. John's father is Henry Prouwder, brother to William and to my maternal grandmother, Catherine Prouwder-Booke. My mother is Maude Prouwder-Caul, née Booke. He seemed to follow along well enough, but then he asked whether the Doucette sisters are my cousins too and I said yes, they are my first cousins, daughters of my mother's sister, Olivia Prouwder-Doucette, née Booke, and then he said shouldn't they be my first, second, and third cousins since there's three of them? I gave up. We had reached Rose's room and the end of my patience.

I knocked and Rose's mother, Eudora, appeared in a narrow space between the door and the jamb. I greeted her, was greeted cautiously in turn, and announced my desire to speak with Rose about an important matter. I was told she wasn't receiving visitors, whereupon I insisted that my new responsibilities to the family overrode such considerations. She demurred, but then tried to bar Zeb's way. I took the advice Louis had just given us and declared that Beck, by virtue of being my colleague in The Work, was entitled to hear firsthand every insight Rose could offer. I thought I might have to remove Eudora's hand from the doorknob by force, but she surrendered and went to announce our arrival. Zeb accompanied me as I entered Rose's boudoir.

She was not in bed this time, but rather fully dressed and arrayed comfortably beside the room's largest window. I imagined the swelling of her belly had increased, but that may simply have been a result of her not trying to conceal her pregnancy any longer. Her bright blonde tresses were adorned with pink ribbons more befitting a schoolgirl than an expectant mother, but she was nevertheless a lovely creature whom I hoped not to distress in the slightest. I thanked her for seeing us and, as this was a clear breach of etiquette, explained that 'Mr. Beck' and I would not remain long. Zeb took notes as I recounted our time in Des Moines and asked whether she and Crowne had ever likewise been delayed in returning to the mansion. Eudora tut-tutted at the mention of his name. Rose claimed that they hadn't, but the sideways glance she made at her mother and the slight movement of her hand across her abdomen made me doubt her, for as surely as a ball which is dropped out a window will hit the ground, Rose's current condition must have been preceded by sexual congress. It seemed to me more likely to have occurred in some far-flung locale than anywhere here on the Prouwder estate.

I took a different tack and asked her about any memorable missions from which Zeb and I could learn. "The molasses flood" was her immediate response, the event so peculiar and horrifying in January of this year that I read of it even in France. Rose described the blackness of the molasses, its overwhelming grip, and the prodigious strength necessary to pull victims free of it. Sigmund Freud, the great Father of Psychology himself, could have drawn no other conclusion but that Rose spoke unwittingly of Crowne and, most probably, the date on which she had conceived his child. Others might condemn the act as one of violence on the part of a black man against a white woman and oppress his entire race for it, but I have seen through that scurrilous accusation and reject it completely. In the Great War I met a colored man, Eugene Bullard, who fought beside us bravely and without blemish in the Escadrille Lafayette. He was, contrary to the false reputation of his people, handsome, strong, fierce yet refined, and in all ways an exemplary man. Although I had only the purest feelings of camaraderie for Bullard, I could well imagine Rose giving herself over to Crowne if he possessed even half the sexual magnetism of my fellow pilot. Try as she might, Rose had failed to conceal her true feelings from the enhanced perceptions one gains from reading Freud; what one says is often far from what one actually thinks!

"Did either of you ever return to Prouwder House before the completion of a rescue? Perhaps to obtain some object vital to your efforts?"

Rose confirmed that they had. Crowne was most clever and had discovered that such a temporary return was possible. If what they required was somewhere on the grounds, Crowne fetched it. If it was inside the house, naturally it was Rose that went to get it. Eudora's expression grew ever more disapproving.

Zeb had been scribbling away in silence, but now he spoke.

"Did he think up some kind of system for where stuff was kept?"

At this, Rose brightened and once again mentioned how clever Crowne was. He had indeed arranged items outside in a sort of clock face pattern. Axes, for example, were at the noon position, which was the northernmost point of the mansion. Bars of all lengths were stationed at one o'clock, cudgels at two, darts at three, and so on. Owing to the length of the alphabet, maps were also at the noon position, nutcrackers at one o'clock, et cetera. Rose chided herself for not devising any system so sensible for the mansion's interior. She began to smile and reminisce about Crowne, but Eudora put a stop to that by saying that if Crowne was so clever, why did he get himself lynched like he had?

Rose's smile was turned instantly to tears. Eudora stood and bade Zeb and me to leave for our questions had pained Rose enough. I was inclined to continue our conversation despite Eudora's directive, but it was Rose herself that intervened. She asked her mother to bring them lunch from the kitchen. Eudora seemed ready to argue, but Rose entreated her to hurry and the woman left with a loud stomping of her feet.

We let Rose compose herself and I apologized for disturbing her. She dabbed at her eyes and relaxed against the back of her chair. "It's all right. No one lets me talk about Jefferson, so I am glad of this opportunity." I admitted I had not known Crowne's Christian name. She added to my chagrin by informing us that Crowne had worked on the estate his entire life and had, in fact, been born in the very stable we could see through her window. She then surprised me utterly by asking how Zeb and I had met. She listened attentively as Zeb gave her an account of the Fanning, Philadelphia, and the farm. "You're fortunate," she stroked her belly, "that there will never be evidence of your relationship as there is of mine with Jefferson."

"What," I ventured, "will become of your child?"

She explained that Jefferson's sister had agreed to adopt it. Boy or girl, it would be named "Pride" and Rose hoped she would be able to count on my assistance in providing for the child, both in terms of mundane needs and of education. I readily consented to do so.

"Jefferson didn't have to die, you know. The mob hadn't caught him. They _couldn't_ catch him. Me, however, they seized immediately. They saw I was with child and correctly deduced that Jefferson was the father. He instantly surrendered himself so that the crowd would let me go. I'm a strong swimmer, even burdened as I am, and soon got myself out of reach in the water. Jefferson begged me to leave, but I treaded water and watched while they beat and hanged him. I memorized the scene. I described to myself the exact number of attackers and onlookers, their sexes, ages, clothing, and expressions. I wrote every detail in a small notebook, such as Zeb is using, and I keep it under lock and key here, in this table. Someday I hope to publish Jefferson's story. I only came back to Pittsburgh for the sake of our child and to make some commemoration of what happened. Otherwise I would have chosen to continue treading water until I became so fatigued that I would drown."

All this amazed me. I'd had no idea Rose possessed such a steely character nor that she'd also been tempted by suicide. "Do you have advice for us?" I asked. Zeb shifted his knee so that it rested against mine.

"Be careful," she said. "Even though doing The Work brings you influence and deference at Prouwder House, do not trust your family too much. They are merely a mob whose names you already know."

We passed Eudora in the hallway as she led a maid bearing a lunch tray. She scowled at us, but I deemed it worthwhile to have endured her disdain in order to speak with Rose. Zeb and I took our own lunch in the apartment: cold cut sandwiches, pickled green beans, and bottles of Coca-Cola which we had earlier placed in the new Frigidaire. While we ate, we reviewed what we had learned. Zeb was quite enthused about setting up a room with all things needful. He began making a list of tools, medical devices, and emergency gear which should be placed there. I knew many of the items were already available somewhere on the estate; it was just a matter of gathering them into a useful location and I promised we would put his plan into action after lunch and a brief "siesta". The latter activity was interrupted by the distinct sounds of footsteps in our common room. Zeb and I got out of bed, pulled on our trousers, and opened the door to find my sister Hyacinth eating scraps of ham casing and the stringy ends of green beans off our plates. Her shoes, dress, and hair were in the same neglected state as when I'd last seen her, but this time she had thickly applied rouge, powder, lipstick, and mascara to one side of her face while scrubbing the other side clean.

I had been hoping to speak with her today, but I was frankly surprised to find her in our apartment. We'd locked the door and, as far as I knew, Zeb and I possessed the only key. "Hyacinth? How did you get in here?"

She spared us not a glance, but studied our plates instead. "There's an 'e' on the end of 'Belle', another on the end of 'Booke', and Candell is spelled C A N D E L L."

Zeb pointed his thumb at her. "She read my notes?"

"*Apparently.*" *I sat down across from her. Zeb cut fresh slices of ham and bread for her, put them on a new plate, and laid out silverware as well before retrieving his notebook from the table. She ignored the knife and fork, tore the meat and bread into bits with her dirty fingers, then arranged the bits into interconnected squares and rectangles. "Hyacinth, Zeb and I are trying to understand the tunnels better. Can you tell us anything about how they work?"*

"*The Work, The Work, The Work.*"

"*Do you still hear cries for help or did those stop when …?*"

"*Help, Help, Help.*"

It pained me to see her in this condition. In better days, Hyacinth was my best friend. She played with great patience whatever game I found, learned, or invented. We explored the mansion and the grounds together, watching the progress inside a robin's nest, or making a private shrine of pretty stones at one eddy of Nine Mile Run. I counted the strokes of Hyacinth's brush through her hair for her, focusing intently on the numbers between sixty and eighty where I had on occasion gotten lost. We battled our cousins in hip-high snow or hid from our nannies. Hyacinth shared with me her discovery of several cedar chests where Mother's or even Grandmother's debutante clothing was stored. She gave me books to read on my own or had me read others out loud to her. She took my side when I insisted that I no longer be made to wear frilly clothes, as was the custom in my infancy. I kept silent when she snuck small glasses of sherry out of Grandmother's cabinet.

Lowell was raised separately from us. He was two and five years older than Hyacinth and I, respectively. Father took him along to Philadelphia when he and Mother began to live most of the year apart from each other. I guess he saw something so similar or endearing in Lowell that he could not bear to leave him behind, something he did not see in Hyacinth or me. When Lowell next visited, he was more like our cousin than our brother and he preferred the company of grown up men over that of children. Father, William, Henry, Louis, and Nathan took him into their offices and their confidences.

A change came over Hyacinth as well. She seemed to be striding into the adult world far faster than my legs could keep up with. She did not gain access to the men's discussions of business or politics, but after the workday, she and Lowell spent the bulk of their time together. I was definitely not wanted and I remember being on the outside of many doors at that time.

"Hy, do you have a key to our door?"

"Only one key. Only one cry for help." She pointed at her plate. "Tunnels, tunnels, tunnels."

Zeb went to check our door and reported that it was still locked. "If she came in that way, she locked it behind her."

I didn't think that likely, given how neglectful she was of even her own hygiene. "Look for secret passageways." Zeb joined me in pushing or knocking on the walls of the room.

"Nothing."

I too found nothing. There were a few secret passageways and rooms in the mansion. Hyacinth and I had discovered them many years before, but they were well known to all the Prouwder children and none of them led to or from this apartment. Hyacinth stood and rested her half–powdered forehead against one windowpane, tracing others with her unpolished fingernail. Zeb shrugged. "I guess she doesn't have anything to tell us."

That seemed true, but her very presence made me suspect otherwise. I had in my pocket the only key to our rooms that

I knew of, our door was locked, there didn't appear to be any hidden entrance, and we hadn't heard Hyacinth move about until she was already in our common room. It was almost as if she'd appeared out of thin air. Suddenly, I knew what had happened. "She came through a tunnel!"

Zeb expressed doubt at my conclusion. "I didn't yell for help and you didn't either."

"She said it herself: 'Only one cry for help.' It isn't us she heard. It's the same person she always hears and I think I know who that is." I drew closer to her, stopping only when she flinched away. "It's Lowell, isn't it? You still hear him or think that you do. All these years you've been wandering the mansion, trying to find the tunnel that will take you to him, but he's gone, Hyacinth. He's dead."

She acted with such speed that she caught me completely flat-footed: hands that had been tracing across our windowpanes were suddenly flush against my chest and with all her strength she shoved me backwards against our table, over it, and then onto the floor in a heap. Zeb rushed to my aid while Hyacinth rushed in the opposite direction, out through the door to the smaller bedroom, then through the apartment door and down the stairs with a clamor of shoes and lunatic rantings.

As quickly as we could, we followed her. I wanted to convince her to give up her mad search and stay where we could care for her. She ran ahead of us down the longest straight stretch of the third floor, then dodged left through a door I knew led only to a small linen closet. The door slammed behind her and I hoped to corner her in there or, perhaps, pursue her down the next tunnel she used, but before we could reach the closet door, one opposite it flew open and disgorged a man bearing a triumphant smile. He dashed into the closet, paused until we very nearly had our hands on the knob, then closed the door between us.

The door was unlocked, as all doors in Prouwder House are, but when we opened it, there was nothing to see but neatly folded sheets, blankets, towels, and washcloths. No secret passageway and no remains of a tunnel either.

"Who in hell was that, Tom?"

"That," I braced myself against a shelf, "was Frank Candell."

GATE

4/13/19

Tom slept good, but I woke up off and on all night wondering if I'd find his sister standing at the foot of our bed or maybe that Frank C A N D E L L running through our door. We had talked the rest of the day before about those two, deciding not to tell Belle and Louis about Frank just yet, and trying to figure out where he and Tom's sister went. I don't even understand how these tunnels work normally, let alone when Tom and I don't hear any yells for help. He says it's science, but to me it's hocus pocus, like that Houdini fellow.

I can't ponder stuff like that for very long without I get a headache, so I turned my mind to a simpler chore: finding a good place to put things we need for our rescues. Prouwder House has three main floors plus the basement and our apartment, so we looked in the middle, on the second floor, for a room that isn't being used much. That floor is mostly bedrooms and bathrooms. (The first floor is public rooms, like the ballroom, dining rooms, art gallery, library, places where friends and business partners can be met and entertained. The third floor is servants' quarters and odd rooms like the gymnasium.) We found a dressing room that's big enough. It's wedged between two bedrooms and doesn't connect directly to the hallway, so we'll have to go through one or the other bedroom to get to it, but there's a small patio outside it and that has a stone staircase going down to the ground, so all in all it's pretty good for our work.

What clothes were in there we stuffed in wardrobes in the bedrooms, along with some hairbrushes, hand mirrors, and the like. That left a pretty good number of shelves and drawers and tables empty. We scouted around and found a couple other sets of shelves in the basement. They weren't being used for much so we dusted them off and carried them up to our "supply room". We crossed paths with Roberts the butler and we had him help us haul one piece into place, but then he made himself scarce. He must have gone straight to Mrs. Prouwder-Caul because she showed up with him in tow just a few minutes later. On the surface she was all smiles and offers of help, but I could tell she wasn't really too pleased about what we were doing because she likes things just so around here. She suggested we use one of the out buildings on the property or a room in the basement, but Tom made a good argument against both those ideas, which was that they weren't "centrally located". He told me when she was gone that he'd decided to start "throwing his weight around" when it came to rescue work.

Tom also kept Roberts hopping until he had broken out in a sweat that made his uniform pretty uncomfortable, I bet. He's not a bad sort of fellow, I figure, but it was good to have the upper hand on him after how snooty he was at breakfast that time. I wished we could put Charles the chauffeur to work hefting and hauling too, but he was off driving somebody somewhere. Marks was off duty, just like James. I'm pretty glad to be wearing my Navy uniform now because it says that I'm doing useful work here, same as anybody else.

With all the storage in place, Tom and I broke for supper and then began gathering things into our supply room. That's where we ran into some trouble between us because Tom wanted to put everything in order of the alphabet like Crowne had done, but I said we should instead put long, skinny things together and round things together. That way, pipes and baseball bats and spears would lean together in one corner and globes or spools of twine or medicine balls would roll around together in another. Tom put an "abby-cuss" in what he called the A section of a top shelf, but even if I thought we needed it, I'd never think to look for it there. Neither of us could make the other see why his system was better, so we knocked off for the day and went "home" to our apartment.

This morning we got back to it and brought a whole lot more flotsam and jetsam into the supply room, but neither of us was any less stubborn about how to organize it, so we hadn't made much progress when we heard an awful din of screams! Tom listened close in that way he can and guessed it wasn't coming from anywhere inside the mansion. We ran out onto the patio, down the stairs, and zigzagged across the grounds until we figured out which way to go. Turned out the source was an old iron gate on a corner of the estate I hadn't seen yet. It was pretty covered with vines and probably hadn't been swung open for ten years or more so I didn't know how we were going to get through it, but no sooner had we laid hands on it than I felt us going down a tunnel.

When we stopped, we had hold of another iron gate, a kind of dirty yellow color, and bolted shut on our side. We were in a long narrow alley between short buildings with plaster of the same dirty-yellow color. Screams and gunfire bounced back and forth between the buildings. Between the bars of the gate was a big area of flat dirt and some grass surrounded by walls. Looked like it might usually be a pretty peaceful place, but right then hundreds of people were running for their lives away from two lines of soldiers shooting right into the thick of them. It was horrible, but even scarier was how many of them were hurtling towards our gate!

Zeb and I threw back the bolts and the gate fairly burst away from its moorings. A stampede of brown faces, arms, legs, and bodies nearly crushed us against the ochre walls to which the gate was affixed. Men, women, and children pressed past us, screaming and clutching at the walls or each other while the retort of bullets continued. Some stumbled but righted themselves; others were borne along by the tide of humanity. Still others fell and became obstacles to those behind them or, worse yet, the first crushed and bloody threads of a human carpet that stretched from one side of the gate to the other. Zeb snagged one half-naked boy away from the deadly soles of his countrymen and held him with the strength of one arm high above turbaned, scarfed, or uncovered heads. He and I scrambled onto a window ledge and a drainage pipe, respectively, thus saving ourselves from being trampled, but such precarious positions left us generally ill-suited to helping others. One elderly lady, bearing the mark of the Hindu and a sari of crimson and gold, clutched piteously at my foot, but before I could assist her she had been carried away by the frantic crowd to a fate I do not know.

Our attention was partly turned from the teeming throng back to the ongoing crack of gunfire which everyone but us was fleeing. Out in a vast area beyond this gate, a great number of citizens ran hither and yon. Bullets that did not strike flesh struck dirt instead and marked the deadly aim of the gunmen. When the crowd dodged right, bullets followed. When they dashed left, bullets likewise pursued them. Always it seemed to be the thickest center of the crowd that drew the most fire. Lying down provided no protection: those who flung themselves onto Mother Earth in hopes of shelter were targeted all the more mercilessly.

I cannot say how long the barrage lasted. For its victims one is justified in saying it lasted the rest of their lives. For survivors it was perhaps ten minutes, but time does not pass in hell. I likewise cannot say why the barrage ended. Had the gunmen reached some quota of bodies? Had they at last recoiled at their deeds or merely killed the man or men they had targeted from the start? Perhaps most ghastly, had they simply run out of bullets? For whatever reason, the firing stopped and eventually no more people rushed through the gates behind and partially above which Zeb and I sheltered. The boy he held aloft struggled to be free and ran away the instant Zeb put his feet upon the ground. We heaved air in and out of our bodies, clinging all the while to the gate we had opened an eternity and mere minutes before.

Out on the field and there in the passage the situation was identical: silent dead, crying injured, traumatized survivors. It was another human carpet, horrifying and overwhelming. I scarcely knew what to do. Not all the bandages in all the vases of Prouwder House could staunch the vast flow of blood. My vision swam from bodies to walls to gate to field and then the sky above. I noticed that it was very early evening. I wanted to ask Zeb whether he also surmised that this was India, but from my mouth came nothing intelligible. Zeb had pressed his brow against the bars of the gate. We clung to metal and breathed. Amid the wailing came the sound of boots in quick march. Brown soldiers in tan uniforms and tilted hats drew into view. They carried rifles with bayonets which they trained upon us the instant they saw us. There was much shouting and a British colonel appeared. He seemed astonished to find us, white men, amid the brown people he'd attacked.

"You there! Who are you?"

We were neither inclined nor mentally able to answer, such was the carnage we had witnessed. It occurred to me that, despite how awful it had been to fail Abraham in Pinsk, we had not been made to endure the sight of his being executed. Now, although we had seen dozens or scores mowed down, we were spared any personal acquaintance with the victims. I thought this was perhaps the only balance of mercy we might find in doing The Work.

The colonel took our silence as provocation. "Arrest them!"

We rushed to lock the gate against this man and the troops he commanded. They thrust their bayonets through the bars and pierced the loose cuff of Zeb's jersey, but left his skin uncut. I was not so fortunate: one bayonet tip caught me on the kneecap and drew blood, but I flinched away and thus saved *myself from a more serious wound. Zeb dragged me another yard off and that gave me time to gain my feet. We ran to the end of the alley and caught up with the slowest of those fleeing the attack. The streets were a pandemonium of screams, people, animals, and vehicles. Survivors reported what had happened to growing throngs of passersby and initial shock began to turn into anger and investigation.*

All this developed as Zeb and I dashed away with little sense of where we were located and even less of where we were headed. We did not, of course, blend in with the locals. Our race alone would have made us stand out, but our height and our American uniforms added to our distinctiveness. Owing to the different branches we had served in, we were distinct even from each other.

I point this out because, as alarm among the general populace grew, so did the number of authority figures. Medical personnel, civilian police, and military men hastened sometimes alongside us, sometimes in opposition to us. I knew it was only a matter of time until the colonel's arrest order caught up with us. I led Zeb down ever narrower and less populated streets. I hoped to keep us out of sight of the troops that had fired on the crowd, but my strategy also brought us more and more attention from the city's denizens. They had likely never seen Americans before. Some stared unreservedly, others hurried inside their homes. It was unclear whether we had put significant distance between us and the site of the massacre or had merely skirted around its edge.

Tired and wounded, we came to a shallow indentation in one wall and stood there panting. A boy about the age of the one Zeb had lifted above the stampede peeked through chinks of boards opposite us. Other children were bolder or shyer in their assessment. Zeb wiped sweat from his brow and said we had better get back to where we started. He'd tugged on a few gates as we ran, but had found no tunnel home. I declared I had done the same, also to no avail. I didn't divulge that I was utterly lost, as that might have discouraged him. I suggested we find shelter and return to the gate under cover of night.

Zeb dug around in his backpack and produced one of the British shillings we had procured at Prouwder House. Mother, although not a member of a rescue team at any point in her past, had begun collecting foreign currency back when she was a girl, first from her uncle William and later from her brother Louis. Her entire assortment she made available to all who did The Work, provided they contributed as much as they withdrew. From among the children observing us, Zeb selected the oldest boy and, by means of not unskilled pantomime, made clear to him that we would pay him for a hiding place. He guided us as stealthily down back alleys as the gaggle of curious children accompanying us made possible until we reached a small shop which combined the sale of dry goods with shoe repair and, apparently, concealment from the police. The boy seemed to relay our request for sanctuary to the shop's owner, who may have been the boy's father, and Zeb surrendered our coin to him.

We were then led into a closet, the door to which was hidden by a display of newspapers. The shelter was cramped and stuffy. Zeb and I could neither sit down nor see much. Some feeble light did seep in under the door so that the bottom halves of our shoes were visible, but otherwise Zeb and I more felt and heard each other than saw. I bade him turn around and I then sought more coins in his backpack because, as surely as the sun rises in the east, people will take advantage of those in need. I wanted to be ready to pay our continued "rent" of this space. By memory and guesswork I extracted another shilling from the depths of his pack, then turned him around again.

He asked me what I thought we had witnessed earlier. We agreed that it was not a battle between armed opponents, but why troops would be ordered to fire on women and children was beyond our imagination. There seemed to be no justification for it and we began to wonder to whom we could report the attack. Anyone that outranked a British colonel might be hundreds of miles away, but the rack of newspapers we were hiding behind gave me at least one idea for a future redress of the crime. Zeb whispered, albeit with little satisfaction, that we had at least been able to save someone this time. The Work was indeed a more nebulous endeavor than I had been led to believe by the heroic stories I'd heard from William and Louis.

A scant hour had passed when we heard a commotion in the shop. There were suddenly many voices, first talking, then shouting and we both tensed up. An attempt was made to open the secret door. That failed, but served as a warning to us and when the second attempt succeeded, Zeb and I rushed out into the shop, the main entrance of which was blocked by three of the soldiers who had fired so mercilessly into the crowd. We knocked the first of them to the ground and the shopkeeper took that opportunity to flee. That left Zeb and me with one opponent apiece. To his, Zeb delivered an abdominal punch which took the man quite out of action. My man had his bayonet ready and thrust it at my gut. I managed to sidestep the blade for the most part, but its tip penetrated my shirt and might have sliced across my skin if I hadn't brought all my weight to bear on the rifle itself. I'd hoped to force the blade and muzzle into the shop's dirt floor, but now the weapon was entangled in my uniform. I gave the soldier an elbow to the nose and he partly turned away, thus loosening his grip on his weapon. Zeb kicked him in the head and we were momentarily free of assailants.

With all them soldier boys knocked down or out, Tom and I hauled ass away from the news shop. We ran where our noses led us, but nowhere looked good. If we couldn't even buy a hidey-hole for money, it didn't seem likely we'd find one for free. I reckoned one of the kids who'd followed us had ratted us out to the soldiers. I just hoped he'd gotten good coin for it 'cause the people around us looked mighty poor off. Why exactly that colonel was so het up to catch us, though, was a puzzler. We hadn't seen anything that dozens of others hadn't and, hell, we didn't even know exactly where we were! Maybe he was just trying to round up everybody that wasn't already dead. Maybe he thought we could make trouble for him in a way the locals couldn't.

It seemed like our only plan was to keep running until we reached Prouwder House on foot, but we did get to catch our breath here and there when we crouched behind barrels or wagons. People got out of our way quick enough, but then pointed and shouted so any cops or riflemen had an easy trail to follow. Down one alley we found a ladder and used it to get up on the roof of that building. This hid us better, specially once we'd pulled the ladder up with us, but it also slowed us down considerable. We jumped from one rooftop to the next where we could, but not every roof looked like it could hold the weight of two grown men and a ladder, so we had to backtrack some, plus we made a ruckus in the houses we were running across and that brought out the people who lived there and *they* brought the cops. Soon we were being chased down below on the street and up above on the rooftops. We were pretty well boxed in once, but Tom got the idea of jamming the bottom of the ladder into the ground and then riding it in an arc over to the next roof. We broke the ladder that way, but escaped the cops for a couple more minutes. It seemed like more and more of them were chasing us. Dogs and children joined in and I saw we weren't going to get away. I just hoped we wouldn't break our necks while trying!

The end of our run came when the space between the roof we were on and the next one was too big to jump. Tom tried anyway, but fell down onto about five cops in the street below. Before I could jump down to help him, about five other cops had caught up with me on the roof and took hold of me by the throat, arms, and legs. Soon after that, we were thrown head over heels into a paddy wagon and from there into a jail cell in the dirty basement of a police station. We always seem to end up looking like criminals when we set off to rescue somebody!

The police who captured us also confiscated our backpacks. They could be replaced, of course, but I imagined Mother would fuss a bit. I still believe it's better to embark on a mission well-prepared, but knowing ahead of time what sort of situation one is getting into and precisely what tools will be required would certainly cut down on expenses. Best to keep things in perspective: a thousand backpacks lost would be a small price to pay to ensure Zeb and I return to Prouwder House safely.

Our cell, dismal as it was, provided the rest we needed

after attempting to elude "justice". Zeb took a few deep breaths, then set about testing the bars of our lone window. I held him back from a similar testing of our cell door, however, for something told me we had nearly reached the end of our time in Amritsar and it wouldn't do to disappear down a tunnel prematurely.

Our location I had discerned from the sign on the façade of that very police station. Although we were presently in the custody of the civilian authorities, I surmised it was the military that wanted us. No doubt some emissary would come to claim us, perhaps the colonel himself. He was certainly the man I most wanted to confront. Back in Pinsk, Major Narbut had, so far as I knew, gotten away with murder, but I hoped the British public would not display as much sang-froid when it came to the massacre of people under their rule. Until there could be punishment for his crime, I wanted to plague the colonel's conscience.

Zeb and I had rather long to wait. A police officer came by to read the charges leveled against us, but, when asked, we did not divulge our names. Threats of violence were made and, worse yet, water was withheld from us, but at every opportunity I insisted upon the colonel being brought to our cell. This was finally accomplished late that night, by which time I had filled Zeb in on the broad strokes of my plan.

The colonel was the same gray-haired, stiff-backed man we'd seen earlier in the day, just as cool and collected now as when he'd been overseeing the slaughter. He was much older than the Polish Major Narbut, perhaps sixty, but his hair was plentiful and he wore glasses above a full, dark moustache. There were medals on his beige uniform and a riding crop in one of his hands. He introduced himself as Colonel Reginald

Dyer and asked our names, but we maintained our anonymity. He promised that our names would be beaten out of us later and asked what we were doing at Jallianwala Bagh. I stored both his name and that of the public garden away for use once we were back home. I hoped my memory was as good as Rose's. "We're here to observe and report," I lied.

"And to whom exactly do an American sailor and pilot imagine they report?"

"To a higher authority," I responded. "What you've done here today will not go unnoted."

The colonel snapped his riding crop against the back of his forearm and drew himself to complete attention. "What I've done here today is to suppress an insurgence against the British Raj, about which I know infinitely more than any foreigner."

"You yourself are a foreigner, are you not?"

"No, indeed," Dyer replied. "Unlike you, I was born here, educated here, and these people are mine to watch over."

I glanced down. "There's blood on your boots, Colonel."

Dyer did not drop his eyes, but rather raised his chin. "You are obviously agents of an enemy government, here to undermine the rightful rule of His Majesty George V. As such you will be hanged. If you cooperate, you may be granted execution by firing squad. What say you?"

Zeb clenched and unclenched his fists, but took no other action. I determined it was time for us to go and took his hand in mine, which seemed to unnerve Dyer slightly. "I say, Colonel, that we have observed all things and are ready to depart. We've seen you and what you have wrought. Remember in the days to come that we were able to leave this cell at the moment of our choosing. We have only waited so that we could hear directly whatever plea for mercy you wished to make so that it *might be weighed against the pleas for mercy you ignored today. Sometime soon we shall return to carry out judgment. No matter where you are at that hour, Colonel, we will reach you. Remain watchful. Do not sleep lest you be taken unawares."*

Dyer's face was utterly impassive, but his voice shook a little as he ordered the guard to unlock our cell and drag us out. By the time the man's key turned in the lock, however, Zeb and I had grasped the bars of the door and disappeared entirely.

Walking back from the gate to Prouwder House, Zeb congratulated me on "a mighty fine speech that had put the fear of God into that limey bastard", but he wondered what higher authority I meant to report the massacre to.

"Why, the very highest, of course!" I replied. "The Fourth Estate, the annals of history, the ultimate judge of all things!"

"Your mom?" he guessed.

"No," I slung an arm across his shoulders. "Tomorrow I'm going to contact my favorite journalist from our very own record of note, The Pittsburgh Post*!"*

TRACKS

4/14/19

I like pressing up against Tom. There's something real nice about being so close to him that his face is all I can see. He's a couple inches taller than me and his face is kind of round, especially when he's smiling, so it's like looking right up at a full moon, but with dimples. His eyes and hair are like those dark patches on the moon's surface, only they don't seem cold when I got my arms around his waist and his arms are around my shoulders. I don't know how close the moon and the Earth get, but I know they never get to rub the stubble on their chins together like we do.

This time, however, we were squeezed together in a booth on the first floor of Prouwder House. This is where guests and business partners can go to make telephone calls back to their homes or offices so they won't be overheard by anybody. Tom was sitting on the bench with the earpiece wrapped around behind me and talking into the mouthpiece right beside my belly. He was squished up against the glass part of the door pretty hard, but I had it worse 'cause I was standing up as straight as I could, which meant my neck was bent sharp and my skull kept knocking against the ceiling. I had all my weight on my left leg and it was starting to cramp up, plus I had to lean hard onto my left elbow and that made it sore pretty quick. I guess whoever built this cabinet never figured two grown men would use it together 'cause most men's business is private.

On the other end of the line was the *Pittsburgh Press* reporter Tom likes, Reginald Bigh-Lyne. He says the guy writes well and he showed me a couple of his articles. One was about labor strikes and the other was about improvements in education for Negroes. I guess they made Tom think this was the fellow who should write about what we saw in Pinsk and Amritsar, but their talk wasn't going well.

"I can assure you," Tom kept saying, "we were eyewitnesses to both massacres."

Turns out, the reporter had a hard time believing we were in White Russia one day, in India a few days after that and now already back in Pittsburgh! Tom, of course, couldn't explain how such a thing was possible without saying we had a magic house that sends us all around the world to rescue people. That would have made him sound crazy.

Just when I thought I'd be crippled up for life, Tom got frustrated with the guy and threatened to take his story to *The Gazette.* That must have pleased the reporter pretty good, 'cause he told Tom to do exactly that and hung up on him. Tom crossed his legs one knee over the other and did just about the same with his arms, pondering what to do next. There were no holes in the cabinet to let sound or air get through so it was getting pretty stuffy inside, but he didn't seem mindful of that.

"Our story is not credible, Zebediah. I should have foreseen that."

I asked him why he didn't tell the reporter who he was. Maybe that would help, but Tom said it was better not to get the Prouwders involved in a newspaper story. They like their secrets, as I've said before. Tom's mom would be especially mad if we told the press about the work we do. I suppose it's a good thing we're keeping these journals at least. I should try to write better.

For the time being, as they say, Tom saw no way to report what we had seen happen to those Jewish men and boys or to all them people in Jelly Bag. We decided to go back to supplying our storage room, but then we couldn't get the door to that telephone booth to open and wouldn't you know it right then we started hearing a cry for help! Tom and I both jiggled the handle and pushed on the door, but neither gave. We had to add our own voices to the call for help we were hearing and hard knocking on the pane of glass besides until along came one of the maids. Agnes, I think it was. She set down her load of sewing and lifted up on the handle to free the door and out we tumbled. We grabbed our backpacks, told her thanks, and ran off down the hallway.

As usual, Tom had the better sense of where we were going, which was outside. We hustled down the stairs of the poor coacher, around the end of the greenhouse, and then sped headlong down the hill toward Nine Mile Run. There are some streets and houses at the point where the run empties into the Mon River. Tom says the area is called Duck Hollow, but we didn't stop at any of the shanties there. Instead we clambered up onto a very low trestle bridge and picked our way from the first tie to the second. Soon as we stepped onto the third, the bridge was suddenly a whole lot longer, higher, and bigger. It wasn't crossing some itty-bitty creek anymore, but a major river, and smackdab in the middle of it, wedged hard between two ties, was the man whose screaming we'd heard clear back in the Prouwder House telephone booth!

I didn't know how the fella had gotten where he was 'cause there wasn't any walkway alongside the tracks, just girders and a big drop into the drink. Tom sprinted like a goat over to the guy and I followed him, but careful. There wasn't much of the guy to be seen. He was like one of those icebergs we saw in the North Atlantic: head, one shoulder, and one arm above the ties, the rest of him dangling below in midair. He was wedged in tight enough that he couldn't breathe very deep or pull himself up, but not so tight that he wouldn't fall into the water if he let go and that was maybe fifty feet down. On top of that, the next train to come along would knock his head clean off while the rest of his body would drop down and get swept away. I doubted the engineer would even suspect he'd just killed a guy and there wouldn't be any evidence either. I kept my ears open and my eyes peeled 'cause Tom and I sure as hell wouldn't have much time to save this guy. The rails already felt like they were rumbling!

Tom took hold of the guy's shoulder and braced his feet, then told me to dig down and get a purchase on the guy's other armpit. The fella himself wasn't much help. He looked at both of us wild-like and, maybe 'cause he was panicked or pinned around his chest, he couldn't get out any clear words. It was just a bunch of 'ughs' and 'gargs'. Slobber dripped down his chin onto the collar of his shirt, which was blue denim and buttoned up to his Adam's apple. (I'm trying to put a lot more details in my journal. Maybe if I get good enough I can write for *The Pittsburgh Press* myself! Miss Barnes would be proud of me. Maybe she would even read one of my stories to her class or assign it to them kids for anna-lisa-sis!)

I bent over and gripped the guy's arm, but I kept watching for a train too. The way our rescues have gone, I figured we had one or two minutes tops to get this guy free and off the bridge. Tom and I both pulled up, but we couldn't work him loose. He spewed more gibberish and yelled for help like we weren't already his last hope. Tom wanted to push him on through and bring him up over the side of the bridge, but I knew we'd lose him for sure if we did that, so Tom got a length of rope out of his backpack and looped it good around the guy's arms, shoulders, and chest. We tried to push him down then, but he wasn't having none of that and said his first clear words, which was a string of ~~ubsenatees ubcenities~~ cusses. I definitely felt vibration in the rails by then.

Tom said the fool was so out of his mind with fear that he might wriggle out of the rope entirely. He seemed even scareder than that Italian guy hanging from the balloon ship. At least you could sort of reason with Ludano. If we couldn't push this fella down, then we just had to pull him up and so we put our backs into it double hard, but it was no use. Tom lay down on the tracks, which scared me to my knees, and reached as far down the man's torso as he could. He wasn't wearing a belt, but eventually Tom got hold of his pants and brought one of his legs up so at least he had three limbs on the bridge. That was as far as we got though, 'cause the man's belly was even thicker than his chest. Tom tried to get him to breathe out all the way so he'd be thin enough to squeeze upwards, but he just kept panting and slobbering and cussing.

"He isn't right in the head, is he?"

Tom agreed and quick wrapped more of the rope around the guy's middle so at least we wouldn't lose ground. "I suspect we'll have to render him unconscious in order to extricate him." I asked how he thought we would do that, seeing as how he would become dead weight soon as we knocked him out. "I propose we secure him to the underside of this tie and then I shall endeavor to asphyxiate him."

I didn't understand every word, but when he clamped his hand hard over the guy's nose and mouth, I got the picture. It took a long time and there was more cussing, some clawing and then finally the guy slumped against the ropes. I got some burns from that on the palms of my hands 'cause I was bearing his whole weight while Tom worked his chest up between the ties. This was as hard as birthing a calf and Tom grunted a lot, but got the man's waist up onto the tracks before he came to. He struggled at first and made more weird sounds, but then he got it that we were helping him and brought both legs into the open. He lay on his back and panted. One of his shoes was gone and his pants were halfway down his ass, but he was safe at last. Tom and I were panting hard as well. There was no way we'd outrun the cops I saw step onto the far end of the bridge!

At least they weren't a train. That's what I'd thought when the headlights of their police wagon first hit the girders around us. They were maybe a few years older than Tom and me. They both carried flashlights as they walked toward us and each kept his free hand on his pistol.

"I bet you a dollar they're gonna arrest us."

Tom thought that was "highly unlikely", but we hadn't met one cop yet that appreciated what we were trying to do on a rescue. Mostly they've been real sons of bitches, if you ask me. These cops shined their lights right in our eyes and asked us what we were doing there. Our slobberer sprang to his feet and tried to run away, but his pants fell down to his ankles and tripped him up. Tom and I caught him under each arm 'cause God knows we didn't want him to get stuck in the ties again. One of the cops said maybe this was the guy they'd been told to be on the lookout for, William Snyder.

The crazy fella seemed to recognize his name at least, though he didn't care much that his skivvies were on display. I wanted to know what he'd done and the taller cop said he was an inmate at the Woodville State Hospital for the Insane down in Collier Township. It hit me then that we were still in Pittsburgh! That hadn't happened before. The river below us could be the Monongahela, the Allegheny, or the Ohio. Tom didn't look surprised. He'd probably figured all this out long before. He's smart that way and when he suggested we get off the bridge, I definitely took his word for it, but the cops weren't keen on letting us go just yet. They had lots of questions about who we were, how we came to be on this bridge, and whether we were connected to this William Snyder in any way.

Like usual, Tom had such good answers that I half believed them myself. He said we'd just been discharged from the Navy and the Air Service, now back home and looking for work anywhere we could when we'd heard this miserable sod screaming for help and a hell of a time we had getting him loose too! I guess most of that was the truth.

"Well," said the sergeant, whose name was O'Malley, "if you're hoping for work here on Neville Island, you're shit out of luck because the feds aren't going to build that ammunition factory after all, now that we got the Armistice." The other one, Patrolman Dewalt, said we should go into law enforcement, like they had, because they were just discharged as well. That set Tom to asking about their service, where they'd seen action and the like and boy, weren't those two cops full of stories! I was getting mighty antsy seeing as how we still weren't off the bridge and like to be killed if a train came bearing down on us, so I started ambling faster towards the paddy wagon even if that meant we were going to be arrested. Better locked up than fitted for a pine box!

We finally got off the tracks and helped Dewalt and O'Malley push Snyder into the back of their wagon. They seemed satisfied with our story, but I still didn't trust them. It wouldn't do to have a local rich guy like Tom get arrested for helping a lunatic escape the asylum, so I was eager to get away as soon as possible. They still had their hands on their pistols however and Tom kept jabbering away about dog fights and strafing runs. I think he liked having an audience, but he also asked a lot about battles these guys had seen. Both were infantry and everything they said about trenches and barbwire and mortar shells made me glad I'd been on a ship the whole time.

Eventually we got around to them saying they had to take this guy back to the loony bin and Tom, without talking to me about it, asked them for a lift into town! They said sure and opened up the back of the wagon. Snyder now had snot AND slobber running down his chin, plus he had stuck one hand into his skivvies and was playing with the toys God gave him. I just about bolted away like a crazy man myself, but Tom climbed in docile as a sheep so I followed him. We were gonna have words about all this later.

"We'll drop yinz off on Liberty Avenue. How's that?" O'Malley said.

Tom said that would be stupendous. I'm not sure whether stupendous means great or stupid and I don't think O'Malley knew either, but he sort of smiled and locked the door behind us. One thing I was sure of was that Tom was sweet on the cop and I said so. Tom scoffed, but I said anybody dumb enough to get into a police wagon of his own free will had to have his nuts where his noggin belonged. Tom said the pot was calling the kettle black, but I ignored him and said we were either going to wind up in a jail cell or a padded cell, no doubt about it. He argued that these were agreeable defenders of civil order, fellow veterans, and native Pittsburghers, so we couldn't be in safer hands. Speaking of hands, Snyder had used his to make himself hard and now had it all on display. I gave him a slug to the shoulder and told him to knock it off, but Tom said he wasn't mentally capable of observing societal norms and should be left in peace. I just turned to look out the bars on the door.

We had crossed the river (Tom said it was part of the Ohio) and were now passing through a hard-packed neighborhood which looked like a lot of jail cells and padded cells to me. I'm glad Prouwder House is on a big estate so I can pretend I'm still out in the country when the mansion itself is out of sight. Why didn't we just jump back to Duck Hollow, I asked. Tom said this was a rare opportunity to enjoy Pittsburgh instead of fighting for our lives in some far-off place and we should take advantage of it. We could see a show, have a drink, or maybe visit a public park. If it pleased Tom to wander around in the choking smoke of all those factories, I wasn't going to make him do it alone, so we went on bumping along brick streets, sometimes in sight of the river, then crossing it again at what Tom said used to be Allegheny City until Pittsburgh took it over a dozen years ago. That didn't seem like a neighborly thing to do and I was glad Waynesburg is too far away for that to happen there. We crossed back over the Al and pulled up in front of a police station.

"Told you so!" I braced for a fight 'cause if Tom and I were headed for a jail cell the way we'd been in India, I meant to knock a few of those cops' teeth loose for having lied to us with smiles on their faces. Tom stayed calm and said we were downtown, right where we'd asked to be. When our cops and a couple others opened the door, I was ready to wade into them with my feet and fists, but it was Snyder that got out first. He screamed bloody murder and got an elbow into one cop's chest, but he still hadn't pulled his pants up right, so pretty quick he was sprawled on the pavement with the other three cops piled on him. I was too surprised to take advantage of the brawl, so I just sat there and watched, like Tom was doing.

The two new cops and Dewalt got Snyder squared away and hauled him up the stairs into the police station. O'Malley stayed behind and thanked us again for saving the man's life. We climbed out of the wagon and shook hands with him. I knew I'd been wrong not to trust him, but Tom didn't rub my nose in it. Instead he asked O'Malley for suggestions on what two discharged servicemen should do in Pittsburgh, even though we were supposed to be from there. He was just making time with the guy, but O'Malley didn't catch on and said there was theaters and movie houses, bars and boxing, all within walking distance. Just don't get drunk and wind up back here, he warned us.

Tom gave him another handshake and a smile like I hadn't seen him give anyone but me before. It made me jealous and I pulled him away quick. I already fended off Nellie Edgerton so's Tom and I could be together; I wasn't gonna let him get all mooncalf over some cop now!

We walked off and started looking at "mark-ease" to decide what we wanted to do. Tom knew just about every alley downtown there, so I just followed along, like usual. I thought about how, if I hadn't ended up at Prouwder House, I might have been living on this street or that and I might even be out looking for a good time right then. If Tom was out too, maybe he and I would have gone to the same show. I wondered if I would have spoken to him, maybe said "Good evening" or asked him if he liked the show. I probably would have been too shy, but if he'd talked to me first, I'd probably be following him all around town just like I was doing right then. Some things have to happen, no matter how you go about them, I guess. Like six plus one, five plus two, and four plus three all add up to seven. You can't change that.

There were plenty of choices. At the Nixon, Cyril Maude was playing in "The Saving Grace", a comedy, and at the Alvin was "The Melting of Molly" with Isabella Lowe and the original cast: "great fun, great girls, and great Mary", according to an advertisement in *The Pittsburgh Press* that we bought. The newsstand we bought it at probably didn't have a hidey-hole like the one in Amritsar. At the Gayety we could see "Puss Puss" with Clark and McCullough. That was on Duquesne Way at 6th Street. If we went to the Davis for vaudeville, we could see Emma Carus, but at the Pitt Theater there was "Mary, Be Careful", a "new play of Youth, Love, Ideals and Realities with a famous cast". There was also The Trail Hitters at the Victoria while Loew's Lyceum had Sessue Hayakawa.

After a lot of talking, we decided to take in Mutt and Jeff in The Woolly West at the Duquesne Theater. Tom talks a lot about being a cowboy or panning for gold, trapping beavers and the like. A lot of city folk have ideas like that. They don't know how awful boring it can be to work with herds of cattle or sheep and what a stinky mess skinning an animal is. I like being in the country if I get to just sit and draw or read. Once you bring in the idea of work, I lose interest right quick. I'd do it for Tom, though, if he decided he wanted to chuck this rescue work and room after room of luxury. I suppose I'd have to go along with him, just to make sure he didn't starve himself to death.

We got to the Duquesne, paid at the box office, and settled into our seats. There was a pretty big crowd even though it was a Monday. I guess there's enough people in Pittsburgh that anything you want to do, the same idea has occurred to lots of other brains too. The seats were comfortable, but the more people that came in, the more I fidgeted around until Tom asked me what the matter was. I kept looking at the huge Germans and Slovaks pouring in and then at the tiny exits we'd all have to go back out of and I told Tom I knew there was going to be a fire in the theater or maybe an escapee from that lunatic asylum who'd come out on stage and start firing a repeating rifle into the crowd so that everyone would rush to the doors and crush each other underfoot until the floor was just as red and sticky as the cushions we sat on.

I was sweating all over and shaky. Tom hove me to my feet and got me outside to the alley before I puked. My knees just about gave way, but Tom had a good hold on my hips and head so I didn't fall over into my own sick. When I was finally empty, I didn't rightly know where I was or what had happened. Tom wiped off my chin with his handkerchief and made me spit until the taste was gone from my mouth. He said I was all right, I just had "shell shock" from everything we've been through the past few weeks. I said, well, you've been through all that too, so how come you aren't shook up like this, but he didn't answer. He just led me to the Tic Toc, a diner at Kaufman's department store, and ordered us coffee, apple pie, and a chicken Waldorf salad. He's pretty good at taking care of people when he sees the need. He asked if I wanted to head home, but I hated to cut our "night out" short, so we took a streetcar to Schenley Park and walked around until we got to Phipp's Conservatory and Botanical Gardens where we found a bench and sat down.

I watched people stroll along the paths and admire what plants were growing there or starting to bud. They looked happy, but for some goddamn reason I started bawling so hard I had to put my head down and cover my face with my cap. Tom could have been disgusted with me, but he just put a hand on my shoulder and said something about the garden of Jelly Bag. That only made me tear up harder, but he talked about Zigman Froyd and the "talking cure" and said it was good for me except it was Tom doing all the talking.

Not too long after that, I was all wrung out and asked if we could go on home. He said sure and we took a taxicab back to Prouwder House. It looked very quiet. A lot of lights were lit and I have to admit it's a beautiful place even though every room leads somewhere dangerous. James the night watchman came around the corner as we were getting out of the taxi and said hello to us. He's one of the few here that treats us normal, him and Belle. He doesn't look down on me or up to Tom. I mean, he doesn't bow or act like he's got manure on his shoes when Tom is there. He just smiles real big like he was doing right then, happy to see other folks still awake. Maybe that's why he's nice to everyone equal, 'cause he's protecting us while we sleep.

In any case, we shot the breeze with James for a while and were headed indoors when we heard another yell for help coming from down the hill just like it had before. We left James staring in confusion and ran off toward Duck Hollow again. I wondered if Snyder had gotten loose from the cops somehow and was running across another train bridge, maybe with his pants slipping down and police hot on his trail. Sure enough, there on the low bridge over Nine Mile Run was a man just about his size, springing from one railroad tie to the next fast as he could go and screaming his lungs out! Tom and I climbed back up onto the tracks and chased him hard. We had just about caught up with him when all of a sudden he jumped over two ties at once, out of our grasp, then stopped and turned around. Damned if it wasn't that Frank Candell! He had a wicked smile on his face that I wanted to punch right off him, but soon as Tom and I stepped onto the ties he had sprung over, we fell through a tunnel, not into the creek, but onto a different set of tracks running crosswise. We weren't outside anymore and we definitely weren't in Pittsburgh either. Sprawled out like drunks, we looked around at a big train station with a glass ceiling and ironwork columns holding it up. "Where are we, Tom?"

"If I'm not much mistaken," he perched himself up on one elbow, "this is the central train station in Munich and those, Zebediah, are communist revolutionaries!"

Monday, the 14th of April

Determining our location was no particular achievement: a train station is perhaps the most easily identified kind of structure on Earth, even more unmistakable than a dam or a cathedral, as the first, without a view of the water it retains, may be taken for a wall, and the second, absent a view of the altar, could be misconstrued as a fortress or perhaps a museum. That this specific station was the main hub of Munich was attested to by its grandeur and the many signs announcing departures from and arrivals in München. One urgent example of the latter was the locomotive which bore down on Zeb and me from just ten feet away.

Shrieks from female onlookers and the mighty blast of the train's horn threw us into action. As yielding was our only recourse, we leapt to either side of the track. This meant that Zeb was now squeezed between one train at rest and one in motion while I had to spring to safety on a platform at the feet of several startled passengers and three armed guards wearing red armbands. The latter trained their weapons on me and called for others to seize the even more conspicuously dressed American sailor accompanying me. I hoped Zeb would not choose to fight or flee, as that could mean a bullet to his back.

Prouwder House receives several newspapers each day and I read them all. During the Great War, rumor held sway over fact, both because of the need for secrecy and the censorship it begets, as well as the difficulty of ascertaining the truth when so many factors are in constant play. It was thanks to newspapers that I knew, amid the general postbellum chaos of Germany, that communist revolutionaries had taken over Bavaria. The men holding me and now hauling Zeb up onto this platform were undoubtedly ill-disposed to welcome our sudden appearance. It was indeed a dicey situation Frank Candell had sent us into, but how to deal with him was a problem for a later date.

Zeb and I were made to kneel with our hands behind

our heads. The senior most guard demanded our names and our reason for being there. Our backpacks were confiscated and searched while onlookers were pushed away or shouted at. The guards frowned at our odd mix of currency, medical supplies, tools, and weapons. I took a chance and declared that my companion and I were American Bolsheviks that had defected from the corrupt and bourgeois West. We were in Munich, I lied, to support the proletarian government of Bavaria. I noticed that Zeb frowned at my words as scornfully as the guards.

My story was unconvincing. We were jerked to our feet and marched past the many termini to a grand staircase and thence to an office which had a commanding view of the station through an admirably constructed arch of glass panes, some of them openable. At a large desk obviously designed for that very spot sat a bureaucrat who pre-dated the new regime. He opted not to take responsibility for further interrogation. Instead he made a telephone call and ordered us transported to "Stadelheim". This was accomplished in the back of a police vehicle, through the bars of which I tried my best to note streets, bridges, and the crossing of the Isar river while Zeb pouted in his corner.

Stadelheim turned out to be a prison, of course, not the luxe hotel I'd pretended to hope for. We were searched again and processed. I gave my name as Owen Bucks while Zeb gave his as Mike Hunt and then we were shoved into a ten foot by ten foot cell from which we quickly determined there was no supernatural escape. Zeb continued to pout. He brought his heels up onto the edge of his cot and layered his forearms onto his knees, all the while giving me scornful looks. "I don't know why you had to say we were Bolsheviks," he groused.

I patiently explained that no better strategy had occurred to me and that he was welcome to invent a better tale for our captors whenever he liked. This did nothing to improve his mood so I sat down next to him and asked how, by the way, he had understood what I'd been saying to the guard in the first place.

"Ich kann Pennsilfaanisch Deitsch schwetze."

I had a moment of such profound disorientation that I could not have identified the man sitting beside me, as if his body, scent, and sound, despite their familiarity to me, did not add up to Zebediah Beck. My mouth hung open in a most undignified manner until he had mercy on me and offered an explanation. "My mom says her maiden name is Thorpe, but it's really Dieffendörfer. She was born out in Lancaster County. Her folks were all Amish, but something went wrong among 'em and my grandma and grandpa moved to Greene County. They changed their name. I spent a lot of time with 'em when I was a kid and picked up their German, which is all they spoke at home. Specially after the war started, though, they hid their background."

I told him that was fascinating and teased him for having perhaps as many secrets as the Prouwders themselves, an idea he has often repeated. This made him smile, whereafter he asked how we were going to extricate ourselves from our current predicament. I admitted that I did not know yet, but that we should remain vigilant for any opportunity. Zeb lamented the loss of our backpacks and the hacksaw one of them contained. I sympathized, but said I'd really just about given up on the idea of carrying supplies with us since they so often became booty for the authorities. It wasn't my intention to give away revolvers to every militia we encountered.

Hours passed, during which we were provided bread, two boiled eggs, a bit of cheese, and tea. We slept, as our bodies could not be convinced, despite the morning sunshine, that it was not night time. It is a good thing that we alone on all the Earth must suffer the consequences of such rapid transit across the surface of the globe; I believe it would kill most people, certainly the aged and the infirm, to travel vast distances at such great speed. If ever a vehicle for that purpose is developed, it will certainly be limited to passage along lines of longitude.

Toward four o'clock in the afternoon, we were roused from our cell, allowed to wash up, and then taken to the Neues Rathaus, or city hall, on the northern end of the Marienplatz. There we met Eugen Leviné, leader of the Bavarian Council Republic and current occupant of the mayor's office in the aforementioned chamber. He had large, almost Egyptian eyes, dark hair which retreated in waves from the shore of his forehead, and a full beard that blended into his high black collar. He wore the same red armband as the guards surrounding us and, other than being seated while everyone else stood, was indistinguishable from rank and file revolutionaries. On his desktop were the contents of our backpacks and he picked over them haphazardly. Our pistols, albeit prone, were aimed at us.

"You say you are Bolsheviks from America," he stated flatly in High German, "but you carry no communist materials. Nothing by Marx, Engels, or Lenin."

"It isn't safe to do so," I explained. "We were in Pinsk recently and were searched by the Polish general there, Aleksander Narbut-Łuczyński. We witnessed the massacre of thirty-five Jewish men and boys who were merely suspected of being Bolshevik sympathizers, among them Abraham Bankausky, a youth of seventeen. Others were even younger."

Whether Leviné had heard of the slaughter I could not tell, but I hoped my report would help establish my bona fides. *Many more questions followed, some soliciting further details of our travels, some pertaining to communist dogma. Fortunately, I have read "Capital" and the "Manifesto", so I was able to talk a good game about dialectical materialism, the bourgeoisie, and the means of production. Unfortunately, Leviné then turned his interrogation onto Zeb, who's had no such exposure to political theory or philosophical discourse. He answered every question in the rude dialect of his maternal grandparents, which was a pain to listen to, even in the short, angry bursts he managed to produce. He spouted simplistic doggerel about the rich owning everything and making all the rules while poor folks die in mine collapses or factory accidents every day, not to mention farm mishaps. He said all that's left to the poorest women is to become whores and for the poorest men there's only booze. Rich folks build churches so that the poor have somewhere to go on Sundays instead of burning down mansions.*

Well, I knew we were doomed. I regretted not employing our "free" time in a quick education on the basic tenets of economics and world order. Now we would surely be shot as the imposters we actually were.

Leviné mulled over what we had said, then rose and embraced Zeb warmly. "You are a true warrior for the people!" he exclaimed. He gestured in my direction. "Take this aristocrat back to his cell."

I protested my allegiance to the cause of the proletariat while the guards seized me by the arms, but Leviné dismissed me as a dilettante and a fellow traveler. "You have never sweated through a single day of labor. Your hands are as soft as kid gloves while Hunt's here are calloused and dirty. He was a sailor made to fight other sailors of his own class, while your aviator's uniform marks you as a playboy who had both the time and the lucre to learn to fly airplanes. I bet there is an American family somewhere willing to pay a grand ransom for your release. If they are unwilling to pay, you will nevertheless act as a deterrent to invasion by Weimar counterrevolutionaries."

I was dragged away while Zeb smirked.

More long hours of captivity passed, made even longer by my solitude. The night was spent dreaming fitfully of vast rows of empty beds in which I sought my boon companion without surcease or success. Where he actually was remained a mystery until long into the next day when he showed up outside my cell, keys in hand. He looked quite pleased with himself and I was as eager to hear his story as I was to escape my imprisonment. In short, he explained as he released me, Weimar troops were assaulting the city and Leviné had only come to power three days before; his hold on the population was shaky at best. In the confused response to the attack, Zeb was able to render two Bolsheviks unconscious and make his way back to the prison. How had he retraced our journey to Stadelheim without the careful observation of landmarks I had made? He hadn't; he simply asked passersby for directions. He called Müncheners "friendlier than Pittsburghers" and generally happy to help anyone with a loved one being held hostage by the Bolsheviks. More strategic use of violence at the guards' station had secured keys to prison cells and "here I am."

We donned workers' overcoats and proceeded south, away from the fighting. Many other locals were likewise fleeing the assault and we joined the throng. As we hurried along, Zeb expressed his surprise that I hadn't already flirted my way out of captivity before he arrived. During an escape from Reds seemed like a poor time to deal with green-eyed jealousy and I told him so, but he wouldn't leave off. I'd been only too keen to spark with "that cop in Pittsburgh", he continued, "so it stood to reason" that I would also bat my eyes at any one of the handsome prison guards at Stadelheim.

He was being absurd and I scolded him for it just as we were forced to turn down a side street to avoid about a dozen Reds with rifles and bayonets who rushed toward us on their way to assist their comrades. Shots echoed off every building around us, but Zeb refused to proceed further until he knew where he and I stood.

This was intolerably ridiculous behavior on his part, but he had dug in his heels with all those long years of experience keeping his balance on board the Fanning *and he could not be moved. I confessed that O'Malley was indeed an attractive man, but why should that matter? Both Zeb and I were free to engage in liaisons as we liked. Our ability to do The Work did not depend on our having exclusive relations and either one of us could take advantage of auspicious situations if we chose.*

The shots grew louder and I was glad the panicked people pushing past us could not understand what was essentially a lovers' spat, risible as it was. Zeb looked more pained now than he had when we'd been at the Centralbahnhof the day before and that in turn pained me immensely. It was actually a relief when a mortar shell hit the home beside us and caused a literal ton of bricks to fall down about our heads!

Zeb, in anguish, had seized me by the lapels of my coat during our spat and used them now to yank me clear of the deadly rain of bricks. He fell upon me in a niche of the opposite building and shielded my poor skull with his broad back. Dust and plaster coated both of us and turned our confrontation into coughs. We freed ourselves from the debris and then set about doing the same for others who had had the rotten luck of being in that wrong place at that wrong time. Some were Reds, others were of indeterminate political sympathies, but none was dead, thank the stars. At worst there were bloody scalps, broken forearms, and crushed toes. Not counting Zeb or me, about seven people had to be dug out of the collapse. Some residents of the home in question dared to look out through the new holes in their walls. One dauntless "Frau" even began sweeping rubble off the floor of her flat down onto our heads, to the considerable consternation of those below.

We tarried among the injured long enough for Leviné to reach the scene. His compatriots had apparently succeeded in beating back the Whites and he was making the rounds, shoring up defenses. He was astonished to find me providing aid to Bolshevik soldiers, both because he'd thought I was securely imprisoned and because he'd considered me no true devotee of his cause. This left him unsure how to proceed. All this I read in an instant upon his countenance. As I've said, my mastery of Freudian psychoanalysis makes it possible for me to discern most men's inner thoughts at a glance.

In the end, Leviné shook our hands, made some inconsequential comments on the battle and the inevitable triumph of the working class, then moved on without ordering I be incarcerated or officially released. In either case, I now felt confident that Zeb and I would find a tunnel home the very next time we sought one. To double our chances of success, however, we chose an actual tunnel as our launching point. One moment we were passing under railroad tracks in

Munich, the next we were emerging from beneath the tracks alongside Nine Mile Run at Duck Hollow.

It was early morning again, although I could not have determined the actual date to save my soul, such was my temporal confusion. Zeb seemed to have gained his second wind and looked determined to carry on with the normal course of his day despite our jump from one "time zone" to another. He also turned out to be determined not to budge out from under the railroad until we had concluded the spat begun in Munich.

"See here," I said, "you can't mean to keep track of my every eye movement from now until we pass into the light eternal, can you? I'm no keener on being your prisoner than I was on being one for Leviné, Narbut– Łuczyński, or Dyer."

Zeb only leaned against a support column and looked glum. I drew closer.

"You can't want to be my prisoner either, I think, as bound on all sides as if you were married to Miss Nellie Edgerton and watched over by your parents and brothers, indeed, by all of Waynesburg."

He kicked at a stray lump of coal fallen from some long-gone train and admitted he would not like that at all. I took his left hand in mine. "Look, we wear these gold rings as a source of revenue in emergencies, but if you won't try to clap my hands in iron, I'd be happy to consider my vena amoris *bound to yours. One circulatory system serving two bodies, as it were. How would that be?"*

He scanned all around us for onlookers, then kissed me as deeply as a human mouth allows until I too needed support from the column beside us. "All right," he said, "but how are we going to track down Frank Candell and what do we do if we find him?"

"For him," I replied while leading him toward Prouwder House, "I have a quite non-metaphorical set of handcuffs in mind!"

LINEN CLOSET

Wednesday, the 16th of April

O ur first order of business after going back to the mansion was, of course, to inform Mother of our return. She took brief notes on our account of the lunatic on the bridge and the communists in Munich and then, with curiosity, agreed to convene Belle, Louis, William, Nathan, and Henry for a tête-à-tête (à huit) at ten o'clock. Rose and her mother I would visit in their rooms later in the day. Thereafter Zeb and I retired to our apartment to freshen up, eat a bit, and change clothes.

We met the others in Great-uncle William's office as it had more seating available and lent itself better to a serious discussion of imminent danger. Belle looked slightly out of place, but several of the gentlemen offered her their seats. She wiped flour onto her apron and plopped down onto the leather settee next to Louis, then readied herself for what I had to say, which was this:

"Frank Candell is alive and making use of Prouwder House at will."

There were gasps and startled looks about the room. Owing to his deafness, William was the last to get the news, but the first to react. "How do you know?" Nathan said for him.

"We," I indicated Zeb, "have seen him both inside the house and on the train tracks down in Duck Hollow. There was no mistaking who he was."

All eyes fell on Belle and Louis. They looked the most astonished. Belle had grasped Uncle's forearm and he had laid his hand over hers.

"You have said," I spoke to them directly, "that Frank died by mishap in California and that he took his own life, but he's still among the living. Was either of you an eyewitness to his fate or did you simply assume he was dead for some reason?"

"Belle was not," said Louis, "but I did indeed see Frank jump on purpose from a great height in California after we had rescued several Chinese miners. I didn't believe he could have survived, but I admit that I didn't see his dead body."

"Why would he do a fool thing like that, Louie?" Belle wiped a tear from her eye.

"Despondency," he replied, "brought on by the years of William's banishment."

Nathan had been translating everything we said by means of hand gestures and finger spelling. William's face darkened and he shouted incoherently. Only his son seemed to understand. "He deserved to be jailed for what he did to me!" Nathan supplied. "I'd shove him off the roof if I had the chance!"

Mother interrupted. "But why has he come back, Thomas? What does he want? Surely he doesn't bear a grudge against our entire family!"

"I don't know, Mother, but he certainly dropped Zeb and me into a dangerous situation. We had nothing to do with his being banished, but he showed no compunction in attacking us. We must all be on our guard."

Mother's Uncle Henry spoke up. "But how did he do that?"

I sketched out for the others what I had already told my mother, but also included the way that Candell had apparently turned railroad ties into a tunnel, despite there being no one in need of help on the other end. "Add to that the fact that he followed Hyacinth into a linen closet and disappeared with her, either to the same place or somewhere altogether different."

"It's impossible!" William said through Nathan. "No man can turn the will of God and God it is that sends us on these rescues! Tell them, Henry!"

Henry looked less than compliant, but William insisted. "Tell them or I will, Henry!"

The younger of the two Prouwder brothers drew himself up in his chair and steepled his fingers before him. They were as long and thin as the man's hair. "As you should already know," he began, "our grandfather, Jan Prouwder, came west from Philadelphia in 1800 and purchased this land. He built the first cabin on the property and lived there with his wife, Mary, and three sons, Caspar, Samuel, and Jacob, the youngest of whom was our father. One winter that Jan and his family passed here was especially harsh. There was much snow, bitter cold, and little to eat.

"One day, just as the sun was setting, a French–Canadian trapper and his Cree wife came knocking at Grampa's door. They were passing through on their way to Ohio and had gotten caught in the snowstorm then raging all about the little cabin. Gramma and Grampa took them in, of course, and shared what provisions they could. The travelers spent the night in safety and comfort with our kin and in the morning, gathered up their belongings to be on their way. They took Grampa outside with them and revealed to him that they were no mortal beings but rather angels testing whomever they

encountered for kindness and Christian spirit. They blessed Grampa and all his offspring. They promised that he and the entire Prouwder family would flourish so long as someone among us continued always to aid those in need. From that day to this, we have heeded the calls for help we hear on this property and have, indeed, flourished."

Mother whispered Amen. All about the room, people were taking in the story, only the general thrust of which I had known before. I wondered how much more, or less, other Prouwders had been told. Zeb certainly looked wholly taken in by the idea that he and I were doing God's work and, although I lean toward a scientific view of the world, I too had to admit the tunnels and travel we'd experienced firsthand were more easily explained by the supernatural than the natural.

"So," Nathan read his father's signs, "Frank Candell can't be using the Angels' ways for evil! You, Thomas, must find out what he is truly doing!"

I reiterated that we all had to remain on alert and agreed to pursue Candell wherever he went.

4/16/19

Tom and I went right from his uncle William's office to his cousin Rose. Her mom was just as unfriendly as she been before, but Tom insisted on getting in. I don't think she would've let *me* in by myself even though I'm doing the work, same as Tom. This time we found Rose out on her balcony. Tom told her all the news. She didn't seem none too concerned about it. Maybe once you've lived through the worst thing possible, nothing else scares you too much. Seeing Tom lynched by a mob would do me in, even if I was never afraid again. Rose is as tough as her name, I guess. She's got thorns, I mean. Maybe that Frank Candell will be sorry, deep and sorry, if he tangles with her!

We had lunch in the kitchen and, boy, was Belle in a bad mood! She like to bite the head off every other cook and serving girl she laid eyes on and dropped our meals off in front of us with a clatter. We ate fast with Roberts the Butler and Charles the Chauffeur, who likewise saw the storm Belle was brewing and lit out quick. Funny how the womenfolk at Prouwder House seem so tough. I guess it's kinda the same in my family, but more low key. Men can be mighty violent, me included, but they don't have *Ausdauer*, as Oma Thorpe used to say.

After lunch, which was good roast beef sandwiches and cooked carrots, Tom and I went back to work laying out our necessities. I decided to give in to him, so we started putting stuff in alphabetical order: axes, bandages, crowbars, dumbbells, and the like, all around the room we'd picked for storing that stuff. Tom was very happy. It pleased him to have won me over to his way of thinking, but really I just didn't want anymore conflict between us. Arguing over other guys most of the day before was enough for me. What do I care if he makes eyes at somebody? I got my own pecker and can do what I want with it, right? That James the Night watchman is mighty friendly and I'm sure he gets lonely wandering around the estate all through the wee hours. Maybe someday I'll take a shift with him and see what's what!

4/17/19

Tom and I went on putting things in order around our supply room today, ending up with winches, yardsticks, and zippers at the end of the alphabet. I don't know why Tom insisted on putting renches together with the winches and washers and wax. He only scowled at me when I asked, so I dropped the issue and did as he told me. We wandered through the whole mansion finding stuff and bringing it all together. I seen a lot more rooms that way and Tom tested me as we went so that I've learned better how to get around now. I'm also getting so I can name all the kin and most of the servants here too. His Doucette cousins flit about a lot. I know there's only three of them, but I swear we saw them alone or together in about seven rooms today. Sometimes they talked to us and sometimes they just read or did croshay or played with whatever came to hand. I asked Tom if we should warn them all about Frank Candell, but he thought for now me and him are the bastard's only target. I made sure to visit B and K in our supply room so that I always have a pair of brass knuckles and a knife on me!

Friday, the 18th of April

Having completed our arrangement of equipment in the supply room, Zeb and I turned our attention today to the problem of using the mansion's tunnels at will. I thought it logical to launch our efforts in the breakfast room, where we first encountered the phenomenon. He and I crouched to either side of the fireplace there and knocked at the tiles all around, much to the confusion of Agnes, who was clearing away chafing dishes, et cetera.

Despite our prayers and imprecations, the entire fixture remained utterly solid and impassable. I tried bringing to mind the particular fire in Chicago that we had jumped into, then imagined any one of what I assumed were the hundred blazes then occurring in the world, to equal failure.

Zeb suggested we try hanging from the climbing rope up in the gymnasium, but neither of us fancied success at the cost of finding ourselves dangling from some other hot air balloon. Instead we returned to the gate through which we had traveled to Jallianwala Bagh, but this time it remained an old, unused gate on the Prouwder estate. Neither of us wanted to try the walls of the chapel or the outhouse, on the off chance that we'd succeed in going back to Pinsk or Des Moines.

We broke for lunch, found Belle just as cross as she had been the day before, and then spent some time with Roberts getting Zeb measured for new clothing. He prefers to continue wearing his naval uniform, but it will wear out eventually so I told Roberts to frequent Pittsburgh's second-hand clothing stores to purchase uniforms that sailors who have been mustered out of service are selling. Roberts has always been rather insouciant, but since Zeb arrived he's become intolerably free of tongue and I felt obliged to 'put him in his place'.

Zeb and I then took another tack: we went back to the linen closet where we had first seen Candell and knocked on every shelf and door. All were unresponsive. We sat down on the floor to contemplate our next move and were surprised by Agnes opening the door. She held a load of bedsheets in her arms and regarded us with studied patience while we made way for her to deposit her burden. Then she shut the door again, sighed audibly, and trotted away.

I admitted to Zeb that I had no idea how to replicate the control that Candell seemed to have over the tunnels.

"Maybe we ain't Christ-like enough to get the angels on our side."

I hardly thought Frank Candell was Christ-like and said so.

"Well, then, maybe he's in cahoots with the Devil."

These last two words he whispered. I smirked, but admitted that was more likely. Eventually we gave up tapping around the linen closet and emerged to find my sister waiting in the hall for us!

4/18/19

Much as I like Tom, his sister Hyacinth gives me the heebie-jeebies! She was right there outside the closet today when we come out, like she knew we was in there somehow. I jumped back, but she barely seemed to notice us. She was plucking at the ends of her hair, then just dropped it and went over to the nearest window, which looked out onto the driveway. She looked weird, like always, half done up and tidy, half de-shelved, but I think she'd switched sides, like the half that was usually dirty was washed up clean and the other half was unbuttoned and scuffed up. I hung back, but Tom stood shoulder to shoulder with her at the window.

"Lies, lies, lies. The road lies on the ground and the leaves lie on the road. The snow lies on the bank and the sun lies on the field." She squinted at herself. "My hair lies on my breast and Great-uncle Henry lies . . ."

"Lies where?" Tom asked her, but she didn't answer. She just spun away from the window, brushed past me, and disappeared into the same damn closet Tom and me had been inspecting two minutes before! I knew enough not to look for her in there, but Tom swung the door open and tried all over again to find where her tunnel had been. It was useless. He came out and pondered. I like watching his face when he's thinking something over like that. His mouth fidgets a lot, but his eyes are calm, like he's peering through miles of clear air at some German biplane. There's nothing for me to do but wait until he's zeroed in on an idea and is ready to tell me about it.

"Great-uncle Henry lies . . ." He returned to the window, then said, "Come, Zeb! We have a further interview to conduct!"

With quickened steps, Zeb and I descended to Henry's chamber, but he wasn't there. We searched until we found him in the library, poring over the family Bible. He, like Grandmother and Great-uncle William, has surpassed three-score and ten years of age and I surmised he was struggling to read the fine print and faded handwriting for he made use of a magnifying glass and the room's brightest lamp. He shut the Good Book as we approached the table at which he sat.

"Thomas, is there Work to be done in here? I'll leave you to it." He began to push away from the table and stand up, but I stopped him with a hand on his forearm.

"No, sir. No cries for help at the moment, except ours for yours."

"Mine? But I have none to offer beyond what I have already told you. I'm afraid you boys are on your own in this matter."

"I think you are indeed afraid, Great-uncle, but of what?"

He patted down the strands of yellow-white hair which he still wore in the style of a Civil War veteran.

I laid his hand onto the Scriptures. "Divine judgment perhaps?"

"God is merciful," he said meekly.

"But also wrathful, Uncle. What have you not told us?"

He glanced at Zeb, who crossed his arms and guarded the door.

"Henry," I pressed on, "while you live, tell truth and shame the devil!"

"Oh! Shame!" He pulled his hand away convulsively and scurried to the window, then pressed his fists to his mouth. "Shame it is that brings this Work to you, Thomas! Not reward for Christian charity!"

"What do you mean?"

"Lord forgive us!" Henry said sotto voce. *"What I have recounted before is, in the main, true. One night, during the last month of 1816, Grampa took in the trapper and his woman, but they were not alone. They had with them a babe, newborn and ill. He perished in the night, despite the entire Prouwder family's best efforts. It was a tragedy which our father remembered all his life and for it we've been made to risk our lives ever since!"*

4/19/19

Boy, it is hard to figure these Prouwders out! After what Tom's great-uncle told us yesterday and then told us in private later, I still am not sure what the truth is. I guess something simlar is true about my own family, what with my Oma and Opa bein' German Amish, but hidin' it when they ~~come~~ came to Greene County. Tom puzzled over it the rest of the day, tryin' to reason out how Frank Candell fits into all of this and uses the house to go where he wants. I think we just got to be quicker 'n him and grab him fast the next chance we get, then maybe slug him until he tells us. In any case, the whole house has been told to be on the lookout for him. Maybe James the Nightwatchman will get hold of him and pin him to the ground until Tom and I come a runnin'.

It's been strange and quiet as far as missions go. Tom is researching his family history as much as he can and I've been whittling some and drawing too. I made our set of rooms cozier today by swiping some sofa pillows out of one bedroom that nobody's using and I also took a framed photograph of Paris out of the same room and hung it in our parlor / dining room. Hope Tom doesn't make me put this stuff back. It ~~ain't~~ isn't stealing 'cause it's in the same house still. More likely it's his mom that'll object, but she doesn't come up to our place. There was an unfaded square of wallpaper behind the photograph I took and that might tip off a maid or Mrs. P-C.

I sent off a letter with $20 to my folks. I told them I found work as a guard on the Prouwder Estate which is as close to the truth as I could come, I guess. They don't know that's Tom's family since he gave them his last name as Caul. I told them they could write to me here if they want. We'll see. Mom writes a little, but Dad never has, although I think he knows how. Maybe one of my sisters will.

That's all for today. Time to cuddle up with Tom! That part is gettin' better 'n' better!

RIVERBANK

Tuesday, the 22ⁿᵈ of April

*Z*eb and I were called away early yesterday after a brief hiatus from rescue work which included Easter Sunday. I feared at first it was Candell's doing since the call for help emanated from the bank of the Monongahela, near the train tracks from which he somehow sent us to Munich. Instead, however, we gazed momentarily upon the river and, without even noticing the change, it became the waves of the English Channel. Even more astounding than that was the immense submarine resting on the beach next to us!

Beach it was, and, after a few minutes of exploration and inquiry, we determined that the strand in question was that of the town of Hastings, in Sussex, England. The submarine had washed ashore six days prior after coming loose from its hawser, by which it was being towed to France as a spoil of the armistice. It being noon or thereabouts, many people were milling around, having fulfilled their duty to attend church. We all regarded the submarine with equal astonishment. Zeb quickly identified it as a German UE II type, namely the U–118. It leaned about thirty-five degrees toward the water some one hundred yards in front of the Queens Hotel.

Onlookers also filled a few rowboats in the waves. We heard again the plaintive cry for help that had brought us there, but it was inaudible to those around us and, Zeb agreed, had a distinctively metallic quality. Clearly, the person we'd been sent to rescue was inside the wreck itself!

I asked a lad in shortpants how one gained access to the sub's interior. He said there was a ladder on the other side and that tours would start up again in the afternoon once there was clear sand between the sea and the sub. Usually, he said, there was a pair of Coast Guards "what took people inside", but they hadn't appeared as yet. I thanked him and drew Zeb away to a spot where we could see a rope ladder dangling from a turret on the sub's deck. The ladder's lowest rungs were tossed about by the vigorous action of the waves, which would hit a man around mid-thigh.

"We'll have to chance it," I said.

He agreed and, hoping to escape the greater part of the crowd's notice, we waded into the Channel and reached the rope ladder. We were quite buffeted by the waves and I almost lost my footing, but Sailor Beck caught hold of me and helped me climb. There were calls of warning from some of the boaters, but our mission necessitated ignoring them and up we went. Zeb, naturally, had much better legs for this work and he it was that found the hatch. An awful stench greeted us at its being opened, besting even the salty spray of the Channel. Zeb led the way down the awkwardly tilted ladder inside until we were at its base and utterly surrounded by darkness and the stifling odor. Zeb was confident of his ability to negotiate the sub's interior despite our blindness, but I overruled that plan of action. It was time, I told him, to try returning at will to the mansion in order to procure the supplies I guessed we'd need, chief among them my Beacon flashlight and also what protection against the smell I could secure. I found a door not far off, focused all my mind on the supply room we'd set up at Prouwder House, and stepped through!

4/21/19

It was a pure wonder to see Tom disappear through that door! Of course, I couldn't rightly see anything in the gloom, but one minute he was with me, the next he was gone. I sure hoped he'd get back all right and it was an awful long time before he did, but all of a sudden, back through the door he came and startled me hard.

"Here," he said, "put this on." He handed me a doughboy's gas mask. The AEF got trained to put them on in just six seconds, but Tom and I took a fair bit longer with ours 'cause neither one of us used them during our service. It was a snug fit and made me 'closet phobic', as they say, but it was a smart thing to do 'cause God only knew what it was we was breathing in that sub! It stank bad in there.

Tom switched on his flashlight and let me take it 'cause I was leading us, seeing as how I'd actually been in a German sub before. He adjusted the coil of rope slung across his chest and we headed down the corridor. The mask made seeing even harder, but we were still hearing that same cry for help and went toward it. It wasn't really a cry, so much as a whimper, but it rang loud enough in our ears. We had to deal with the darkness, like I said, and the stench, plus the damn tilt of the deck! It's hard enough to walk through a sub when it's level. You're liable to crack your fool head open on a bulkhead or a pipe or a valve, but at least the U-118 was steady. We went down another deck after passing through the con and some quarters. Here was the torpedo room and when we finally worked one more door open, there were the men we were looking for!

Neither looked at all good. One was passed out completely and the other barely moved when he seen us except to kind of wave at us. We got over to them quick and seen they ~~was~~ were the Coast Guard boys that had been leading tours. That was a damn stupid thing to do, I figured, but there was no point in chewing these poor guys out. Who knew how long they'd been inside, without the strength to leave. Tom said hello to them and got busy checking them out.

"We was overcome," the conscious guy said. He was no older than me, with a round face and a turned up nose. "I'm William Heard. That's Moore."

"Can you walk?" Tom asked, but Heard just shook his head.

There was nothing for it but to carry the saps out on our backs. That was made double hard on account of the gas masks and breathing bags we was wearing, but I got Heard up onto Tom's shoulder with grunts from both of them and then I took Moore, who was bigger and dead weight to boot. We inched our way back where we came from. My guy got a fearful knock on the head as I was squeezing us both through the closest door and I had to put him down completely when we got to the ladder leading to the upper deck. Tom laid down on the floor above and lifted as I pushed Heard up by the butt, then we three did the same with Moore. All of us were breathing terrible hard by then and still we had a long way to go before we reached the blessed open air!

Moore, luckily, had roused a little by the time we got to the main hatch and he climbed the ladder to the surface about a quarter under his own power and then helped Tom pull Heard up and out. I skedaddled up the ladder quick as I could, which turned out to be too quick 'cause I fell back down a couple rungs and twisted my goddamn ankle. Finally we was all up top and people took notice. Some women shrieked and clutched their hands to their mouths. Kids ran back and forth. A few men went out into the waves to help us fetch the Coast Guard boys to safety on the beach. I retched, but Tom, of course, looked like he'd just stepped off his yacht or something. He's got that gift.

With all due haste we four were taken to a hospital. Many were the thanks and back claps given to us along the way. The physician on duty pronounced Zeb and me fit, thanks to our use of the gas masks, but he confided in us out of earshot that Moore and Heard's prospects were dim.

"That wasn't rotten food, was it, Doc?" Zeb asked. "Smelled like batteries to me."

The doctor nodded gravely and said the two young men were not likely to live out their natural span of years, due to their exposure to those fumes, which had probably caused abscesses in their lungs and brains. Only an autopsy would confirm that diagnosis, of course. Fortunately, no one else had spent nearly as much time inside the deadly vessel. Its sudden appearance and note-worthiness had been a small windfall for the town, which would provide the funds necessary for a celebration of returning servicemen. "Indeed," he remarked, "young Moore and Heard will be counted among the casualties of the Great War."

We clasped the hands of the men we'd rescued and were warmly thanked, but it was a bitter end to our mission. They were handsome boys, lucky to have survived their various battles and eager to tell us about some of the action they'd seen, but now doomed to early deaths without knowing it.

I decided, perhaps recklessly, that Zeb and I should remain in Hastings for the time being and we secured an excellent room at the aforementioned Queens Hotel. I had American currency aplenty and at Lloyd's Bank I was able to exchange much of it for pound sterling, which Mother will be glad to see.

We washed up and began taking in the sights, one of which, it seemed, were we ourselves! Word had traveled fast and passersby greeted us in every street of the Old Town. Shopkeepers and waiters did the same, recognizing us by our American uniforms. The class of those thanking us rose until the mayor himself put in an appearance just as we were setting out for Hastings Castle, the first that William the Conqueror built on English soil, in 1067. The mayor insisted that we be given the key to the city and, on the morrow, after a fine night's sleep and a splendid breakfast, that was accomplished. We made a few remarks in front of City Hall, something along the lines of continuing cooperation with our 'British cousins', and then shook hands on all sides. We stood for photographs and generally had a gay time of it.

Until Zeb opened his mouth, that is.

I don't have anything against anybody, not even Germans. I figure them boys were doing their job, same as I was, and, after all, I got German Amish kin, ain't I? Brits even more so. It was their ships we was protecting out there on the Atlantic, at least some of the time, and I drank with them plus did some other things they was plenty willing to do, even more than Americans, though not as much as the French or what seemed like every man in the Azores!

So, it wasn't ~~predujice~~ prejudice that took hold of me when the mayor introduced Tom and me to a reporter at the *Hastings and St. Leonard's Observer.* He was polite at first and I guess he wrote a good story, but something in the way he managed to turn *our* rescue of *his* compatriots into how great Great Britain is got my dander up. He made some crack about that German sub not knowing it was dead and striking out at good English boys post mortem, then went on to claim that the British Empire was responsible for 'restoring peace' to the whole world. I said something about how 'good Irish boys and Indian boys' might not feel the same. You'd have thought I'd pissed right onto the man's desk for how angry he got. He dug at us Yanks for being 'rather late to the party' when it came to putting down the Huns and *I* said maybe Limies could've beaten the Germans by themselves if so many of them weren't busy making sure the sun didn't set on all the lands they thought they should be in control of.

Well, that caused a big ruckus, you can be sure, and Tom tried to head off the fight me and that reporter was puttin' our gloves on for, but it was too late. This guy spewed a bunch of bullshit about boys from right there in Hastings making the 'ultimate sacrifice' for King and Country and I said that was poor comfort to the women and kids shot to death right there in Jallianwala Bagh on account of that same King and Country.

The reporter threw a punch. I threw one back at him. Somebody from the mayor's office hit Tom, which got me seeing red, so I laid that guy out. Me and the reporter traded blows again and then, for some reason, one of the onlookers punched the mayor even though he hadn't done anything and two other rubberneckers laid into each other with screams about money that one owed the other. There was so much scuffle so quick that Tom and I thought it best to just get out of town right then. We ran from all the fists flying about and dashed back to the submarine, which seemed pretty damn peaceful in comparison with the fights that was following us to the beach. We ran into the English Channel and then out of the Monongahela River.

The bank was steep, but we got up it and then made an inspection of all our cuts and bruises and swollen knuckles. I was hurt worse than Tom, but seeing him with a split lip just about made me want to keep him safe at Prouwder House forever and never let him go on another goddamn rescue. Of course I can't control him and he can't control me either. Next time, however, no matter where we get sent, I'm going to make him wear a goddamn helmet!

Roofline

Monday, the 21ˢᵗ of April

Mother was indeed pleased by our contribution of British sterling to her little bank of foreign currency. She was quite displeased, *on the other hand, by my report of the reporter Zeb and I spoke to and subsequently scuffled with in Hastings. Such publicity, she emphasized, was not only beneath our station, but also dangerous: not even all Prouwders knew the entire truth about The Work, let alone outsiders. God has chosen us for His special mission, she insisted. Under no circumstances may we give interviews to the press! In fact, she suggested, we should take pains to conceal our true identities by adopting* noms de guerre, *as it were, and avoiding photographs as well.*

I pronounced Zeb and myself duly chastised and we returned to our apartment with the breakfast Belle had given us. Zeb said we had gotten a worse "licking" from Mother than we had from the entire populace of Hastings and reminded me of the names we'd given the Communist authorities in Bavaria: Owen Bucks and Mike Hunt. I agreed that we would make use of those names again and not rely on Prouwder prestige to curry favor with the police, the military, or, even more fearsome, hotel maître d's.

After breaking our fast, we enjoyed a day of reading, tending to our supply room, and spooning. Zeb was especially keen on perusing the newspapers to see whether any of our recent rescues have been immortalized in the press. I reminded him that the world is very large; it is unlikely Americans will ever hear of small events in India or even Great Britain within the week of their happening. Technology has no doubt reached its pinnacle and I shouldn't think life one century from now will be appreciably different, except in the minutest detail. Zeb has read more of H. G. Wells and Edgar Rice Burroughs than I. He therefore entertains quite counterfactual ideas about the future which are of little use, in my opinion. I must admit, naturally, that he and I are currently involved in a series of experiences the likes of which run in opposition to the common man's apprehension of the world, so I must leave some space for adjusting my own suppositions.

In any case, by evening, we had settled ourselves into our little apartment with only each other's respirations and the ticking of the clock as accompaniment when suddenly, at 2130 hours, there came a tremendously loud explosion which shook our tympanic membranes to their limits!

We had not doffed our "Work" clothes yet, so we had only to snatch up our knapsacks and we were ready. The boom seemed to have originated outside the mansion. We perceived a plume of fire just beyond the roofline, so, we reasoned, the quickest route to the scene would be to scamper across the shingles to a place I knew of where there is perhaps only six feet distance between roof and ground. Zeb disliked the height at first, since our apartment comprises the entire fourth floor of the mansion, but once we had passed through one window of our parlor, his sailor legs were surer than mine at negotiating our path.

There was a 'widow's walk' partway along our route and it significantly cut the time we needed to reach what turned out to be the catastrophic crash of the largest airplane I have ever seen! There was no hope for whoever remained alive deep inside the fuselage, which was caught up in ferocious flames, but two men had been thrown clear of the wreckage and a third called piteously for help from the edge of the conflagration. Zeb and I dashed to his side, protecting ourselves as well as possible from the heat. The man was conscious, barely, and pinned by one of the aircraft's wings. Zeb was able to lift it on his own while I pulled the man free and across several yards of grass. Thank God for Zeb's prodigious strength! His work on his father's farm stands us both in good stead.

Zeb turned loose of the wing and dashed over to one of the two men now writhing in pain and shock several yards away. He carried first one and then the other to the spot of safety where I had laid my own man. The mansion was nowhere in sight, as I expected. It was deep night, wherever we were, and we panted beneath a waning gibbous moon. Soon enough, many men came running toward the wreck with cries of horror and anguish. The flames illuminated them on one side only, while Zeb and I were lit full-faced. We waved and called to them; they rushed to our sides. Their uniforms and accents made it immediately clear that we had already returned to Shakespeare's "sceptered isle", and what's more, these were men I knew!

4/23/19

Tom called several of the Limies by name and they did the same with him and shook his hand. They quickly identified the three guys we'd pulled away from the reckage and a couple of them ran back where they'd come from to fetch stretchers while others moved in a circle around the burning airplane to see whether anybody else was still alive somehow. There was a lot of excited talk, but I caught that there were at least seven guys on the plane when it took off, so maybe four of them were dead. I hoped they'd been killed right away by the crash. It's a hell of a thing to think of burning to death. I wouldn't even wish that on that Polish prick, Narbut, or that British bastard, Dyer, though seeing them get shot up wouldn't bother me a bit!

The stretchers were brought. Tom and I took the ends of one and carried away the guy we'd pulled out from under that wing. Somebody said his name was Westall. The other two survivors were Ward and Adkins. We trotted through the field as fast as the darkness let us toward buildings in the distance. One of them was apparently the building that the airplane had clipped on its way down. For some reason the pilot couldn't get as high as he needed to right away. There was four hundred gallons of fuel on board. That's why the whole thing was burning so intense. It looked like hell on Earth, I tell you!

We got inside one bunker and piled our guys onto beds along the wall. Mostly the people there were giving them first aid, but one doctor came pretty quick and started in with his stethoscope, etc. We'd just been in a hospital in Hastings the day before and here we were again, watching young guys maybe going to die. Tom had something like the same idea; he pushed me outside and we went back to the reck thinking we could help put it out, but really there was nothing we could do about that. The other airmen had come to the same conclusion. There was no water nearby and even a bucket brigade would've hardly made a difference. Sides, there was nothing but dewy grass anywhere near the airplane, so it wasn't like we had to save a building. The dead was already dead.

I didn't rightly know what we should do next. I had a feeling we could get back to Prouwder house if we ran off in the direction we'd come from, but Tom was licking his lips and looking around at all the guys and I realized these were his kindred spirits: flyboys. They were just as crazy about being up in the air as Tom was that time in the Bellevue hotel. It seems like me and him have been doing this work for about twenty years already, but really it's only been three weeks! Before that, he was with these guys and Americans and Frenchmen fighting German pilots in the skies over Europe. It can take three weeks for a man to get the drink out of his system, easy, so I figured Tom was still hooked on the excitement he got from flying one of these same goddamn bundles of kindling up among the clouds. You wouldn't say the same about me: there's nothing romantic about being on a destroyer.

A guy came up to us then, one we hadn't seen before, and he was stonished to see that he knew Tom. "Caul? I'll be damned!" he said and gave Tom a ~~viggerus~~ vigorous handshake as well as a cuff on the arm.

"Sinclair?" Tom answered. He gave the guy half a hug and me a sideways glance, but didn't introduce me.

"I thought you'd been mustered out," said this Sinclair. "What are you doing in England?"

Tom said we were on a trip and asked about the base. Neither of us rightly knew where we were, except in the general sense.

"The Number 2 School of Navigation and Bomb Dropping. We're testing new airplanes, like that Handley Page there." He pointed over his shoulder to the flames. "Damned rotten luck. Those poor blighters. We're losing good pilots in the peace almost as fast as we did in the war."

"Yes," Tom said back, "all the sorties those men had survived only to perish on a training mission! Rotten luck indeed."

"As you're clearly not keen on returning to the States soon, old boy, perhaps you could stay on and be a trainer?"

I saw more enthusiasm in Tom's face than I ever had before. That's why everything they said to each other has stuck with me so good.

The airman pointed his thumb at me. "Who's the matelot?"

Tom looked at me like he'd forgotten he brung me along. "Hm? Oh, that's Beck, my . . . traveling companion."

"Pleased," Sinclair said without offering his hand.

I said yeah and spat into the grass to my left. Tom stared at Sinclair with ardent. (That's a new word I learned from a book about expending your vocabulary in the Prouwder library here. It means passionate or burning, but maybe that was just the flames reflecting off Tom's face.)

Sinclair invited Tom to get a drink in the officers' club. "But you can come too, Beck, as our guest." Two's company and three's a crowd, I thought. This was just like Tom and that cop all over, only he already knew this fucker and had history with him. No way I was going to sit around and watch them rekindle their ~~relatives relations~~ relationship!

"I got to take a piss," I said and pointed toward the edge of the field where Tom and I first showed up here.

They both looked at me without saying anything, so I run off into the dark and came back to Prouwder house. Screw Tom Caul and whoever he's screwing!

Sinclair and I headed back to the bunkers. I hadn't known him particularly well during the war; he was just one of many Royal Air Force pilots with whom we coordinated attacks, but now he had survived all the dogfights and was helping shape the future of aviation. It was tremendously exciting and Sinclair spoke with spirit about bigger and bigger aeroplanes that were on the horizon. He was certain that the role of pilots would expand, not only in war, but also in keeping the peace. He assured me there would be a constant presence over every country: British, and to a lesser extent, American, planes watching out for enemy troops, enemy weapons, enemy entrenchments. No one in Europe, Asia, or Africa would look up without seeing an RAF aircraft in the sky, all day and all night, ready to strike wherever necessary to prevent aggression.

It reminded me, I told him, of how the Holy Spirit is typically represented as a dove, flying above human figures.

"Exactly," he clapped me on the shoulder, "but a 20th century dove made of good wood and steel!"

We settled into seats in the club. As we were its only customers, Sinclair did the honors and poured us out shots of whiskey.

"To absent friends."

We toasted the dead and settled into a discussion of all the pilots we knew in common. Some had already returned to civilian life. Others were right there, training new pilots and providing essential experience to the designers of new aircraft. We also discussed advancements in the Mears parachute and traded what we'd heard about Leslie Irvin's "rip-cord" system, as demonstrated in his free-fall jump earlier this year. We had another shot of whiskey each and fell into speculation on future developments for the Lewis automatic rifle. Sinclair told me some of the ways in which the Handley-Page was progressing in the dropping of bombs, although, he said, details were only to be shared with RAF personnel. He smiled enticingly. I was quite tempted.

We eventually rejoined the others at the wreckage. The mood was somber on one level, but no one among us had not already seen many crashes, many deaths. Above our stratum of grief was a lively discussion of what had gone wrong with this particular flight: weight, lift, darkness, flammability, and pilot error were each given their due. The substratum of our conversation, near the protean magma of existence itself, lay the bedrock conviction that life was short, unpredictable, and made to be enjoyed. Sinclair stood very close to me.

In time I became fatigued even though my pocket watch lagged those of my companions by five hours. Sinclair led me to the barracks where we lay down on cots assigned to men who were now dead. He took my hand and caressed it in his. I did the same to him and fell asleep.

After coffee and eggs the next morning, which was actually just several hours later, Sinclair and I washed up, then joined the inspection of the fuselage. It had sputtered out at some *point in the night and now the grisly work of extracting body parts was underway. I pitched in, but the fewer details of our efforts, the better. Afterwards, a tractor was employed to drag the burnt and broken biplane back to the main area of School Number 2, where investigations would try to determine the exact cause of its destruction.*

I was introduced to Major James Lake, who feigned remembering me from some action or other during The War. I saluted him and Sinclair explained how I had rescued Westall, Ward, and Adkins from the crash. I naturally downplayed my involvement, wondered briefly where Zeb had passed the night, and expressed my enthusiasm for being back among pilots. Sinclair prompted me to give the Major a précis of my career with first the French and then the American flying force, which I did. The major laid his finger over his lips while he listened and then invited me to speculate on the cause of the crash. I did what I could along those lines, relying mostly on a similar, although non-fatal, experience I'd had in 1917 in which my SPAD had failed to gain altitude. I'd ended up in the tops of an oak and had barely managed to scramble out of my plane before it tumbled upside down to the ground below.

"Quite," the major pronounced. He turned to Sinclair. "See to it that Caul here joins us, at least in an unofficial capacity. Now, if you'll excuse me, I have rather distressing telegrams to compose." He saluted us and strode off.

"Well!" Sinclair smiled, "What do you think?"

I explained that I had family obligations to see to and scanned the surroundings for Zeb.

"Nonsense!" Sinclair drew me along for a more extensive tour of the school. "Mater and pater haven't seen you for years and you are clearly in no hurry to return to your staid life in

the States. Send them a telegram and tell them you'll be staying in Jolly Old until autumn, at the least."

I promised to consider the idea and he showed me what he could of the base, then excused himself with a squeeze of my biceps and said he had duties to attend to, but that I should make myself at home, as it were. Other officers and enlisted men helped me find my way and I had the great privilege of seeing some of the designs for future aeroplanes. I shared a luncheon with other pilots, some of whom I knew, others of whom were new to me or known only by reputation.

There was no sign of Zeb. I wondered whether he'd struck off on his own or gone back to Prouwder House. I rather hoped, I'll admit, that he'd somehow 'shut the door' behind him, giving me an excuse to remain in Andover. Perhaps, I thought, I should send my own telegram, informing Mother of my decision. As much as I was fond of Zeb, as much as The Work provided us all the adventure we could hope for, part of me was glad to be on my own, steering my own course, and free to fly.

After luncheon, Sinclair asked me to accompany him into Andover. We requisitioned a vehicle and set off, bumping along the roads and admiring what signs of spring April in England offered. Sinclair narrated our ride, pointing out native flora or historical points of interest as we came across them. It was a pleasure to listen to him. Not only his voice but his entire manner exuded breeding, culture, and education, so in contrast to Zeb, whose struggles with logic and language are sometimes piteous.

"I shan't marry, I think," Sinclair was saying. "Better to spend my life among the good lads of the RAF, striving to strengthen Great Britain and protect her, our only wife. Per Ardua ad Astra, as the slogan goes. What about you?"

I realized with a little shock that everyone in my family married and said so.

"Well," he lightly squeezed my thigh, "there are plenty of lovely young women in Britain who've never married and, truth be told, have fewer prospects along those lines now that so many fine young men will not be returning from the war. A handsome man like you could do quite well for himself. You could even have children, if you're so inclined, and still spend the bulk of your time chumming about and flying."

I agreed that such a life might be quite pleasant. I studied Sinclair's profile. He was striking. His chin was a bit weak, but his mouth was genteelly sensual and his nose set off from his smooth brow with a mission. It was indeed easy to imagine him soaring "to the stars" and the idea of being his copilot pleased me.

In the town, Sinclair picked up a newspaper and we stopped at a headquarters where he made a report on the crash. One of the crew, it turned out, was a local and would be buried the next day after a ceremony at St. John the Baptist Catholic Church. Andover was, it seemed, rather used to sudden deaths and the quick disposition of the deceased. I suspected the same was true of hundreds of towns across Britain, given the recent ravages of the Spanish Flu and the European Conflict. 'Pestilence and War,' I thought, 'riding ahead of Death.' Famine, on the other hand, Sinclair and I held off by stopping in at a small fish and chips shop. This, he explained, would be a better choice than anything the officers' mess would dispense and represented the best cuisine that the lower classes had ever offered up, in his opinion. The shopkeeper wrapped our meals in newspaper and we took them with us, then wended our way back to the School.

That evening we supped apart from the others, but joined many men in the officers' club for whiskey afterwards. These were alumni of Cambridge, Exeter, Leeds, Manchester, and Oxford. My own intention to study at Penn had been put off in favor of service in the Lafayette Escadrille, but I had long ago decided my education at Sewickley Academy made me an intellectual match for nearly all the other pilots I met from 1916 on. To be frank, many college-educated members of the upper set are simply incurious and regard a bachelor's degree more as confirmation of their class than as training for a rigorous mind. Still, perhaps I could somehow manage to enroll at Penn or the University of Pittsburgh and begin my studies. It wouldn't do to be a Prouwder man of the 20th century without a sheepskin!

Discussion of the crash gave way to broader topics such as the creeping scourge of Bolshevism, the ongoing Paris Peace Conference, proposals for a League of Nations, all of them being interspersed with technical talk about the future of aviation, especially the school's attempts to develop long-range electronic navigation. That last item seemed farfetched to me and I said as much. Better by far to establish ground markers of sufficient size and luminosity to enable pilots to find their way from, say, Andover to Berlin, day or night.

Sinclair interrupted with a headline from the newspaper, "American Servicemen Save Coast Guard at German Sub", then read to us the entire, albeit small, article. I was chagrined to learn that my name and Zeb's were included. Mother had been right to object to our speaking to the press. Not everyone in my own unit had known I was a scion of the Prouwder family, let alone these Brits, and I was momentarily uncomfortable with this disclosure. At least Hastings was not far off; our recent *presence there required no special explanation, as Jallianwala Bagh would have done.*

"It seems rescues are your calling, Caul!" Sinclair proclaimed with great mirth. Per the demand of the group, I recounted our adventure on the beach and the sad prognosis for Heard and Moore. Some embellishments and omissions were necessary, of course. These men were more interested in what one of their peers had done, so I minimalized Zeb's role. He wouldn't mind, I reasoned. We all remained in the club trading stories until the wee hours, then turned in.

Sinclair surprised me in the darkness with intimacies I hadn't expected. He was terribly nervous about them and brought them to an equally unexpected end, without reciprocation. I slept well enough thereafter.

The next day was the funeral: weeping parents, a priest, a fiancée turned into a widow, and many young flyers in stern faces and stiff uniforms. It was a life much to be recommended, despite the danger, and the pièce de résistance came in the afternoon: my return to the skies in a Sopworth 5F.1 Dolphin. The clouds parted before my propeller and the ground approached or receded with every movement of my stick. Best of all, there were no German Fokkers to watch out for or shoot down. I landed only when my fuel level forced me to. What Zeb has missed while tossing about the ocean in his tin can! I resolved to get him up in the air some day for a proper joy ride.

As the evening wore on to night, Sinclair became inexplicably jittery and cross. He avoided my eyes and drank to excess. Nevertheless, it was a surprise when, as we were returning from the officers' club to our cots, he suddenly drew me hard by the elbow into a dark copse. I asked him what the matter was. In an utterly demeaning way, he shook me by the arm and pointed his finger into my face. "See here," he said, "you've gotten the entirely wrong idea about me and you must stop it. What you did last night was despicable. I'm going to be married next year, a dear girl from the village, and she is just waiting for me to set the date, so no more of these perversions. Do you quite understand?"

I couldn't say that I did. Sinclair had made overtures, not I, and what contact there had been between us came at his instigation, not mine. He had furthermore been entirely interested in pleasing himself, not me. All these thoughts put me in a combative mood and I in turn put that mood into my words. "Remove your hands from my arm and my face if you do not wish to leave these woods with a bloody lip and a black eye."

He paused, assessed my intention and ability to deliver on my threats, and turned me loose. I began to stride away and the coward took the opportunity to hit me on the head with his fist. Fortunately, my senses were made keen by our confrontation and my adrenaline had spiked as well. I fended off the bulk of his blow, delivered one of my own to his solar plexus, and shoved him to the ground. I tried to walk away, but he clung to my leg.

"Please, Caul! Don't say anything about this! I beg you!"

I kicked his arm off me and strode away, pausing neither at the barracks nor the officers' club, but continuing on to the site of the airplane crash. I bore left from there and hoped the tunnel back to Prouwder House was still operational. I saw that I had mistreated Zeb by remaining in England so long and resolved to appreciate both his willingness to share The

Work with me as well as his loving devotion to me personally. The future of aviation could go hang itself!

The tunnel worked as I had hoped and deposited me back on the estate, where it was mid-evening. I took in a deep breath of admittedly sooty Pittsburgh air and entered the mansion. At this hour the Doucette girls were often at the piano in the parlor while Grandmother and Aunt Olivia looked on. Great-uncle William, unperturbed by the music, would be trying to win this argument or that with his son and brother Henry. Other Prouwders in residence might be playing cards or backgammon. I passed along the main corridor, calculating where I would most likely find Zeb. He shied away from the Prouwder gathering unless I accompanied him. He was more likely in our apartment or the house's main library, so I headed there. I had just passed the kitchen and was about to climb a staircase when Mother and Belle came in a rush behind me.

"Thomas! Oh, thank the Lord! We've had no word and we've been so worried!"

"Well, I'm back now, Mother. Where's Beck?"

"But that's just it, Thomas! We don't know! The most dreadful thing has happened!"

"What is it?"

Mother generally liked being the bearer of bad news, but Belle jumped in. "He came back two days ago, Tom, and right in front of our eyes, that damn Frank Candell stepped out of the vestibule, grabbed him by his knapsack, and yanked him clean out of sight! We got no idea where he kidnapped Zeb off to!"

VESTIBULE

Thursday, the 24ᵗʰ of April

I rushed from the women along the main corridor to the vestibule and flung open the inner door. The room, perhaps fifteen feet by fifteen feet, was empty, without tunnels, and the outer door was closed. I opened the large closet where visitors' garments and much of our winter gear are stored. It too was empty, but I ran my hand behind every coat and under every pile of scarves until I had satisfied myself there was no tunnel in operation there either. I came out of the closet just as Mother and Belle reached the vestibule. They assured me they had searched every nook and cranny, but I nevertheless lifted the lid of the deacons benches and touched all around under ice skates and boots caked with dried mud. Nothing. I went on to the doorman's station, much smaller than the closet, and likewise touched every oak panel there, along with his chair, table, lamp, and cabinet of keys. Again, nothing.

My hands were dirty. Belle wiped them with her apron. "No luck, huh?"

I shook my head.

"I hoped you'd find something, but I didn't feel anything either."

Mother spoke. "We alerted James to be on the lookout for any signs of Mr. Beck on the estate. He's been tireless in his search, but hasn't found anything yet. Should I summon him for you?"

"No." I put my hands on my temples and rubbed them while squeezing my eyes shut, all in an effort to think toward a logical solution. "You both saw Candell kidnap Zeb. How did he do that? Zeb's too strong to be taken like that."

"Well, Frank's no lightweight, Tom. I've seen him wrestle a steer to the ground and he got Zeb off balance right away. It wasn't more than a few seconds and they were gone."

"Did either of you see anything of where they went? The slightest clue may be very helpful."

Mother shook her head. "We were coming along the corridor. It was perhaps eleven o'clock and Mr. Beck was just outside the vestibule. There." She pointed through the doorway to the burgundy and white tiles of the hallway. "It was just a moment. Mr. Candell emerged, grabbed Mr. Beck by the knapsack, and pulled him backwards. By the time we reached this spot, both were gone. I thought they had passed through the front door to the outside, but it was closed, just as it is now."

"Why did you think that?"

"Well," Mother continued, "it was a quite reasonable assumption, Thomas. I'm not so personally familiar with The Work as you, of course, but I have paid attention to it for decades and—"

"It was cold, Tom!" Belle interjected. "You just made me think of it! We got in here right away, but even from the hall I remember feeling a real cold draft around my feet. You know I hate the cold. I'll put my feet up on the stove sometimes, just to get them off the floor in the winter. The girls all laugh at me for doin' it, but I'd stick 'em right into the oven if I could."

"Why, yes!" Mother went on. "I recall being startled that the front door was closed, not only because Mr. Candell and Mr. Beck were so suddenly gone, but also because it felt as if the door were open. There was quite a steady wind."

I dashed out of the vestibule, back down the corridor. Mother and Belle called after me, but I had no time to spare and ran on. I reached the kitchen where a smattering of cooks and maids, having washed the dinner dishes and set them out to dry, were wiping down countertops. Others were already sitting down for a cigarette or a bite to eat at the end of their long workday. They perked up and watched me closely as I ran to the icebox and flung it open. The several shelves held pounds of butter, bacon, bottles of milk, various cheeses, but no tunnels.

"Mr. Caul?" one of the women said behind me. I ignored her and ran my hand around inside the cabinet and the somewhat depleted block of ice. Nothing. Mother and Belle came in just as I was opening the door to the yard.

"Icehouse!" I called behind me and ran outside. To my right was the vegetable garden, not yet planted with new seeds. To my left were the long upward slope of ground, the icehouse door, and the small flight of brick stairs that led to it. The door was unlocked, of course. I opened it and heard the screen door of the kitchen porch slap shut behind Mother and Belle at the same time. Just inside my door was the switch that turned on the electric lights hanging over a second, longer staircase. These I took two at a time, gripping the iron handrails as I descended, until I stood upon the straw at the bottom. The chamber was large but low-ceilinged. In a pit underneath the thick layer of straw were vast slabs of ice harvested from the Monongahela *and hauled on sledges up to the mansion during the winter. Sides of beef, pork, and lamb, wrapped tightly in strips of muslin, hung here and there. Ice cream cranks sat to one side, in proximity to large bottles of cream.*

I wandered about. No tunnels. No cries for help. There was no colder spot on the estate. If the chill that Belle and Mother had felt was not a clue to Zeb's whereabouts, I had no idea what to try next. It would take me days to touch every wall inside the mansion. If one added in the myriad chests, laundry chutes, crawl spaces, and fireplaces, plus the grounds themselves, it could take me much more than a week to find Zeb. He could be frozen to death by then, if he weren't already. I choked with desperation.

"You have to create *the tunnel, Thomas," said someone in the opposite corner of the chamber. "You can't wait for it to create itself."*

I hadn't heard anyone descend the staircase. Belle certainly wouldn't, given her bum hip; she always sent the other cooks to fetch icehouse items. Mother herself, although she was quite healthy, might hesitate to negotiate the stairs I had flown down.

"Hyacinth?"

She emerged from the shadow cast by one large slab of mutton, her arms wrapped around her chest and her hair carefully braided on one side while loose on the other. "Pray, Thomas."

"What?"

"Be not forgetful to entertain strangers, for thereby some have entertained angels unawares." She drew closer.

"I don't understand, Hyacinth. Please speak plainly."

She idly touched the slabs of meat as she passed between

them. *"It isn't the house that opens the tunnels, it's the angel, and he's listening to both ends. He hears the cries for help and prepares the way for someone to render aid. Pray, Thomas."*

I quietly began the paternoster, feeling foolish for doing it here in the ice and meat and straw, but hoping to appease her enough that she would give me saner instructions. She interrupted my murmuring by gripping my elbow and laying her head against my shoulder.

"No, Thomas. Not like that. Pray because you are desperate for help. Pray because Zeb is missing and near death. Pray because you are bereft and panicked and frightened beyond all measure!"

From somewhere –I didn't know where– she pulled out a meat cleaver and swung it with all her might at my throat. I barely dodged the attack, and, shocked to my core, stared wide-eyed as she swung again. I was nearly frozen in place by the conviction that years of self-neglect and grief had completely undone her mind, but her next blow nicked the side of my knapsack and I retreated quickly.

"Christ, Hyacinth! Stop!"

She advanced, powered by insanity and swinging wildly. I retreated farther and tried to put a side of beef between us, but she swung beneath it and nearly lodged the blade into my kneecap. I backed up faster. She pressed her attack.

"Hyacinth! Don't!"

Her movements were hard to predict and her footing more secure than mine as we moved deeper into the straw. I'd soon be trapped in the same corner she'd emerged from. Although I was a grown man, Hyacinth now induced in me the terror of a little boy whose older sister has already gained her adult height and strength. She'd always been kind to me, but any games of rough and tumble were decidedly hers to win. Worst of all, her face was totally impassive as she swung at me; she might not even care who I was anymore!

She came within an inch of my lip and I cried out involuntarily. That incoherent yelp was followed by several hysterical calls for help. I somehow hoped my mother could come and save me. I flailed backwards and fell…

…and fell and fell and fell! When I finally landed, it was not on the hard icehouse floor, but on even harder rocks. One particularly jagged edge caught me on the back just below my knapsack. I cried out to the clear blue sky above me and only slowly recovered enough to roll off to one side. All around were more rocks, ponds or puddles, and small patches of lichen. Upon one nearby peak was a glacier. Nowhere were there signs of inhabitation.

I stood warily. The sun was still quite low in the sky and a rather constant wind blew this way and that. It was as cold here as it had been in the icehouse. The outer edge of the nearest puddle was frozen while the water in its center rippled with the wind. I panted, both as an aftermath of the fight with Hyacinth and in reaction to the thin air all around me. I guessed I was at least two miles above sea level. It was impossible to tell where I was exactly, but I judged I had jumped some twelve hours ahead in time to central Asia. These were probably not the Himalayas, but some other, lower range of mountains.

I caught sight of Zeb. His white uniform stood out from the gray rocks all around him, some sixty feet from my position. The going was slow; rocks broke or slid out from under my feet with every step and my back hurt as well. It was clear that Zeb was lying on his side, not moving. I prayed Candell hadn't killed him. If he had, I might just lie down beside Zeb and let exposure do me in or give myself over to a life spent seeking hellish revenge. His ankles were bound with rope, as, behind his back, were his wrists. What skin was visible had turned purple and white. I touched him and called his name, but he was unresponsive. His face was turned toward the ground behind one of the largest rocks in the area and I dreaded seeing it. As gingerly as I could, I cut his wrists free and pulled him onto his back. There was blood all along his lower side and his face was terribly blotchy.

His eyelids fluttered, but did not open, and he seemed to say "Tom", but no actual sound issued forth from his horribly chapped lips. For the time being, he was alive.

I hurried to cut away the ropes around his ankles. He was in no shape to stand or walk. I dug my feet below the rocks around me and found steady ground, bent my knees, and got my arms under Zeb's back and thighs. He was nearly dead weight and lifting him was a dreadful chore. I lost my balance and had to put him back down quickly, to which he reacted with a scowl and a mute curse word. My second attempt was more successful, but my knees popped ominously and I was forced to stand still for quite a while to make sure they wouldn't give out. Slowly, laboriously, I turned back where I had come from and shuffled away. I dared not lift my feet, but rather slid them forward as close to the earth as possible, pushing rocks out of the way with my ankles. This was painful and I saw I would not be able to cover the entire sixty feet with Zeb as my burden.

Without realizing it at first, I had begun to pray. My voice was barely any louder than Zeb's had been and my prayer was no formal thing, just the constant plea of "Save us, Angel. Save us." I closed my eyes despite the increased danger of tripping and focused hard on imagining a tunnel home. Only when I heard straw beneath my feet did I open my eyes to discover we had returned to the icehouse!

Mother was there and Belle as well. They clutched their hearts and I fancied I could hear their own prayers echoing around the room. "Put him down!" they cried, but I shook my head. If I did so, I knew I wouldn't have the strength to pick him up again. When I reached the bottom of the stairs, James clattered down them and took half my burden. The women clucked behind us as we made our way to the top, one precarious stair at a time. From the icehouse back to the kitchen went by in a flash and Zeb was placed on a settee brought next to the stove. Belle stoked it. Mother began to chafe Zeb's hands between hers, but Belle told her no, Zeb needed to warm up as slowly as he'd frozen. She had me remove his shoes and socks very carefully. The sight of his frostbitten toes made my vision blur with fear, but Belle asserted she had seen far worse.

She summoned bandages and two of the maids still on duty hustled off to fetch them. We made an inspection where blood showed through Zeb's clothing. "Scrapes," she said. His face, she found, was not as bitten as she expected. Apparently, I told her, he'd taken what shelter he could behind a rock and buried his face partially below it. "Good idea," she nodded.

Lotion was brought, but Belle preferred lard and administered it gently on all Zeb's exposed skin. Bandages were applied over his scrapes and she scooted everyone out of the room before telling me, "You lie down close next to him and let your body heat warm up his back while I wrap yinz up in a couple blankets. Then I'll make some tea for his insides."

I hesitated a moment, but Belle told me to hurry up and

then undid my own shoes and socks as I lay down. When we were tucked in, she lowered the lamp in the room and took a seat in the servants' dining area. "Now we just wait and hope, honey. Lord! My hip hurts! I am never going down those damn steps again!"

4/26/19

It's Saturday now and now's the first time I been able to hold a pen well enough to write in here. I'm on the sofa in our set of rooms and Tom's been waiting on me hand and foot since he got me back from that damn mountain. Speaking of hands and feet, mine still hurt, but I'm hoping when the doctor comes back tomorrow he won't decide I got to have anything amputated. My fingers are safe though I might not get feeling back in a couple of them ever, he says. My toes are another matter. They look like hell, a few of them, and might have to come off. Whatever he takes off me I'll be sure and take off that bastard Candell if I ever catch him! He'll thank God my willy was safe and tucked between my thighs!

It rankles me that I don't even know where I was that whole time. Candell pulled me there and knocked me out cold and that's how I woke up too! Cold and all tied up like a hog, only Candell branded me not with hot iron but a constant wind. Tom has been looking in his big atlas, trying to puzzle out where we were, but to my mind, I was just outside trying to bury myself under the biggest rock I could see and crawl to. Good thing I'm right handed cause my left side is all scraped up from me inching over them rocks to the best shelter around. I wanted to get free and tried hard to work my wrists and ankles loose, but who knows? Maybe it was better for me that I had to stay put where Tom could find me. If I'd gone hiking around, I might have fallen to my death or been impossible to find. I just wish we could carry some mechanical thing that would tell us where on Earth we are, like a pocket watch, but for location instead of time. That sort of ignorance itches at me worse than my fingertips.

Tom tells me his sister Hyacinth showed him he can make tunnels whenever he wants, but he sure hasn't been able to do it since we got back to Prouwder house. He's been trying, but I'm not sure he can do it without somebody swinging a cleaver at his head. He's kind of "bound up" when it comes to feeling things, I'd say. Comes from being a pilot maybe. Only fellers that can beat down their fear would ever have the nerve to take one of them contraptions up in the air. That sure ain't isn't me! I guess I held myself together well enough when the *Fanning* was in bad seas or chasing down some German sub, but otherwise I'm pretty close to the surface when I get mad or horny or want to tell a guy how much I love him. If I ever have to go find Tom cause he's in danger far away, I'll blast a tunnel right through a wall, easy! I'd like to blast my dad's shotgun right through Frank Candell too!

Fortunately for both me and Tom, there's only been one rescue in the last couple of days: a woman in a runaway cart. I didn't go cause I was fast asleep, but Tom told me he ran out here onto the lane leading up to Prouwder house and right away jumped up into the cart and got hold of the reins. He played up how pretty the woman was, how fancy dressed, and how grateful, covering him with kisses and such, but I know he did that just to have a bit of fun with me cause he was stripping down and getting into bed with me at the time and pretty soon he was covering *me* with kisses, which was alright with me. Sometimes a kiss is a whole lot warmer than even a whole pot of tea, huh?

My secret fear, though maybe Tom has the same one, is that next time Candell might not take me or Tom but one of his family instead. That'd be a hell of a thing, trying to find Mrs. P, lost somewhere on an island in the Pacific or up to her neck in African quicksand! We got to hurry up and find *him* before that happens. Tomorrow I'm set on getting up out of this bed and helping Tom talk to Belle and Mr. Booke about where Candell might be. In the meantime, I'm gonna sleep with one eye open!

THE SURGERY

Monday, the 28ᵗʰ of April

*D*r. *Edmund Redler came today to amputate two of Zeb's toes, the result of his lengthy exposure to cold atop that mountain in Central Asia. He tolerated the operation admirably, having been administered two injections of procaine by Dr. Redler's young assistant, Dr. Kenneth Sexton. The procedure took place in the delivery room on the second floor. It has been used for many years as a "laboratory", to make a pun of it, and is well equipped. I myself was born there and Dr. Redler has by and large ushered the last forty years' worth of Prouwders into the world within its walls. Dr. Sexton has only recently joined Dr. Redler's practice and brings with him knowledge of many medical advancements which he was only too glad to discuss with me both before and after Zeb's surgery. I think he envisions a future as "court physician" to our family and has made every effort to leave a good impression. Certainly his shock of blonde hair and steel-blue eyes do so, but I suppose I am not to notice such things if I am to remain on good terms with Zebediah. Sometimes I think it would be best if he also had dalliances or at least the desire to have them; his dedication to me chafes somewhat.*

That was an unkind thing to write, especially as I am currently sitting at his bedside, overseeing his recovery. Had Zeb never befriended me on the Fanning, he would not now be hobbled by amputation and would have no memory of the frigid ordeal which necessitated surgery. The Work would have passed to some other Prouwder and I might now be training for the new airmail service.

I must turn my mind to practical matters, to wit, the Frank Candell problem! He, Hyacinth, and, to a far lesser extent, I, have all developed the ability to summon tunnels at will. Mine came only by dint of extreme fear and I have as yet been unable to replicate it. Hy travels them not out of fear, but by means of her insane grief over Lo's death. He perished over three and a half years ago, but she imagines she still hears him calling for help. She cannot save him and may be doomed to a lifetime of trying.

Candell likewise seems unmotivated by fear. Instead, it appears to be an ever-increasing hatred or rage which lets him command the tunnels. I hope Zeb and I continue to be his only targets, although it is Great-uncle William who banished him from the mansion in '06. How can he have sustained his appetite for revenge these thirteen years? Why has he not acted sooner? I deduce that revenge is not his motive or, more accurately, that his revenge has grander parameters. He is not intent upon redressing his own mistreatment alone, but something fouler perhaps. What that may be, I cannot yet discern. I shall endeavor to "get the jump on" Candell. Perhaps I can whip up enough mortal dread to create a tunnel right into his lair, wherever in the world that may be. Unfortunately, that prospect makes me more giddy than fearful!

4/28/18

So, they cut off my two smallest toes. Ain't that a helluva thing! Now I'm bedridden and all bandaged up. I swear, peace is doing worse to me than war ever did. It's fair to say I'm feeling sorry for myself even though some of the boys we hauled home over the Atlantic had lost most of their damn faces in battle, not to mention the poor bastards that got sent to the bottom in their tin cans! So I just better knock some sense into myself and set about healing up quick. I don't want Tom having to go out on rescues all by his lonesome. He had a comfy chair brought into the hospital room they got here at the mansion and he's hardly stirred from it what with taking care of me. Still, I hate it that I might never be that fast or sure-footed again! No use crying over spoiled milk.

Tom's also kept himself busy learning first aid from the doctor that helped the surgeon. Sexton's his name and damned if he doesn't look more German than me! They've been practicing bandages and splints and Turner kits, some of it on me, some of it on each other. Sexton taught Tom to listen to a guy's heartbeat and lungs, plus feel around in his gut. I had to bunch up my sheets watchin' that and I sure wouldn't mind playin' doctor with Tom once we're back in our apartment. Just now they were running their fingers down each other's spines. I half thought they'd give each other a "short arm" inspection next!

Doc says I can walk about tomorrow, but I shouldn't wear tight shoes for a couple weeks. That's the old doc, I mean. Tom says he's the one that brought him into the world. Hard to imagine Mrs. P-C being young enough to have kids, but I guess she did, huh? Hyacinth I've met right at the foot of me and Tom's bed, but there was an older brother too, Lowell. He died in the Army fighting Pancho ~~Via's~~ Villa's men in Nogales sometime in 1915. Tom says "Hy" and "Lo" did the work before he was killed and Rose and Crowne took over, but I don't quite follow that story 'cause why was Lowell in Arizona in the military if he was still doing rescue work out of Prouwder House? Tom ~~don't~~ doesn't usually miss out on steps in his thinking like that, so I guess this is another family secret. One of about a hundred! Tom's so smart that sometimes he's convinced nobody *else* is smart enough to know when the wool's being pulled over their eyes. Oh well. He'll tell me in his own good time, I suppose.

4/29/19

Christ! Looks like Tom and me learned first aid just in the Nick of time 'cause today we went to Atlanta on a rescue that could've taken place in one of them trenches in Belgium, it was so awful!

We were up here in our rooms about three o'clock when we heard an explosion. It wasn't as big as that plane crash the other day, but it sounded like it was inside the mansion, which gave us both a worse feeling than seeing flames out on the estate. I'd say we rushed downstairs, but that wasn't something I could do, so Tom hurried on ahead. There was shrieks for me to follow and they took me to the front door of Prouwder House which is in a little room (not so little!) they call the Vest of Buell, maybe 'cause it's hung there or something.

Anyway, I got that same feelin' of rushing away

somewhere soon as I stepped into the place. I got to admit I was half-scared I'd end up back on that mountain where Candell left me, but instead I was in a different house's entryway where there was a whole mess of broken glass and smoke in the air, plus them shrieks. They were coming from a colored servant woman on the floor. Tom was there, trying to get hold of the woman's arms. Her hands had been blowed clear off and she was not only screaming but also pounding her feet on the floor. A second woman, white, was also laid out on the floor, plus there was a middle-aged man running down the stairs. "Maude! Maude!"

I didn't rightly know what to do, but Tom yelling put me in motion. "Grab her other arm!"

It was a mangled mess I took hold of. I'd never seen a woman injured that bad and not too many men either. There was blood on the floor, on her dress, on her face.

"Raise her arm and squeeze!"

Tom wrapped a Turner kit on the arm he was holding, then went to work on mine. Other people came through the door. Some were servants and the rest were neighbors or passersby. One of them screamed out "Ethel!" and started cradling the maid's head in her lap. Both their faces were the color of ash and Ethel seemed to faint away. Somebody ran off yelling for the police and then there was somebody on the telephone down the hall calling for an ambulance.

Tom scooted over to the man of the house and what was probably his wife. Her face was burnt up and blood streamed out of her mouth. Tom and the man turned her to one side so she wouldn't choke on the blood. She moaned something awful. I seen men get burned on the *Fanning*; if it was bad, they'd holler and cuss, but if it was real bad, real deep, they just moaned like that woman.

We waited and waited for help. It seemed like the hours I spent on that mountain, but it was probably only ten minutes or so. Cops came through the door, which only then I noticed was hanging half off its hinges. They cleared people out of the entryway, those that weren't seeing to the women. Some went out on the porch and others huddled in the parlor. I figured this was the worst thing they'd ever seen and wished it was also the worst thing *I'd* ever seen too, but that ain't the case.

I could tell from the way people talked that we were in the south somewhere and I thought of that fellow, Crowne, that got lynched down here. Out through the door I saw lots of nice houses, not some marina near Biloxi. Still, it seems we usually run foul of the authorities one way or another, just for doing our jobs. One of the cops, an older one, was talking to the pudgy-faced husband and called him Senator. I didn't know if that meant we'd be all right or see federal government levels of trouble.

The ambulance came and a doctor plus two burly men hurried into the entryway. They conferred with the Senator and he oversaw them lifting his wife gently onto a litter. He shook both our hands, said he was Thomas Hardwick, then followed the doctor outside as Mrs. Hardwick got slid into the back of the ambulance. They all drove off at a fast clip to the right. Ten minutes later, I know because I finally seen the clock there in the entryway, a wagon came for the servant woman. There was no doctor, just some black guy in overalls with the reins in his hands. Ethel was told she had to get up and walk to the cart, but Tom lifted her up in his arms and carried her out. A couple colored ladies climbed into the wagon and made a bed of sorts for her to lay on. Her cart set off in the opposite direction, maybe to a hospital for colored people.

Tom and I hung around and talked to the police, who asked us for a statement. Tom gave our names as Michael Hunt and Owen Bucks. He said we were veterans out seeing the country we saved from the Hun, just passing by the house when we heard and saw the explosion. The cops told us a lot more than we told them. This was a package bomb, they said, pointing at remains of wrapping paper, wood, and shrapnel around the entryway. One of them even picked up the envelope and showed us how it was addressed to Senator Hardwick in Sandersville, Georgia. I figured that was where we were, but then the cop said it must have been forwarded on to Atlanta because this is where the Senator was so I finally knew why Sandersville looked like a big city even though I'd never heard of it!

The cop said it was just bad luck that Mrs. Hardwick was there when the bomb was opened and went off. He didn't say anything about Ethel, who had even worse luck being the one that opened the thing. Hardwick should have to open his own damn mail, I thought, but I kept that to myself. Tom talked like the cop already, the same molasses accent. He's good at that. He did the same thing when we was with my folks down in Sycamore. They didn't notice 'cause they didn't hear him talk before. I suppose his real accent is what I hear at Prouwder house, but maybe he's only putting that on too. Maybe I haven't ever heard him talk exactly like himself.

Well, I'm tired now so I'm going to sign off, like I used to do when I was manning the radio on the *Fanning.* Hobbling around on just eight toes makes every footstep feel like two!

Tuesday, the 29th of April

Zeb aided me well, despite his own malady and only partial training in First Aid. He's got a fearful temper, it's true, but otherwise he has a steady disposition and isn't one to balk at whatever The Work requires of him. I should perhaps investigate treatments for battle fatigue, however; if we continue to see horrors such as today's, he may need psychiatric care. I myself am able to repress unpleasant memories so that they do not interfere with what must be done in the moment, but not all have that ability, of course.

As soon as he and I returned to the estate, I began to investigate what had made the good Senator a target for assassination. He was defeated in the fall and will not be returning to Congress, which means the motive for killing him must be retribution for some prior act. I made for our library, where various newspapers the family subscribes to are kept. That may indicate a level of organization the library does not actually possess, for various sections are scattered about the house in bedrooms, sitting rooms, nooks and crannies. Mother, for example, shares with her sister a penchant for the society pages, but eschews the "funny pages" over which Olivia snorts. Her daughters share that awful habit, but they are also enthralled by every dress advertisement they see. Great-uncle William is strictly interested in the business section and consumes its every word like poppy seeds fallen from his toasted bagel. Great-uncle Henry, on the other hand, reads the obituaries assiduously and circles those of persons known to him. He attends funerals nearly every week. For him it is not morose, but comforting. Grandmother can no longer read print, but she will peruse photographs and illustrations, often remarking that she must share this or that item with Grandfather. She never actually takes a newspaper back to her suite, however, which tells me she knows at some level that Grandfather's obituary appeared years ago.

It is my first cousin once removed Nathan that I sought out. He was, fortunately, not occupied with William's demands, but free and at home. I found him in the secondary library at the far end of the mansion's third floor. It is a small space without much in the way of resources, but it does have a superior view of the valley below us and plenty of light to read by. Mother disdains Nathan's cigars, so this is where he usually comes to enjoy them. I greeted him and he offered me one of the Arturo Fuentes he had on hand. Generosity is a hallmark of his character, in stark contrast to his father's miserliness. We lit our stogies and puffed away for a while before I brought up the matter on which I wanted Nathan's counsel, for he is a great follower of politics. I outlined the events of the day, my encounter with Senator Hardwick, and the attack upon his household, leaving out gruesome details, of course.

Nathan peered out the window and stroked the sandy-blonde beard adorning his jaw. It is an enviably thick and well-groomed thing that makes him very nearly a Doppelgänger of King George V or the late Tsar Nicholas of Russia. He asked me a few rudimentary questions and then posited that Hardwick's sponsorship of the Immigration Act last year may be the reason *he was targeted for death. The Act, as Nathan explained, made possible the deportation of undesirable aliens, specifically anarchists, communists, labor activists, and the like.*

"So," I mused, "the bomber was very probably a foreigner."

Nathan agreed and began to peruse the stack of newspapers in the corner of the room. He pulled several issues and laid them out for me. "Luigi Galleani is behind this, I'd wager." He went on to recall for me several of the attacks for which Galleani and his followers were responsible. They stretched back two decades or so, Nathan thought. I thanked him for his help and we finished our cigars while discussing the state of politics. My time in the war and, prior to that, my occupation with childish things, had left me ignorant of many fundamentals, but Nathan was giving of his knowledge and forgiving of my deficiencies. Indeed, I think he enjoyed teaching me, for Great-uncle William scoffs at Washington and strongly favors a completely "hands off" policy from lawmakers. I think Nathan, were he not a Prouwder, might have pursued a career in public service, but his father is so domineering that he would never have permitted it. Behind the scenes is how William prefers to work. Nathan was forced to study accounting at college, not law, as I surmise he would have liked. Ah well, families!

After our conversation, I made a beeline to the day's accumulation of mail. There was nothing suspicious among the letters, packages, or periodicals the postman had brought. Nevertheless, I made sure that Agnes, one of whose duties is the sorting of mail into slots designated for each permanent resident of the mansion, would be on the lookout for anything fitting the description of the package which brought such horror to the Hardwick home. She is especially on alert against anything stamped "Gimbel Brothers Novelty Samples". I told Mother as well and she promised to warn everyone here, including James, the night watchman. Our home is rather secluded, but we are prominent citizens and, like Messrs. Carnegie, Frick, Heinz, and Mellon, not unacquainted with death threats. The number of men patrolling the grounds will be doubled for the time being.

I tried to give Zeb all the information on Galleani that I had gathered, but he was in a contentious mood, no doubt on account of his feet, and rather perplexingly took the side of those trying to effect change in society. How he can have seen firsthand the terrible injuries brought on by anarchists and not be as utterly repulsed from their cause as I is incomprehensible! I told him I would count it among my life's greatest accomplishments if we were instrumental in bringing that blood-thirsty bastard to justice. He countered that Candell was no anarchist, but had nevertheless maimed Zeb in his quest, so what did I think of that?

Truly, there is no arguing with an ignorant man, so I let the matter drop and curried favor with Zeb by reading to him from "Huckleberry Finn", putting on this accent or that as the passage demanded. Mark Twain is a great source of good humor and let us put the issue of social criticism aside. Soon enough, Zeb was quieted and, having already written in his own diary, fell asleep. He snores beside me as I write these words. He dreams of visiting upon Frank Candell the same injury he himself has endured, but I, perhaps to my damnation, would rather cut off the villain's head than his toes!

BIGELOW
BOULEVARD

Thursday, the 1ˢᵗ of May

*W*hat a splendid day we've passed, one I've been looking forward to for quite some time! The Flying Circus was in town today, as well as Admiral William S. Sims, president of the Naval War College and commander of US naval forces during the recent conflict. He is a great man, but modest, an "admirable Admiral", as it were. He arrived this morning to throngs of well-wishers and was cheered the entire route between Penn Station and the William Penn Hotel. Great-uncle William, Mother, and I met him at the luncheon given in his honor at the Chamber of Commerce at noon. Aunt Olivia and the Doucette girls were also in attendance and later took part in the selling of Victory Liberty bonds. I find Olivia contrary, but I must admit she is still a great beauty. Her daughters are no less comely, albeit dimwitted, and the four of them were popular purveyors of bonds. They did much to repay the nation's war debt. Our family, naturally, has contributed a fair sum toward that end as well.

I wish Zeb had had the opportunity of attending. No doubt he would have liked seeing the man who did so much to *modernize the Navy and keep him safe. Unfortunately, he was needed for The Work and remained at Prouwder House in case a rescue was called for. This he did gladly for he's a very good sport. He reports there was one call for help, but it was of little interest and quickly resolved, despite his handicap.*

The part of the celebration to which I had most looked forward came not to pass, which was a disappointment. I had risen early and was on hand at Penn Station to see the arrival of the Flying Circus. Some of the aviators were known to me, either personally or by reputation, and I accompanied them to Thornburg golf course, where they assembled and tuned up their machines, Nieuports mostly, but also some Fokkers captured by our side. There was to be a mock battle above the Monongahela in the afternoon, but our dirty Pittsburgh rain forced its cancellation. I should invest in an airplane of my own, the very latest, so that I can indulge in flights whenever I wish or perhaps provide some service to the population. Rides for children or mail delivery come to mind. Perhaps I could survey the city from the air so that municipal authorities would better know where to build new homes or industries.

In any case, William, Olivia, and Mother returned to the mansion after the luncheon and I agreed to chaperone Ernestine, Josephine, and Pauline until we all convened again in the evening for speeches at the new Syria Mosque on Bigelow. Great-uncle Henry is a member of the Ancient Arabic Order of the Nobles of the Mystic Shrine and donated a great deal of money toward the construction of this venue, although he tends not to go in for public events, preferring the private side of the Shriners. William opposes secret societies and browbeats Henry about his support of them, but this is one instance in which Henry stood up to his older brother and exercised control over his portion of the Prouwder fortune. I haven't given much thought to what I could do with my portion. I suppose I'm content for now to let it grow under Mother's aegis. Perhaps later I shall find a worthy person, organization, or institution and become its benefactor.

The girls and I took in the sights and I treated them to ice cream cones. They mostly conversed with each other, as usual, unaware of the attention they were garnering from potential suitors all around us. On the surface, Olivia seems still to consider her daughters little girls, but I wager she is secretly sorting through potential sons-in-law with all the not-inconsiderable power of her intellect. It will be interesting to see whom she folds into the Prouwder clan. A Carnegie, a Mellon, or a Frick would not be beyond her plans, perhaps even a Roosevelt, so long as he were handsome.

But, back to today. Senator Philander Knox came to speak at the Mosque in the evening, as did Major General Leonard Wood. It was Admiral Sims, however, who most engaged the audience with his tales. He expressed great respect for Pershing and decried recriminations against him. Truly there is trouble in our great nation and one hopes the press will continue to be watched closely, although the United Kingdom has recently relaxed its censorship of newspapers.

I had a brief opportunity to speak to Senator Knox about the bombing at Senator Hardwick's home, although I naturally revealed nothing of my personal acquaintance with the attack. He expressed his horror and vowed to further the fight against undesirables among us. He then turned the conversation to my service abroad. I made a few remarks, striving to be as modest as Admiral Sims, and alluded to my fervent desire to see the anarchist faction destroyed utterly. Although Cousin Nathan has allowed himself to be cowed out of a career in politics, I will not submit to Uncle William's or Mother's judgment in this regard. Who knows? Perhaps someday, after some future war, Senator Thomas Caul will be addressing just such a crowd as was gathered tonight!

I managed to disengage myself from my family after the speeches, motion pictures, and musical performances so that I could spend more time with my fellow pilots. They were as disappointed by the weather as I was and regretted not being able to demonstrate their skills for the public. As enthused as I am about aviation, it seems unlikely the general population will ever get the chance to see airplanes in battle. Despite Sinclair's visions of a Pax Britannica based on air power, I rather think the heyday of dog-fights has passed. This Beast of War will be tamed into delivery of the mail, et cetera. If pilots battle in the future, it will no doubt be faster and higher than those on the ground can see.

Disappointment had naturally led to drinking among some of the pilots. It takes courage to fly and alcohol plays its part in all aspects of the activity: preparing to take off into the sky, celebrating one's safe return to Earth, and consoling oneself about untimely deaths among one's brethren. Some flyers had indulged in too many beers among Pittsburgh's Germans and came away with broken teeth or cracked ribs. Others ran afoul of large gangs of sailors roaming the streets. I myself saw only the ordinary complement, but my vision wasn't doubled by drink!

It was pleasant to end my day back in bed with good old Zeb. He is as loyal as a hound.

KILDAY WAY

5/1/19

Well, ain't I a slob? Tom and his whole family went off to town to see the festivities and rub elbows with Pittsburgh's upper crust, leaving good old Zeb here at the mansion to rescue the whole damn world. I bit my lip and said sure, I'll stick around, as if I had a choice, but what they don't know is that, as soon as Mrs. P-C had left with her uncle, her sister, and them three girls I can't tell apart, I made the stable boy give me one of the horses they hardly use anymore and rode off to the "point" where the Mon and the Al come together to turn into the Ohio. Belle saw me leaving and nodded ~~conspeara conspiriter~~ like we was in cahoots. She tells me stuff when none of the Prouwders is around and no other servants either. She sees we're two of a kind now, her with her hip and me with my feet, both wounded for the Work!

Anyway, downtown, there was lots of men on horseback and lots of sailors too so nobody took notice of me. I paid a guy to tie Blue up in his backyard and he fed and watered her to boot. I gave him another two bits later on, but first I went wandering around. There was a parade for that Admiral, Sims is his name, and people cheered so hard you'd think he won the war in the Atlantic by himself! He never came on board the *Fanning*, I'll tell you that, even when we passed in review for Woodrow Wilson. He wasn't there when we were hanging on for dear life during this storm or that and I don't remember him helping attack the U-58 either. Tom's all for men like Sims though. He gushed about him once he finally got home. I suppose that's what his experience in the war was like: him alone, high above the men on the ground. I can't forget that I'd probably be lying in a bed downstairs with the other servants if I wasn't in one up here on the fourth floor with Tom himself.

I had a beer and a sausage at a joint in Deutschtown, which is on the north shore, far away from where the planes were supposed to be flying. One swabby gave me the eye and I thought I'd have gone off with him if I was still in the Azores or Queenstown, but now I'm with Tom, so that's that, as they say. I've sunk my anchor with him and there's no more drifting around for me.

I wanted another beer, but I needed to keep a steady keel in case I heard a call for help and had to ride back to Prouwder House on the quick. There was plenty of drunks around without me joining in. I heard school was called off on the south side so the kids could take in the air show, but it was just a regular Thursday on the north side. That didn't keep the Germans from downing whole pitchers of Fort Duquesne Pilsner, Iron City, or something even closer to home. I guess they're drinking up before Prohibition takes hold next year. Germans worked hard against Temperance, but now that we've been in a war with them, they're beat here too. Pennsylvania went for Prohibition in February, but you'll never get the lager away from my Opa Dieffendörfer!

There was flags and bunting everywhere I wandered. Just about every shop window had a sign getting people to buy up victory bonds. The Heinz factory was going full tilt. I like their ketchup. I hear they got pretty good bosses there, free doctoring, a swimming pool, and classes for women. Maybe if this thing with the Prouwders doesn't work out, I'll try for a job bottling pickles or something.

I was thinking about that when I heard one of them calls for help Tom and I are used to now. It didn't sound too far off, but who knew where it might take me. I could end up in China through one of the Prouwders' china cabinets or jump onto that bear skin I saw in one room and find myself up in Canada fighting a grizzly! I took off like a shot back toward the house where Blue was tied up, but funny thing, the yelling didn't stay in front of me. Instead it started falling away behind me until I finally turned around and headed back where I'd been. Not too far from there was an alleyway and halfway down that three guys was beating the tar out of some sailor. It didn't take me too many steps to come up behind the smallest of the three and smash his head against a brick wall. Then I saw the sailor they were thrashing was the very one that had given me the high sign back in the bar. He was doing okay with one of the louses that had jumped him, but there was still two going at him and his face was bloody from cuts above both eyes and his lips.

Lucky for me, those two hadn't seen me lay out their

buddy yet, so it was a shock to both of 'em when I got my arm around the next guy's throat and drug him away from behind. He was flailing about, trying to get free or punch me in the face, but he passed out before either of those things happened. These poor saps don't know how many dirty fights I been in with my brothers!

Now that the odds were in our favor, guy number 3 tried to make peace or win me over to his side, saying that the sailor was queer and made a pass at them. Fellows are stupid like that sometimes. Kimball, for instance. Me and him did plenty together on the *Fanning*, but soon as I met Tom and got serious about him, Kimball started shooting his mouth off about us like as if he had never had me right in that same damn mouth!

Well, this guy was so intent on explaining why he and his pals had jumped the sailor that he lost track of the sailor's fist until it landed right in his gut. I could've taken part in the beating, but I say fair is fair and that's one on one, not two on one. The sailor, whose name is Albert, gave the other guy a knee to the nose when he was bent over gasping for breath, then I pulled him away and we left the alley. He lives all the way up in Troy Hill and when we got to his place, I did some of that first aid to his poor beat up face. He told me he got a job at the Eberhardt and Ober Brewery. Seems to me like a hard slog uphill after a long day's work, but he likes it, he said. His boarding house is run by a woman named Mickey or McKee or something and there's a couple other brewers living there, but he has his own room. He got friendly after I patched him up and damned if I didn't want to have a lie down with him, but I saw where that might go so I said my goodbyes and headed back toward town to pick up Blue.

I came back here and hung out reading until Tom got home. He was all fired up about the planes he'd seen and then he got real sweet with me. I don't know what two guys should be like. If I'd been stupid enough to stay in Sycamore and marry Nellie I'd know we was supposed to keep ourselves to ourselves, like they say at every wedding, but with Tom it's just not clear and there's nobody I can ask about it. I guess we'll just figure things out as we go, but I suppose I shouldn't get too angry when he smiles at cops or pilots and the like 'cause even when me and him were getting cozy together, my mind went some to Albert, wondering what he'd be like.

I want to be loyal, but maybe I'm just a dog.

STREETCAR

5/2/19

H ell of a thing we saw today. A truck ran into a streetcar over in Rankin, which is a town near the estate. Me and Tom were right on the scene, even without the house sending us there, 'cause he wanted to make a call on the mayor of Braddock. Since Tom watched them speeches yesterday, he's got some idea of being in politics. It's a mystery to me why he would want that since he's not hurting for money. Seems the Prouwders could also buy any law they wanted, but Tom muttered something about service and off we went with Charles the chauffeur at the wheel of the family's brand new enclosed Model T. Charles gave me a dirty look when I climbed up and sat down next to Tom, but I was invited, wasn't I? I don't think Tom's mom knew we were heading out, but she can hardly tell him no after the fact, especially since we maybe saved one kid's life.

Right as we were passing Hawkins Avenue on Second in Rankin, there was a huge crash and we all three snapped our heads to the left to see a truck smash into the front of a streetcar. Plum through the windshield of the truck came something big that at first I thought was a barrel or a bundle of clothes. It hit the pavement and went limp. Two other bodies flew out of the truck and likewise smacked the ground.

Tom yelled for Charles to stop and barely waited before jumping out the door. I followed him around the end of the Model T, opening my knapsack as we ran. Already I could see blood and then everything seemed to slow way down. We got to the boy on the street and saw he had a whole bunch of cuts on his neck from the plate glass he'd just gone through. It was awful, but Tom took the bandages I held out for him and between the two of us, we got the worst of the bleeding stopped. Lots of spectators came a running and we handed them more bandages, but Tom had to take over 'cause most of them were sort of seized up with horror.

Two of the three guys in the truck were just kids, basically. The driver was older than us. He had some cuts. I saw it was a Caruso Brothers automobile truck and it turned out this guy was one of them Carusos. Andrew, I heard. It was the youngest, Willy, that was hurt the most and he got taken to the hospital pretty quick. I don't even know if he survived, but I sure hope so. He's about as young as that poor Abraham over in Pinsk. Why the hell people don't have a guaranteed number of years they get to live I sure don't know. We don't all got to live as long as that Vanderbilt guy, but you'd think 30 or 40 would be something God could agree to.

Anyway, Willy went off to the hospital and Andy and the other kid, Walter, I think, went home. Nobody in the streetcar was hurt even though the whole front of it was wrecked. It sure made me almost scared to get back in the Model T, I'll tell you. Glass all around us that could turn into knives at our throats, given half the chance. Plus, there's nothing holding you in the damn thing. You might even be going 30 or 40 miles an hour and no tie to the seat you're on! At least with a horse you can squeeze its ribs with your legs or jump off if he tumbles.

On the good side, I guess you could say, the mayor of Rankin and then the mayor of Braddock came along and shook hands with Tom. People on the sidewalk also patted him on the back. Some knew he was a Prouwder. They're famous in these parts, of course, but I don't think Tom had been well known before the war, seeing as he was pretty much a kid. What would it mean for me and the Work if he went into politics, I wonder?

Friday, the 2nd of May

Our first aid training continues to benefit us. Today Zeb and I were able to render aid in a motor vehicle collision. I believe I shall enlist good Doctor Sexton to further our skills beyond bandages and treatment for shock. I'd like to be able to set bones and put dislocated shoulders back in place, for example. Sutures would also be a good idea. I wish that Zeb would take an interest in the medical field. It would be good for him to lead in some aspect of The Work since I may busy myself more and more with pursuit of office. My encountering both Rankin Council President Price and Braddock Mayor Quinn was fortuitous. I could easily schedule a meeting with Edward Babcock, the mayor of Pittsburgh proper, but it's probably better to work up to that. I will need a broad base of support if I'm to win elections. Perhaps I really should earn a college degree as well. My acceptance at Penn was deferred for the war, but I'm certain I could enroll there this fall.

More immediately, all my attempts to locate Frank Candell have failed. I simply cannot drum up the emotion needed to manifest a tunnel at will and I do not relish the idea of Hyacinth attacking me with a cleaver again. Zeb is much more volatile than I; perhaps he could master this aspect of our endeavor.

It's hard to believe, in a world as big as this one, that there isn't somebody to rescue every minute, but I guess I should be glad for "quiet" days, huh? Not like a car crash is quiet, but I figured helping those Caruso guys was just a freebie and that Prouwder House would send us off to Egypt or something. Maybe there really is an angel working behind the scenes here and maybe he sees when we need time off. Why would an angel help that bastard Frank Candell though? He cain't be a good guy in anybody's eyes, let alone God's, but apparently he comes and goes as he wants, free to yank sailors across the globe and leave them freezing their toes off on a mountain top!

I drew a bunch today. I like writing in here and I try to improove, but it's my sketch book that makes me really remember stuff. I drew the crash and put them three guys in it, laid out on the street. It was a kind of gruesome picture, but I still liked drawing it. I've read lots of books with pictures. Maybe I could do work like that in my free time. I wouldn't even have to leave the mansion. There's already a drawing room here somewhere. I've heard people mention it, but I haven't found it yet.

I've tried my hand at making tunnels, like Tom has,

but it hasn't gone any better for me than it has for him. I was in our supply room one time and sort of had a queer feeling like a tunnel was close by. Everything went blurry for a second and I thought it was pointed outdoors somewhere, but then it was gone and I was just in the supply room, not Timbuktu. I didn't tell Tom about it 'cause maybe I was just dizzy or something. He's good to me, but sometimes it's pretty clear he doesn't think I'm as smart as him. He's got more education, I know. He finished high school and I stopped after eighth grade, but Becks are definitely the smartest people in Sycamore. My dad keeps whole books of facts about horses in his head and Mom does the same with recipes. She can eat anything and tell you every ingredient in it, plus make it for herself at home. My brother Clement is a miserable cuss most of the time, but he designed the cabin he and his family live in and I got to admit, it's swell. It's a whole lot better than that cabin Frank Candell got sent out to live in. Course now it's in bad shape, neglected and all, but even when it was new, I bet it wasn't as tightly jointed as Clement's place.

Those Doucette girls get schooling here at the mansion. Tom did too when he was younger, then he went to Shadyside academy for high school. I think it's a Miss Bridges that teaches those girls. Maybe I could hire her to give me class. Tom didn't go to college, so I could catch up with him, education wise. I'll look into it.

Saturday, the 3rd of May

A busy day. The most rescues we've had so far in our time doing The Work. We were taken further and further afield, first to Wilkes-Barre, where some forty miners were overcome by 'black damp'. I knew we were in for a dirty job when Zeb and I were called to the mansion's coal room. I had him leave the kerosene lamp behind for fear we might encounter explosive gas on the other side of the Tunnel and we took our flashlights instead, plus gas masks. Seconds count, of course, and we didn't dawdle, but the right equipment can make all the difference.

Most of the men were able to exit the mine under their own power, but Zeb and I were obliged to assist or carry the rest, making at least three harrowing trips into the depths. Those who got out first naturally alerted personnel on the surface and aid was rendered swiftly.

5/3/19

Gas! Tom and ~~me~~ I started the day off rough with a call to a coal mine, but we got everybody out. No sooner had we come back to the basement of the mansion than we heard another call for help from the kitchen! I figured it was Belle herself, but it was a pretty quiet voice and the more we heard it, the more I decided it was a man's. It was coming right from the oven, hot with biscuits getting baked. Belle and the other cooks was startled when Tom and I came running in, especially 'cause we was dirty with coal dust, but she saw we were heading for a rescue and once we focused on the oven, she opened the hot door with a rag and barked at the other women to turn their backs and run out of sight. People who work here know weird stuff happens, but it isn't good for them to see it with their own eyes, I reckon. They dashed away like chickens from a hound dog and Tom took hold of my hand while sticking his foot into the oven. Lucky for us we didn't have to get burnt inside! A tunnel opened up right away and as we were going through it, Tom kind of tripped over or kicked something.

Suddenly we was in a small kitchen and saw we'd knocked some guy right out of his own oven! He didn't have his lit at all, but had just stuck his head in there, breathing up the gas. Damned if life ain't short enough for some people but they got to end it early. F'ing fools, I say.

Tom got the gas off and I went around opening windows. When I was done with that, I turned back to the two of them. My eyes bugged out to see Tom was kissing the fellow right on the mouth! All kinds of thoughts run through my head at that, but before I had time to slug either one of them, Tom took a deep breath and I saw he wasn't kissing the guy so much as blowing hard into his mouth. The guy's chest rose up and after a minute or so he was pulling air on his own. We lifted his arms above his head to help him out, then found his telephone and told the operator to send an ambulance. There was a newspaper on the table there so we saw we were in Los Angeles, out in California, but I had to run outside and find out the address, which was 835 on South Maple.

We carried the guy out to the street and met the ambulance there. Some other people who lived in his building came out and told the ambulance guys his name, which was something like Booler. They said they would take him to the receiving hospital, but I don't know what its name was. When they were gone, Tom said we could wander around some and see the city. It's a booming place. There are a whole lot of cars and people and buildings, streetcars too. It was just mid-morning, but two thirds of the curbs were already taken up by cars, mostly Fords and Pontiacs. We went where our noses led us, which was up to West 8th. You'd think there couldn't be any west streets out there since the whole city is right up against the ocean, but we found one and looked at shops the whole way to South Hill. We was hungry since we hadn't got any breakfast, so we stopped in at one place for ham and eggs. Nice to have the US Dollar as the money!

Tom told me a little about the motion picture business out here and we wondered if we'd see Chaplin or Fairbanks or Mary Pickford. Tom said they started their own company this year, Artists united or something. I looked up at the top floor of the building across the street and thought maybe I'd seen Buster Keaton swinging around up there for the cameras, but it was just some birds. Tom said the whole motion picture fad would be over in a couple more years. I didn't agree, but I didn't say so. Not everybody gets to travel around the world and have adventures like us, so pictures is all that most people have. He doesn't understand that.

Well, after our meal we went on up Hill and that's when we saw car crash number 2!

It's worth pondering whether the power behind The Work foresees the disasters it sends us to. How else to explain our presence at the intersection of Seventh and Hill this morning? We'd only just arrived there when I observed exceptionally erratic driving on the part of one vehicle. It swerved left and right, careened off one curb, and then plunged into cross traffic. Other automobiles were able to avoid a collision, but it was clear the shop door dead ahead would not dodge out of the way. Fortunately, my instincts had already set me in motion. I dashed alongside the car, leapt onto its aptly-named running board, and yanked the door open. The sole occupant resisted me strenuously and drew a revolver, but when I slammed my foot upon the brake, he lost hold of it, the engine stalled, and the car stopped just one inch from a lamppost.

A patrolman was quickly at hand. He rousted the driver, who reeked of liquor, and sat him down roughly upon the street. A woman on the sidewalk had nearly fainted from fright, but the gathering crowd saw to her. I pointed out the weapon and the patrolman confiscated it before questioning the driver. He gave his name as George McLaughlin and this was indeed the name found on the vehicle's license plate. He further claimed to be a resident of Venice, California, but his accent exhibited the very same 'twang' Zeb and I had heard in such great supply in Des Moines, Iowa. Naturally, he could have been a recent immigrant to the Golden State, but when I confronted him about his accent, he confessed that he was in fact a salesman from Burlington, Iowa, by the name of Miles Bressler. The policeman placed him under arrest on charges of public intoxication, carrying a concealed weapon, and suspicion of automobile theft. So is one undone by one's own words, n'est-ce pas?

Zeb and I decided we had had enough of the sunny West and made our way back to the would-be suicide's apartment, the door of which was fortuitously still unlocked. Once we'd opened the door of the oven, we walked hand in hand back to the kitchen of Prouwder House. Only Agnes was present. She is perhaps the most unflappable girl I've ever met and gave us only a wry look, despite the extraordinary way we'd just arrived. Zeb rather hurriedly shut the still-hot door of Belle's oven, said "Ouch", and then sucked at the burned spot on his finger. We were somewhat in a stalemate with Agnes, unsure of what to say, but then Belle came hobbling in and sent us all scattering with orders for Agnes and the news that lunch was served in the dining room for us.

Neither of us had an appetite, so we retired to our apartment and washed coal dust out of our hair and off our faces. I held Zeb's finger under the cold water tap and refused his request to apply butter to it. He complained that he was now down to one good limb, so I coddled him a bit and pointed out that he had at least one additional very adequate appendage left besides his unburnt hand. He struggled to understand the word 'appendage' until I cupped the member I had in mind and then we spent a pleasant hour "resting".

Do we got a set number of rescues we got to do to satisfy Prouwder house? We had four today and the last one came when I could have gone for another go-round with Tom in bed! But there we were, nice and naked, when suddenly we start hearing a whole lot of voices crying for help. We jumped up. Well, Tom jumped up and I groused along behind him. We got dressed, grabbed our gear, and set out. Pretty quick we saw we had to head down the hill to them railroad tracks again. I tell you, we might as well have a short run of track laid out closer to the house, just to save time. I guess trains and streetcars are pretty dangerous places is why we've gotten called down into Duck's Hollow so much. I just hoped we weren't going back to Munich 'cause Tom read to me in the newspaper about how the Reds there had executed a bunch of nobles and then got killed off themselves. I also didn't want to find another fat guy wedged up to his neck on some railroad bridge.

Where we went instead was France. It wasn't Frenchmen we were sent to help, but poor American soldiers that were riding in an Army truck when it got knocked over hard by a train. Three of those guys was already dead and eight more were broken or tore up bad. It was evening there, so Tom had to use his flashlight again to help us see what we were doing. Lots of broken bones and muscles run through with truck parts, not to mention that every one of them had been knocked hard on the head. The train was still coming to a stop when we got there, but soon its crew was on hand to help us and somebody got sent off to fetch doctors.

I really do got to try to catch up with Tom as far as this first aid goes. He's a quick learner, which I am not, but if he gets Doc Sexton back to the mansion, I'll do my damnedest to master what he has to tell us. I should draw what I'm supposed to learn, wrapping bandages, putting on Turner kits, and the like.

Tom asked one of the least injured doughboys where we were: La Ferte St. Aubin, southeast of Orleans. (I asked him how to spell all that Fran say.) He hates it even more than I do not to know where we've been and he hung a big map up on the wall of our main room with pins in it for every rescue.

It was quite a while until the last hurt soldier was taken away. Tom and I helped push their truck off the road and then waited for the train to get underway again. He suggested spending the night in Orleans, but it was about thirteen miles off and I still ain't regrown those two toes of course, so I said no. Instead, we shuffled along the track until we saw the Monongahela on our right and then climbed the hill, which was mighty hard going for me. The mansion was lit up, but I was winded and needed to piss, so we both walked into the trees to do our business. I don't know why it's like that, but when one guy starts peeing, any other guy with him up and decides to do the same.

That's how it was that we were in the dark of the woods, kind of out of sight, when we heard somebody creeping through the leaves in front of us. I figured it was James the nice night watchman and I almost called out to him as if to invite him to come and piss with us or something, but then I saw it wasn't the shape of James, who's tall. This guy was shorter, but stout, and the way he was walking made it plain he was trying not to be noticed. James strides around pretty loudly. He told me he has scared away bums just by being confident and noisy like that, without even having to say "Clear off!" to them.

No, this guy was Frank Candell! I hoped maybe James would be on his trail, ready to crack him over the head with the policeman's billy club he carries, but it was just me and Tom watching real quiet. We stayed still as long as we could, then followed slowly and carefully, trying to hide behind one tree and then the next.

Candell crept on and from where he was and which way he was headed, there was only one place he was going to: that old cabin that Tom's great-great-grandpa Yawn had built as his family's first home on this property. Tom knew that too and he must have hoped we'd catch the bastard inside with no chance of escape, same as me. On we went. There was sounds of the cabin door being forced open and then closed again. We went a little faster then, figuring Candell wouldn't hear us from inside as easy.

I peeked in the one small window on this side of the cabin, but it was dirty and inside was dark, so I couldn't see much. Candell looked like he was crouched by the hearth off to the left, but I couldn't be sure. There was no way we could rush inside without fighting the door first, but there was nothing for it but to try. Tom and I got hold of the door's edge and pulled with all our might. I heard Candell yell, but then I slipped backwards on the threshold stone and fell on my ass in the muck. Tom jumped over me and tussled with the guy for a moment before he got thrown to the floor. He let out a cuss and I felt that dizzy way I do when a tunnel opens. It closed up right quick and Tom said, "He got away!"

I was so mad I kicked at the threshold stone with both my heels and low and be hold it flipped right up on its side! I would've figured it was packed deep into the mud and leaves, but it came up easy, like it had been put in place recent. One of my feet held it up, but the other one plopped down into a hole beneath it and I sat up to look down into it.

"Hey, Tom, bring your flashlight over here." I kind of poked around with my foot while he stood up, brushed his pants off, and came to the door.

"What is it?" he asked.

"I don't know. Turn that thing on and let's have a look."

He did that and I got my foot out of the way.

"Christ have mercy!" he said.

I peered into the hole and saw what my boot had been poking at. I would've been happier to see a lit stick of dynamite down there than what I did see 'cause half-buried in the earth was the tiny skeleton of a poor little baby!

"Tom! Is that-"

"Yes, Zeb. I believe it is."

THRESHOLD

Sunday, the 4th of May

Zeb and I examined the hole he'd uncovered. Aside from the skeleton, which was undoubtedly the French-Canadian trapper's child, we found scraps of fur and a small strip of bark. There appeared to be writing on it, but we could not read it by the light of my bulb. We conferred for some time before deciding to transfer the contents of Zeb's pack into mine and then carefully place the skeleton in his bag. To him it seemed somewhat disrespectful to move the child's remains, but I argued that this was no proper burial place to begin with. I also feared Candell might hide the skeleton in some other location rather than let us have it. Perhaps he did not even know of the skeleton's existence, but the doorstone would not have been as easily displaced had someone, presumably Candell, not already dislodged it from a century of dirt, leaves, and roots. The skeleton very likely held importance for our erstwhile colleague in The Work and I was determined to know why!

We met James on the way to the mansion. I told him to be on the lookout for Candell, especially in the vicinity of the cabin. He promised to keep a sharp eye out and, although he was clearly curious about the contents of the bag Zeb carried *like a serving tray, he did not ask. He is a good servant, as was his father before him.*

Since it was quite late and we were fatigued, we retired to our apartment directly. We took the precaution of securing Zeb's backpack beneath our bed because I thought Candell or even Hyacinth might steal away with it, although I could not guess to what purpose. Perhaps Candell had discovered the child's grave while he resided in the cabin and simply decided to leave it there. Perhaps he'd found the skeleton elsewhere and hidden it away under the threshold for some unknown reason. I considered the possibility that he was motivated to extort money out of us, but how could anyone now living in Prouwder House be held accountable for a child's death a hundred years ago? If blackmail were indeed Candell's intention, why had he not already made his accusation and demanded payment for his silence? I had many questions and the beginnings of a plan, but sleep overtook me.

5/4/19

It was creepy to sleep right above a baby's dead body, but my own body needed rest so there was no arguing with myself. Tom tied my backpack to the legs of our bed so as that Frank Candell couldn't steal it back. I was more afraid of Tom's sister, to be honest. She's just as creepy as a skeleton, if you ask me. I could imagine her getting hold of that skeleton and waking us up with it dancing in her hands. She's a piece of work. I'd rather have all my brothers and sisters watching me sleep than just that one sister of Tom's!

Anyway, we snoozed real good after all that had happened the day before and woke up just at the end of the time breakfast is served here at the mansion. Tom sent me down to the kitchen to fetch plates of eggs and toast from Belle while he guarded the kid. We ate and then he went off to talk to his mom. I didn't let that backpack out of my sight and spent some time sketching out the cabin's threshold and the hole the kid was buried in. I have a pretty good memory for things I've seen and in this case my memory was good enough to give me the shivers. I made the hole extra dark with one of my charcoal pencils and made it look like the moon was shining on the upturned stone. I didn't even draw the skeleton itself, but I think I made it so anyone looking at this sketch wouldn't want to peer down into that hole!

When Tom returned, he said most of his family was going to church. When they came back, he wanted to gather some of them together for a meeting. That wouldn't be until after lunch. I was glad he decided to stay with me and watch over the backpack so I wouldn't be alone with it. We got it untied from the bedframe and then took it into our big room where there was more sunlight. I sure didn't want the thing laid out on our "dining" table, so Tom put it on the rug and then rummaged around inside until he found that piece of bark. When he hauled it out, we held it up to one of the windows. It was still hard to read, but we made out "Pierre" and "1816". They'd been carved into the underside of the bark strip and the grooves were partly packed with dirt.

I asked Tom if that was the name of the Frenchman's baby, but he said he didn't know since Henry hadn't mentioned it. My ma and pa had a baby that was stillborn and he's buried at the top of the hill behind our house with a little grave marker. They sure wouldn't have put him in the ground right in front of our door. It wasn't right that people would be stepping on a grave every time they came into your house or left it! I said that was a mighty weird thing to do with a baby's body. Tom nodded and then seemed to be staring at something real far away. I turned and looked at the wall, but there was nothing interesting on it, not even a picture. Just some old wallpaper, kind of green and tan, with oak leaves and acorns on it. He sort of said "Pierre". At least his lips moved like they were saying that, but you couldn't hear his voice or anything. He gets that way sometimes, calculating this or that. I wanted to ask him what he was thinking about, but he can be ornery if you interrupt him, so I just left him to his pondering and took up my sketch pad. I drew the skeleton just as it was, there on our rug. I even put in Tom's feet and shins, standing behind the poor thing. It's a pretty grisly picture, but ackrit. Least I think so. Tom didn't say anything about it. He just up and left the apartment without so much as a buy your leaf.

> *Examination of the skeleton, at least as far as I, an amateur, could conduct it, yielded no particular results. The baby's skull was intact, as was each bone. That suggests a death unmarred by violence, such as succumbing to illness. I may ask Dr. Sexton to take a look. "1816" suggests the babe died in the very year The Work began. It may refer, of course, to the child's birth, but he could not have lived to see 1818, I think, such is the size of his skeleton. Most likely, 1816 is the year of both birth and death.*
>
> *I sought out what records there are of our family in its*

earliest days, leaving Zeb to his sketching. He is, as I have noted before, quite talented with the pencil, pen, and paintbrush. He has an eye for the depictive arts. Imaginative, abstract art, however, lies beyond him, which I happen to think is all to the good. Some of the canvasses I saw in Europe were awful things, full of disjointed bodies and faces shrieking in horror or devoid of recognizable subjects entirely. Rubbish.

Records of our family tend to be heavily mercenary. Generations of Prouwders like my mother have duly noted dates of birth and death, as well as income, expenses, inheritances, and the like, as befits our roots among Dutch Protestant businessmen. Documents of a more personal nature are rather lacking, at least in the main library, which is where I went from our apartment. I found no diaries there. Perhaps none was ever written or, as I think more likely, they've been kept hidden in boudoirs, attics, or hope chests in Prouwder homes around the city. Many may have been destroyed after their authors' deaths. I must take pains to ensure that does not happen with the journals Zeb and I keep! I did, at least, confirm that no Pierre is listed as a descendant of Jan Prouwder, which lends credence to the story of the trapper. Henry seemed unjustifiably guilty. Infant mortality was quite high back then and Great-grandfather Jan had no medical training. Why should the French-Canadian have blamed him for the boy's death so bitterly that a grave was made of the Prouwder threshold?

One other item I found was of extreme interest, but I shall not reveal it here for now, lest Frank or Hyacinth read this entry. I will need confirmation of it from one of three who are in a position to know!

It took forever for Tom's kin to get back from church,

even though they just go to the one they paid to have built in Prouwderville. They all had lunch together and he brought me soup and salad 'cause I stayed home to "babysit". Tom said he wanted to get them together in his uncle William's office, along with Belle, but she wasn't going to be free until two o'clock, so that was when we'd meet up. He drummed his fingers on the table while I ate. I kept my eyes off the poor creepy thing, but Tom kept looking at it, then out the window, then back again. He was mighty puzzled, I could tell, and that ain't something that sits well with him.

Finally it got to be that time. I put my dishes in our little sink while he laid the skeleton on an old piece of linoleum and then slid that into my pack. Off we went and met Tom's mom and grandma along the way. Belle was the last to get there and somebody made room for her on the settee so all the women got to sit down. Louis, William, Henry, and Nathan was also there. Tom's grandma made excuses for her husband not being there. I think he's dead, only she don't remember it. Pry nobody wants to correct her. I agree. Let her be.

Tom started off with telling everybody about the rescues him and me have been on, especially the ones with Frank Candell involved. He talks "eloquent". I can see how he'd be a good politician. He made a real good story out of me losing my toes. I'd feel sorry for myself even if it wasn't me it happened to!

I think this might have been the first time all these people got together to talk about the rescue work. I could see Mrs. P-C wasn't real keen on having her mom hear about all this and it wasn't exactly clear to me why he'd made sure she came. At the sort of right moment, Tom got me to hold one end of my backpack and out he slid the skeleton baby. Mrs. P-C gasped and her uncle William barked something I couldn't understand, then pounded his fist down on his desk. Belle was stoic. She's seen stuff like that before, I bet. Louis was the one that looked fit to cry, but it was Grandma Booke that spoke.

"Pierre? Maude, is that Pierre?"

Grandmother startled all of us with her question. I hadn't yet shown the bark strip to those gathered in William's office. Nathan relayed her words to William, who scowled even more deeply once he'd been told.

"Catherine! Be quiet!" he said to her in his mangled way. Decades of decorum fell away and suddenly my great-uncle and grandmother were just older brother and younger sister again. She ignored his outburst as she had probably begun doing way back in 1860 or so on the occasion of her debutante ball. She leaned forward, lifted her eyeglasses, and examined the infant's remains closely. I drew out the epitaph and held it so she could inspect that as well. She nodded.

"Yes. Pierre. The fur trapper's baby." She sat back and peered at the pattern on her sleeve with an interest equal to the one she'd just shown for the mysterious corpse lying before her. Such are the vagaries of her mind at seventy-five years of age. She seemed disinclined to say more, so I turned to William, whose face was red with anger. He continued to pound the ink blotter in front of him and squeezed his lips together so forcefully that I feared he was utterly incapable of speech at that moment. Mother, on the contrary, had gone pale. If she understood what Grandmother was referring to, it was likely a

story she'd chosen to bury long ago and her *grave was no doubt far deeper than the hole in front of the cabin's door. I would get nothing out of her, but I now had my own theory on what had happened so long ago.*

"William," Nathan signed as I spoke, "you maintain that our family was blessed by angels for our charity and magnanimity. I do not think The Work is a blessing. Evidence to the contrary is all around us. Here sit Belle, half-lamed by a gunshot, and Louis, made miserable by years of hazard. You yourself were deafened by the roar of Krakatoa and not far from this room is Rose, unwed mother to a mulatto child and traumatized eyewitness to her . . . partner's lynching. At any moment we could be visited by my sister, mad from pining for my dead brother. I am unscathed, but my dear Zeb has already been maimed by his involvement with our family and every convocation reveals the Sword of Damocles hanging over Prouwder infants. The child before us is the wellspring of all this injury and death and I think one of you knows why."

I crouched and touched her hand. "Grandmother, what was the name of Jan Prouwder's wife?"

William interrupted with a shout. "Mary Elizabeth Miller! A good woman and a better matriarch than can be found on God's green Earth today!"

Grandmother laid her hand upon my cheek. I wasn't sure she knew precisely where she was, let alone why, but she smiled at me kindly. I regretted the role she would have to play in my revelation of the truth as it had been made clear to me by my research. "She wasn't born Mary Elizabeth Miller, was she, Grandmother?"

"Oh, my no. She was born–"

"*Catherine! Please!*" This time it was Henry that interrupted her.

"*-Máire Sibéal Muilleoir. Irish she was, from a wee village called Glencolmcille. I'm Catherine Mary, in her honor.*"

"*And a good Catholic?*" I prompted her.

"*Well, I'm not, but Grandma was. Oh yes! She taught us all the Rosary, in secret, you know, for Father didn't like it.*"

"*And she's not buried in the Prouwder family cemetery?*"

Grandmother shook her head. "*She lived to be eighty years old. Did you know that?*"

"*I read that recently, yes, but not where her grave is.*"

"*She insisted. She and Father argued about it terribly. You can ask Henry or William, if you see them. They fought, but* Mamó *-that's what we called her in private- won out. She got her way and was buried in Saint Mary Cemetery, over in Lawrenceville. Do you know where that is?*"

I nodded and kissed her hand, then stood up. "*Jan Prouwder hid his wife's religion. He made her change her name. Today such a marriage might be frowned upon, but even more scorn would have been visited upon our ancestors back in 1799.*"

"*But, Thomas,*" Mother said, "*the fur trapper was probably Catholic himself. What can all this have to do with us today?*"

"*He likely was,*" I agreed, "*but when he came in need to our door, he did not find the charitable welcome William wishes he had. Instead, Jan Prouwder heaped all the outrage he himself feared onto the family at his door, condemning them to the storm outside. It was not illness which did the child in, Henry. It was the cold. This child,*" I pointed, "*froze to death.*"

Henry hid his face in his hands.

"*I put it to you,*" I continued, "*that the French Canadian buried his son Pierre under our doorstep to serve forever as a punishment for what Jan Prouwder did that day in 1816. We continue to labor and suffer for the original sin of our family, which is hypocrisy."*

William scattered several items from his desk onto the floor and swiveled his chair away from the rest of us. Just then the door to his office was flung open violently and Frank Candell appeared with a pistol in his hand!

CABIN

Tom sprang toward the bastard, but stupid me was distracted by the red ribbon flapping through the air as it followed the knob it was tied around. The door smashed into the side of a bookshelf, one of them that line just about every wall in that office. It made a real big noise, bigger than any slamming door I ever heard before, which was another distraction to me. Mrs. P-C shrieked and flung herself in front of her mom. Tom's got the quick reactions of a fighter pilot and grabbed hold of Candell's arm lickety-split. He got the gun away from him, but Candell's a helluva fighter himself and punched Tom on the head so hard that he fell to the floor. I was finally in motion when the door slammed shut again. The ribbon was caught between it and the jamb, plus there was a funny click and then a scream from the hall. *Jesus*, I thought, *how much can happen in thirty seconds?*

I ain't as quick as Tom, but I knew enough to try to follow Candell, only the door turned out to be locked! That isn't supposed to happen here in Prouwder house on account of the work we do, but that was the situation. I peered into the keyhole and sure enough there was the butt end of a key in there. I started to ask Tom or one of the others for a pen or something to push it out with when I finally seen some of what was happening behind me. Tom and his cousin Nathan were holding onto that old guy William. He was clutching his upper arm and then the smell of gunpowder hit me and I realized he'd been shot!

Louis, Henry, and the two Prouwder women were frozen in place, but Belle was hustling across the room, untying her apron as she limped along. She got William's arm wrapped up tight and barked orders around like we was all in her kitchen. She told Nathan to telephone for Doctor Redler and told Tom to hurry up and get that door open, then lifted the old man's arm up so he wouldn't bleed as fast, I guess. "Louis! Louis!" she yelled. "Don't just sit there! Get ready to chase Frank down!"

I wasn't having any luck with the door even once Tom got me a pen to work the key with. He told me to stand back and was fixing to kick it off its hinges when suddenly there was another click and the door swung open, calm as could be. Out in the hall was that one maid, Agnes. She just looked at us plain-faced, like she had when Tom and I was stuck in the telephone booth. She hadn't even lost hold of the towels she was carrying. She laid the key in Tom's hand and then said, "Millicent fainted."

Tom and I came into the hall and saw a different maid laid out on the floor next to a potted plant. *Must've been her that screamed,* I thought. Agnes didn't seem the screaming type of girl. Millicent's stack of towels was all over the place.

"Mother?" Tom called back into the office, "could you see to her?" Mrs. P-C got up from the couch. Her mom didn't seem at all upset. Tom and I took off running toward the nearest staircase and Louis wasn't too far behind us. When we got to the parlor, Tom's aunt Olivia and his three cousins were frantically beating at curtains on fire, more of Candell's work. One set was already on the floor, doused with lemonade from a pitcher. Roberts the butler was there too, only he wasn't nearly as helpful as the Doucettes. He seemed more intent on cleaning up the lemonade spill than keeping the mansion from going up in flames! One thing I can say about the women in Tom's family: none of them is dainty that I've met so far.

Tom and I yanked other burning curtains down from their rods and stomped them out, which didn't do my pitiful feet any good, I'll tell you! It didn't seem like the fire had gotten much of anywhere beside the curtains except for one sofa that was also getting eaten up by flames. It was a big heavy mahogany thing. I got one end and Tom got the other, but it was too much for us. Olivia and her daughters joined in quick and we six carried the thing out past the poor coacher so it could burn to cinders without destroying the rest of the place. That stuffed suit Roberts just stood in the big doorway and shut the doors behind us when we came back in. Wouldn't surprise me if'n he maybe didn't care much if the mansion burnt down.

Louis showed up, then Mrs. P-C came downstairs with Millicent under her wing so to speak and turned her over to women from the kitchen. All of us searched from room to room, looking for anything else Candell had set on fire. We didn't find anything. Probably the parlor was his only stop after he run away from the office. James came in then with blood all over his scalp. It looked awful, but heads bleed a bunch and the scrape on his crown wasn't all that bad, it turned out. Tom asked him what happened and James confessed that Candell had gotten the drop on him while he was patrolling the grounds.

"He'll head for the cabin," Tom said. Louis nodded in agreement, then Tom and me took off running into the woods.

There were wounded to tend to and a house to guard, but the immediate threat was Frank Candell. I trusted that he was making his escape, not circling around for another attack, but if Zeb and I couldn't catch him, we'd exhaust ourselves and our servants in keeping watch. I wished for weapons, but there was no time to retrieve the pistol from William's office nor supply ourselves with brass knuckles and blackjacks from the equipment room. James had lost his billy club somewhere when he was waylaid by Candell, so we didn't even have that to utilize. Into the woods we plunged, unarmed.

Zeb's disability slowed us up somewhat, but I surmised this race would go to the smart, not the swift, and I tried to plan ahead for when we'd confront Candell. His assassination attempt didn't seem well-conceived. That suggested he had acted impulsively or at least ahead of whatever schedule he'd devised for torturing us. Killing William -if William was indeed his target- would have been easier to accomplish had Candell waited until they were alone. He knew, of course, that doors in the mansion remain unlocked at all times so as to facilitate The Work and he'd gotten past James before; doing so again in the dead of night would not have been a great obstacle to one who knew the lay of the land as well as Candell did.

Something had prompted him to act and I could only assume it was our removal of the baby's skeleton. That suggested in turn that he was well aware of its presence under the cabin's threshold. Could he possibly be drawing power from it? I scoffed to myself, but his ability to use the tunnels apparently at will begged an explanation. I had, of course, also summoned a tunnel, under great duress, but mortal fear didn't seem Frank's modus operandi. He was much more likely to be inspired by anger, I thought. Anger at William for banishing him to the cabin seemed rather too thin a fuel for such wide-ranging trips around the world. Not to mention that his banishment had been imposed over a decade ago and had lasted four years until Candell faked his death. There had to be more to the story!

We reached the cabin and sacrificed any advantage of surprise by forcing the door open. I hoped Candell had no other gun at his disposal, but made sure to shield Zeb with my body as we stumbled inside. Candell was there. He crouched at the cold hearth and let a malevolent smile spread across his bullish face. I leapt for him, but again he was quicker and disappeared into the fireplace. Zeb and I felt the pull of the tunnel and raced after him.

When we emerged, the scene was familiar. We stood in the remains of the home in Chicago which marked our first rescue. Candell ran down the street with a speed one wouldn't expect in a man his age and a laugh which echoed off neighboring houses. I knew I could catch up to him, but Zeb could not and I didn't want us to be separated. Since Candell appeared to summon tunnels at will, he could easily send himself, and me, wherever he chose or, much worse, send Zeb off to some other unknown place of peril, thereby forcing me to stop my pursuit *and start a global search. We had to stay together and wear Candell out.*

He turned and ducked into the narrow space between two homes. We turned as well and saw him clamber up a tree, then leap into nothingness. I helped Zeb onto the lowest limb, felt the swirl of space around us, then saw that we were no longer in Chicago, but rather a large forest. I recognized the deep-green firs of Sweden where I had rescued a little blonde boy from starvation and exposure. I took Zeb's hand in mine and, before the air had completely settled down, jumped with him in tow.

We landed with grunts onto the floor of the Italian bell tower where we'd last seen our hapless rope-clinger, Ludano. He wasn't there then, of course, but rapid footsteps on the staircase indicated Candell was fleeing the scene. How he was able to lead us through rescues he hadn't participated in puzzled me, but we couldn't stop chasing him yet and I began to form an idea for catching him.

Candell was nowhere to be seen when we emerged from Tempio di Santa Maria della Rotonda, but I guessed his next stop and led Zeb around the corner of the church to a long blank wall. Zeb's mangled feet were beginning to slow him down seriously; I hoped Candell was fatiguing as well. We laid our hands on the foundation of the temple and felt yet another pull through the atmosphere.

It almost seemed we passed through the wall itself. On the other side of it was Pinsk's cathedral, where we had narrowly escaped a Polish firing squad. Zeb looked stricken by our return to the spot where so many young men and boys had been massacred. He swore under his breath and said, "I'm gonna bust the bastard's jaw for this." He pointed ahead of us to where Candell was racing away. The smile was now gone from his face as he glanced over his shoulder. Zeb took off after him with renewed vigor. I think no one who saw him at that moment would have guessed he had recently had two toes amputated!

"He'll go to India next, won't he?" Zeb asked as we ran.

I shook my head. "Des Moines."

"Ah, yeah!" Zeb scanned the street while I kept my eyes on Candell. "There!"

He ran to our right and I followed. Beside the home we were approaching was a small structure whose purpose was clear, despite the fact it was an even more dilapidated example than the one we'd used at Mrs. Carter's home. We got somewhat hung up at the privy's door and I worried we would lose the momentum necessary to carry us farther, but our pause lasted only long enough for Zeb to say "I hope we don't end up underground" and then we were in Iowa.

Candell was closer than ever and I risked separating from Zeb in order to tackle the villain. I almost had my hands around his waist, but he whirled and punched me in the head for the second time that day. A woman's scream came from inside the house and I thought I saw someone at the window, but my vision was temporarily obstructed by stars of pain.

There was no large iron gate anywhere nearby, but Candell made do with the one in the neighbor's white-picket fence. "Come on!" Zeb helped me to my feet. "He's headin' for Jellybag!"

"You go there and keep chasing him! I'll be waiting!"

Zeb looked confused, but responded to my push and vanished through the same gate as Candell. I, on the other hand, fought my dizziness and dashed across the street I'd called home for nearly a week. Up ahead of me was a large pond where Zeb and I had spent time skipping rocks with

Little Barbie or pointing out fauna to her. I reached its edge and focused all my adrenaline on opening what I hoped would be our final tunnel today.

The world responded without my even moving and I found myself beside a significantly larger body of water next to a German submarine lying askew. I concealed myself behind the curve of the bow and had not long to wait before I was face to face with a very astonished Frank Candell. He began to say "What?", but my fist to his jaw cut him off decisively. He fell to his knees, got a second blow to his cranium, and collapsed onto the sand!

Tom is smarter than anyone I've ever known and a good thing he is too, 'cause I was wore out by hobbling after Frank Candell. Jallianwala Bagh looked just as awful to me as it had the first time I saw it, only now all the bodies were gone and most of the blood too. I think I saw plenty of bullet holes in the walls, but there wasn't time to look at them too close 'cause I figured I was trying to drive Candell into an ambush.

How he knew where to go, I got no idea. Maybe all these weeks he's been tracking us after our rescues. What a louse, using other people's tragedies for his own benefit. It still boils my blood to think he stood on the same ground where poor Abraham met his end! In any case, he outpaced me *-damn* these feet of mine- and got to the side of a big rectangle pond before disappearing. I wasn't sure where he had gone 'cause Tom and me have been on so many rescues in the last five weeks that they all kind of smash together. I got to the same spot, felt like I was falling into the water, then showed up back in

Hastings where that U-boat still is. I was just about to get tide water covering my feet, which wouldn't have felt good at all, when I heard a few punches and grunts around the curve of the sub. I sure hoped Tom was getting the better of Candell and hurried over to see that was exactly what was happening!

He was beat, but the two of us pinned him hard into the beach anyway. I wanted to knock him unconscious and maybe drown him in the Channel, but Tom had questions for him. Like I said, he's smart. He got right to the point.

"How have you been using the tunnels?" he asked. "Who was Pierre to you?"

Candell spat wet sand and blood out of his mouth and glared up at us. "Why in hell should I tell you?"

"Because," Tom panted, "your days of attacking us are over. I have a *very* strong feeling you won't be able to use that skeleton once we've destroyed it, whereas my companion and I could quite simply drag you into the surf and drown you right now, then get away with it easily!"

Tom is smart, but he was also a fighter pilot. Sending men down to their deaths is something he did plenty of in the war. Me, I just sent a lot of potatoes to their deaths in my belly!

Candell took him seriously. "My brother," he spat again.

Me and Tom looked at each other. "How can that be?" I asked. "He's been dead a hundred and three years. You're still here."

People had started to draw closer to us. "His father

was my father. Francois Candell. Pierre was his first child and I was his last."

"You're not half-Cree though, are you?" Tom asked.

Frank shook his head, which made more sand stick to his face. "Different mothers, but he told all us kids about the Prouwders and what they had done!"

Tom relaxed his grip on Frank a bit. "I know Jan sent them away. I'm sorry. We're all sorry."

"Screw your sorry! Prouwder sent them away in a *blizzard*. Both Pierre and his mom froze to death and my father lost some of his toes and fingers to frostbite. You all got what was coming to you!" He looked up at me and chuckled. "All this time you've been telling yourselves you're special and blessed. Angels! Hah! You're demons! Cursed things and I'll never be done getting my revenge on you!"

I looked at everybody getting closer and closer. Police was sure to be called. "Tom, let's go. Let's get him back to the mansion and deal with him there."

He nodded in a sort of absent way and we hauled Candell to his feet, then drug him into the waves. A tunnel finally came, but I sure felt spent and I bet the other two was also. We showed up, after a real long time, on the bank of the Monogahela, right where that train bridge is, in Duck Hollow. I admit I relaxed too much and Tom did too. We were pretty stunned by the chase and what we'd found out. Candell took his chance, broke away from us, and dove into the river.

I figured he was going to use another tunnel and get away into the Atlantic or South Pacific, spend the rest of his days by some lagoon with half-naked native women all around, but instead he just got pulled along by the current. He was trying to swim to the other shore, but we watched him flounder as he drifted toward the Ohio and then he disappeared under the surface. I hoped we was rid of him for good!

Monday, the 5ᵗʰ of May

James and Great-uncle William are recuperating, thanks to Doctors Redler and Sexton. The latter also examined Zeb's feet and pronounced him more or less still on the mend, despite yesterday's exertions. We have moved poor Pierre's remains far from the estate and will bury him with Christian solemnity at some point soon, once Mother has made the arrangements. Secrecy is paramount, she asserts, and I agree. She was naturally distraught by the attacks, so I've decided for the time being not to divulge what Frank Candell told us. Perhaps that wasn't even the truth, but another lie on his part. I feel I have overlooked something important in the matter, but it escapes me for the moment.

I did tell Belle and Louis what apparently became of their erstwhile companion. They've believed him dead before so they were not terribly distressed by the news. I must admit, minus an actual corpse, his demise is nothing to rely on. We shall all remain vigilant.

At least there are many pairs of eyes keeping watch over Prouwder House. Two of the dearest belong to my Zeb. He quite surprised me at lunch by mentioning, merely in passing, that today is his birthday! Number twenty-one, as a matter of fact. So, for the next six months we shall be the same age. I scrambled about and secured him a set of paints, water colors to be precise, which I presented to him at supper. Belle was an angel of short notice and made him a War Cake of molasses, corn syrup, raisins, cinnamon, cloves, nutmeg, et cetera. I think she likes Zeb more than me and I admit I am terrifically jealous! We both ate with gusto and thanked her profusely.

There were tender intimacies afterwards. My mind wandered as much as my hands and lips. Jan Prouwder married a Catholic woman, but hid that fact even though he must have loved her. Others who followed in The Work have been transgressive as well, although I know nothing of the kind about Jan's son Jacob and his wife, nor about William and his late wife Sarah. I wonder about the connections among Belle, Booke, and Candell. Was there something of Zeb and me in Louis and Frank?

There is something else I have realized, but I cannot bring myself to discuss it here. Suffice it to say, I love Zeb and he loves me. What shall happen to us is not for us to know.

Must dash. Heard a call for help from the attic. Hope we go somewhere beautiful!